FATHERS AND SONS

Warren Troost, the model senior naval officer, and his son Andrew, torn between rigid family tradition and rebellious personal desire . . . Tony Trapasso, working for the C.I.A. in waters far more murky than he ever sailed through as a submarine commander, and his son Mike, flying to flaming glory in the air over Vietnam . . . Jacob Miller, moving from command of a mighty aircraft carrier to the highest circles of power in Washington, D.C., and his son Sy, trying to follow in his father's footsteps and prove his manhood in a war where the old rules and the old ways no longer worked . . .

These men, and the women they loved, bring to life the years of struggle in the tidal wave of war abroad and unrest at home that were the 1960s. . . .

ON STATION

NAVY
ON STATION

ROGER JEWETT

A SIGNET BOOK

NEW AMERICAN LIBRARY

A DIVISION OF PENGUIN BOOKS USA INC.

PUBLISHER'S NOTE

This book is a work of fiction. Names, characters, places, and incidents either are the product of the author's imagination or are used fictitiously, and any resemblance to actual persons, living or dead, events, or locales is entirely coincidental.

SIGNET TRADEMARK REG. U.S. PAT. OFF. AND FOREIGN COUNTRIES
REGISTERED TRADEMARK—MARCA REGISTRADA
HECHO EN DRESDEN, TN, U.S.A.

SIGNET, SIGNET CLASSIC, MENTOR, ONYX, PLUME, MERIDIAN and NAL BOOKS are published by New American Library, a division of Penguin Books USA Inc., 1633 Broadway, New York, New York 10019

First Printing, November, 1989

1 2 3 4 5 6 7 8 9

PRINTED IN THE UNITED STATES OF AMERICA

This book is dedicated to the beloved memory of Walter and Eugene Strolovitz, and to Cliff M. Cheifetz, who supplied me with many of the reference books I needed to write this novel.

1

ON APRIL 19, 1960, just as the second watch was coming to an end, Chief Petty Officer Juan Gomez, the first of the five men for the mid-watch, entered the *Concord*'s control room for the number two main machinery space. Here two turbines driven by high-pressure steam generated by two boilers fired by superheated oil turned one of the aircraft carrier's four huge propeller shafts.

Gomez, a short swarthy man, with twenty years' service, always arrived for his watch a few minutes early. "A beautiful night topside," he commented to Charles Hansen, the CPO on duty; then he moved toward the opening from which the thick glass protective round viewing window had been removed. He looked down into the cavernous space and listened to the sounds of the machinery.

The control room, suspended sufficiently high above the deck from the bulkhead in a corner, allowed the engine men in it to have what amounted to a bird's-eye view of everything in the brilliantly illuminated "number two main" as it was called by the men. There were three more identical spaces on the CVA 60, an eighty-thousand-ton aircraft carrier named after the Battle of

Concord. Together the four engines delivered 270,000 horsepower, which could move her at thirty-five knots. But now she was making fifteen knots at the very most, Gomez judged by the sounds he heard coming from the machinery below. He, like all of the old-timers, had learned to *read* the condition of the various pieces of machinery by listening to their sounds.

Satisfied with what he was hearing, Gomez looked at the instrument panel, where everything from the revolutions per minute of the number two shaft to exact temperature in the firebox were displayed on a variety of dials and gauges. From this room the engine men controlled the speed of the ship, in response to the orders from the bridge.

"Fifteen knots," he remarked, looking at the speed indicator and satisfied that he'd been on target.

Then Hansen said, "Been steady that way this watch, and according to the log, the one before too." He had a slow southern drawl. "Any word about liberty?"

"We'll have some time ashore," Gomez said, moving back to the windowless space.

"Yeah, but how much?"

Gomez shrugged. "Time enough for you to drink and screw, Charley." He was still looking down at the machinery when he caught sight of wisps of black smoke coming off the equipment close to the burner basket, a large metal screen that filtered the spray of superheated oil before it entered the firebox.

"Listen, just because you got married before we left the States and became a virgin again, that doesn't mean the rest of us old guys—"

"Madre mía!" Juan shouted . . . but it was too late. A sudden swoosh of fire burst into the machinery space. Black smoke was everywhere.

"Hit the alarm!" Gomez shouted, breaking into a

fit of coughing. His eyes teared and his throat hurt. "Can't find it," Hansen answered.

"Get the hell out of here," Gomez ordered. "Everyone out through the escape hatch . . . Go . . . Go." He counted four men. "Charley, get the fuck out of here!" he yelled, feeling his breath tighten. "Charley?" He dropped to the deck and felt around until he found him. "Christ, Charley—" He began to drag him toward the escape hatch, now totally obscured by the black smoke. His blood pounded in his ears. He felt as if his chest was being squeezed. He bumped into something that gashed the right side of his forehead. The blood poured down his face. He could feel the heat of the fire coming through the deck. Then suddenly he lacked the strength to move. He shook his head. He knew he wasn't going to make it out. "Rose," he said, whispering the name of his wife. "Rose." And just before he let himself be sucked into the swirling blackness, he managed to conjure her face into his dying brain.

Captain Jacob Miller sat down in his swivel chair on the *Concord*'s navigation bridge. The *Concord* (CVA 60), an eighty-thousand-ton aircraft carrier, was steaming into the eastern Mediterranean toward the Israeli port of Haifa, ostensibly for a courtesy call, but really to deliver a dozen Crusader jet fighters to the Israeli Air Force.

Though the delivery was a "top-secret operation," the *Concord* and her two escorts, the DD *Holmes* and the *Murry*, were constantly shadowed by either Russian submarines or TU-95s, turbo-prop-driven long-range bombers used mainly for antisubmarine and reconnaissance operations.

Since 1800 the radar and the sonar had reported

nothing on their screens. But they were steaming only fifty miles off the Egyptian coast and Jacob was almost sure that Egyptian fighters would attempt to make a few low-level passes at his ship before they reached Israeli waters. To prevent that, he had four fighters flying CAP at twenty-thousand feet that could be vectored onto any bogey by the ship's tactical air controller.

Jacob had recently turned fifty, and had taken command of the *Concord* six weeks before in Norfolk, the ship's home port. This was the first time in his career that he had commanded an aircraft carrier. It was a necessary step on the way to making flag rank, and perhaps somewhere up ahead in the future, the real possibility of becoming the chief of naval operations. Having fought in World War Two, and in the Korean War, he certainly had the combat experience. He wasn't just a *paper pusher*. He almost smiled at his own thought. There were dozens of officers with the same qualifications. Whether he made CNO or not was up to the fates and to politics, from which even the Navy couldn't escape.

Jacob had come onto the bridge because he wasn't sleepy, though it was almost time for the mid-watch, and because it was his habit to visit the bridge just before turning in. Even as he noted the escorting DD *Holmes* on the starboard side and *Murry* on the port, Jacob thought about the letter he'd finished writing to his sister, Miriam, before he had come to the bridge. Her letter had been delivered aboard by a carrier-on-board-delivery aircraft the day before. Despite the geographic distances that separated them, theirs had always been a close brother-sister relationship, which had been made even closer when Miriam had married Tony Trapasso, a friend of Jacob's.

Tony, according to Miriam's letter, was on another

trip to Saigon, with his usual stops in Hong Kong and Tokyo.

The most disturbing portion of the letter was Miriam's comment that their mother, now in her late eighties, had to be put into a nursing home. Jacob was well aware that the best of them, and his mother was in the very best in the city, was nothing more than a holding place for the elderly before they died. He'd told his sister that he would foot the entire bill and, in addition, he would pay for their mother to have twenty-four-hour nursing care.

The rest of his letter consisted of chitchat about his son, Simon, who was at Annapolis, and her son, Michael, and daughter, Ruth. Mike was pre-engineering in Pennsylvania State and had joined the NROTC and Ruth was a senior in high school and thinking about going to Vassar. Jacob had also written that he'd run into their mutual friend Warren Troost, who like himself was a captain, though senior to him, and whose son was also in Annapolis.

Having mentally gone over what he had written to his sister and being satisfied with it, Jacob filled his pipe, lit it, and smoking contentedly, thought about events of the day. The ship's ETA in port was 0800 the next morning and by 1000 the American ambassador and his party, which included the deputy prime minister, the admiral of the Navy, and several of his aides, would come aboard for a reception and tour of the ship.

Jacob shifted his position and was about to return to his sea cabin when the watch officer, coming up behind him, said in a tight voice, "Captain, we have a fire in number two main."

At the same instant the fire bell sounded three

times, indicating a fire in the aft section of the ship.

Jacob winced, then ordered, "Sound fire quarters and notify damage control central."

Almost instantly the Klaxon began to blare. As soon as it was silent, the watch officer came on the 1MC. "All hands, fire stations . . . All hands, fire stations . . . All hands, fire stations."

"Did the men in the control room get out?" Jacob asked, leaving his chair. His eyes went to the bridge clock: it was 2358.

"Two are missing. COPs Gomez and Hansen."

At the same instant, one of the bridge phones rang. A yeoman answered it. "Damage control central, skipper, reports firefighters are already on their way."

Jacob ordered a reduction of speed, then quickly drafted a message to be radioed to Vice Admiral Harry Foster, commander of the Sixth Fleet at Gaeta, Italy, advising him of the situation aboard the *Concord*; then he did the same for the skippers of the two escorting destroyers.

A man holding a phone said, "Skipper, damage control says, it has shut down the flow of oil in number two main and asks permission to shut down the ship's ventilation system."

Jacob took the phone from the man. "This is the captain," he said. "What's the situation down there?"

"Bad, skipper," the damage-control officer said. "We've got an oil fire going with heavy black smoke. It's hard to get to, and the ship's uptake and ventilation system are pulling that smoke all over below deck."

Jacob realized he had no chance of making the saluting point by 0800, much less conduct a reception and tour of the ship. "Close down the ventilation system," he said, "and I'll just keep headway to cut down the uptake."

"Skipper, maybe we'll get lucky."

"Maybe," Jacob answered, looking aft, where a huge column of black smoke was already beginning to trail the ship.

The phone rang again. One of the junior officers answered it. "Captain, the XO can't make it through the smoke to the secondary conn. He says he'll keep trying."

Jacob nodded; then to the officer of the deck he said, "Move all the aircraft out of the hangar to the flight deck."

"Aye, aye, skipper."

Jacob picked up the phone linking the bridge to the chief engineering officer and ordered a reduction of speed to 1400 rpms.

"That will just give us steerage way, skipper," the EO commented.

"That's all I need right now," Jacob responded, and as he put the phone down, the DCO was on another phone.

"One of my teams was able to get into number two main," he reported. "But they were forced out by the heat and smoke. Mainly the smoke, skipper."

Jacob acknowledged the report. "We're down to holding steerage way," he said.

"Once we get the main fire out, we're going to have a problem with secondary fires, especially in the uptake flues."

Jacob agreed and put the phone down. On various levels above where the fire was burning were storage tanks holding tens of thousands of gallons of jet fuel and storage areas for various kinds of ordnance; a secondary fire breaking out in any one of those areas would be catastrophic.

Already the aircraft handlers had moved several of the planes from the hangar to the flight deck.

"Skipper, the *Holmes* and *Murry* ask if we need their assistance," the OOD said.

"Thank them and tell them that we're managing. But ask them to stand by in case the situation changes."

"Aye, aye, sir."

Jacob moved back to where the captain's chair was, but he didn't sit down. The fire would mean an investigation by a board of inquiry. It would comb the monthly Hull Report and if it should find that the fire resulted from his negligence, then his naval career would come to a swift end. . . .

"Skipper, the radio officer has a message for you from the Secretary of the Navy," the OOD said.

"Coded?" Jacob asked, facing him.

"No, sir."

Jacob went to the phone bank and picked up the one connecting the bridge and the radio room. "Captain Miller, here. Read the Secretary's message to me."

"Yes, sir. The message reads, 'Can you maintain operational status?' Answer requested immediately."

Jacob waited for something more.

"Sir?" the radio officer questioned.

"That's it?" he asked, feeling his anger rise.

"Yes, sir . . . that's it."

Jacob breathed deeply. Apparently there wasn't any interest in Washington about the men, or the condition of the ship. All Washington seemed to be interested in was whether or not it could maintain its commitment to NATO, which stipulated that two American aircraft carriers would be in the Mediterranean at all times. "Answer," Jacob said more harshly than he intended, "unable to say until fire is out and damage assessed."

"Aye, aye, skipper," the radio officer responded.

"Skipper," the OOD said, "the XO has finally made it to the secondary conn."

"Let me speak to him," Jacob said.

The OOD handed the phone to him.

"Pete," he said to the XO, "you take the conn, I'm going down to number two main. Hold her as she goes."

"Aye, aye, sir," the XO responded.

Jacob turned, left the bridge, and hurried toward number two main. The smell of smoke was everywhere and became more pronounced the closer he got to the fire. Even the lights in the passageway were dimmed by swirling gray smoke.

When Jacob reached the bulkhead door leading to number two main, a dozen firefighters, wearing protective suits, and under the direct command of the DCO, were preparing to enter it.

"Skipper," the DCO said, "I've got three firefighting teams inside working."

"Good. Very good!" Jacob answered, suddenly remembering another fire at sea in December 1944, when he had been air group commander and skipper of a fighter squadron aboard the *Alamo*. Then the fire resulted from the planes in the hangar breaking free from their tie-downs during a typhoon. The ship was so badly guttered it was returned to the States for repair. . . .

The bulkhead door was swung open and the firefighters, armed with hoses that delivered foam, hurried into the dense black smoke.

"Skipper, the XO reports two bogeys . . . bearing,

eight-five . . . range, twenty miles . . . altitude, fifteen thousand," the man at the phone reported.

An instant later the Klaxon screamed general quarters and was immediately followed by the OOD on 1MC. "All hands, battle stations . . . All hands, battle stations . . . All hands, battle stations."

"I'm on my way back to the bridge," Jacob snapped, and began to run.

The man and the phone relayed the message.

Jacob ran down the passageway, coughing from the smoke, and up the many flights of steps to the bridge.

"They're holding at ten miles," the OOD said as soon as Jacob appeared. "Our guys are vectored on them."

Jacob went to the phone bank and called the secondary conn. "Pete, I'm back on the bridge. I have the conn. Better stay where you are."

"Aye, aye, sir," the XO answered.

Jacob returned the phone to the bank and looked at the radar display. The two bogeys were still there.

"Our guys could make them sweat a bit," the OOD said.

Jacob shook his head. "We don't want any more trouble than we already have. I don't want any trigger-happy Arab to start shooting."

The OOD agreed.

Jacob moved to the forward part of the bridge and looked down at the deck. All of the aircraft, including those jets that were going to be delivered to the Israelis, were on the deck. There was nothing secret about them now, especially if those bogeys were equipped with infrared cameras.

"Skipper, DC reports the fire in number two main under control," the OOD said.

Jacob turned toward him. "We're lucky," he said in

a low voice. "Very lucky." He glanced at the clock. It read: 0215.

The OOD smiled. "Yes, I think we are."

Jacob checked the radar again.

The bogeys were turning.

"Very lucky," Jacob repeated a third time.

2

TONY TRAPASSO SAT in the rear of an air-conditioned limo driven by a native Vietnamese employed by the American embassy. This was Tony's fifth visit to South Vietnam. But this time he was part of someone else's operation. He was there to make a cash delivery and evaluate Admiral Pham Khan.

A man in his early forties, Tony, wearing a white shirt, dark blue tie, and gray silk suit with three points of a white handkerchief showing just above the edge of the jacket's breast pocket, looked like a very successful businessman. His sideburns had just a touch of gray, enough to give him an air of dignity.

Commander Peter Graubard was seated next to Tony. Graubard, a member of the American naval attaché's staff, like himself was involved in various covert activities. Tony never had mentioned the fact to any of the people in the military with whom he had worked over the past years that he had once been a naval officer, a lieutenant commander . . . the skipper of a submarine and the recipient of the Navy Cross. He much preferred to be a man without a past. That way he never had to explain or defend his connection to the Mafia.

Graubard had made it very clear during their first

meeting some months before at the embassy that he had "no use for Company men who only fuck up wherever they're sent." And now, assigned to Tony, he sat in resentful silence, looking out of the window at the crowded streets of Saigon.

Tony leaned forward and, pressing a button, raised the bullet-proof glass partition between the front and rear of the limo. "Commander, did you run a check on your contact?" Tony asked. "I mean, a real check. The Vietnamese military has more admirals and generals than—"

"I've worked with Admiral Pham Khan before," Graubard snapped. "I know the man. He'll deliver what he says he will."

Tony didn't challenge Graubard. But he still didn't like the idea of having to drive out of Saigon to meet Pham Khan, especially with a briefcase filled with a half-million dollars in fifties and hundreds. The admiral's loyalty had a high price attached to it.

"I've used his men to blow ships and bridges in the north," Graubard said, still looking out of the window. "Even as far as Haiphong." He had a definite southern accent.

Lighting a cigarette, Tony questioned, "And every mission was confirmed?"

Graubard turned from the window. His eyes narrowed. "What's that supposed to mean?"

"Did you confirm—"

"Just how the hell was I supposed to do that?"

Tony shrugged and blew smoke toward the glass partition. "You could have initiated the missions—"

"*Did* initiate, Mr. Trapasso."

"You initiated the missions but Pham Khan could be pulling your chain about their success, or even whether they were carried out. You weren't there to authenticate any of his claims."

Graubard's face reddened. "I have photographs back in the embassy."

"Of all the missions?"

"Some."

"They could have been faked," Tony answered.

Graubard glared at him.

"You can't be sure they weren't faked, can you?" Tony patted the attaché case on his lap. "This is supposed to buy us a clean Mekong Delta. I just don't think—"

The limo rolled to a stop.

Tony pressed the intercom button. "What's wrong?"

Smiling, the driver turned around and shook his head.

The next instant four men carrying AK-47s and wearing black pajamalike clothing rushed at the car from an alleyway and shot out the tires.

Tony pulled Graubard to the floor and took a snub-nose .38 out of a leg holster. "You got one of these?"

Graubard shook his head. "There are weapons here," he said, and opened a compartment under the seat. "Here—Christ, there were supposed to be—"

"The driver probably made sure there weren't," Tony said. He'd fought it out with the Vietcong on two previous occasions in the uplands. "Now, listen . . . those pajama boys will shoot the locks off the doors any moment. As soon as they do, I'll go for the guys on my side and then I'm getting out. You follow and pick up a weapon."

Graubard was wide-eyed and very pale.

"You with me?"

Graubard nodded. "What about the money?"

"We're going to have enough trouble trying to save our asses without worrying about the money."

There was a sudden burst of rifle fire on either side of the car.

The instant the shooting stopped, Tony pushed the door open, saw the two black-clad men, and squeezing off three rounds at one, he moved the .38 left and blew the top of the other man's head off with one shot. Then he was out of the car on his belly, with Graubard after him. "Get that other rifle," he yelled, pulling the weapon out of the hands of the first man he had killed.

The two men on the other side of the car fired through the open door.

"Where's the driver?" Tony asked.

Graubard shook his head. "In hell, I hope," he growled.

"Take the rear," Tony said. "I'll belly my way around the front. When I yell *go*, you come up firing. . . . Okay, start moving." Tony wiped the sweat from his eyes with his sleeve. The gray silk suit he wore was splattered with dirt. He began to crawl. He couldn't see the driver and hoped the driver couldn't see him. He paused, took a deep breath, and after he exhaled, he shouted, "Go!" Squeezing the trigger, he scrambled to his feet. The burst fractured the bullet-proof windshield.

The driver ran from the car.

Tony squeezed the trigger again.

The driver stumbled. The back of his white shirt stained red. He struggled to regain his feet, then collapsed.

Graubard cut down the other two men.

"Get their weapons," Tony said. He opened the door opposite the driver's side.

A man fell halfway out of the car.

Tony frisked him. "A thirty-two Beretta," he said, putting the weapon in his back pocket.

"I got the money," Graubard called, reaching into the rear of the car.

"Come on, let's get the hell out of here," Tony said. "It's a long walk back to the embassy."

"We just going to leave the car here?" Graubard questioned.

Tony shook his head, went to the rear of the car, and unscrewed the gas cap. "We're not going to leave anything for the friends of these bastards." Standing to one side, he struck a match and threw it into the gas tank.

The car burst into flames.

"Okay, let's get the hell out of here," Tony said; then he added, "I don't think those photographs you have back in the embassy are worth a shit."

Graubard didn't answer.

3

THE RECEPTIONIST LOOKED up, fluttered her eye-lashes several times, and before she could speak, Warren said, "Mrs. Troost is expecting me . . . I'm Mr. Troost." He was wearing his uniform.

The young woman's cheeks and ears reddened. She punched out several numbers on the switchboard. "Tell Mrs. Troost her husband is here." She waited a moment, nodded; then, looking up at Warren, she said, "She's expecting you. Please go right in . . . through the door and turn left; her office is at the end of the hallway, on the right."

"Thank you." Warren walked through the frosted door on which the nude figures of two women were etched into the glass. This was his first visit to the new offices of the magazine *The Complete Woman*, of which Hilary, his wife, was part-owner and publisher.

The walls of the hallway were decorated with framed covers of previous issues of the magazine, several very expensive modern paintings, a few very dramatic photographs of famous contributing authors, and a dozen full-color eleven-by-fourteens of nude men and women. *The Complete Woman* had evolved over the last few years into the equivalent of a women's *Playboy*.

17

Warren entered the office and Hilary's secretary, Joan Polk, a woman about his age, who had been with Hilary for several years and knew him, stood up and came out from behind her desk to greet him. "Welcome to New York. It's so good to see you again." She kissed him on both cheeks.

"Good to see you again too," he said, kissing her cheeks.

She stepped back and looked at him. "You don't look any different than the last time I saw you . . . perhaps a bit more healthy than the men I'm used to seeing around here."

"Time at sea will do it all the time," Warren said. Until six weeks ago he'd been the skipper of the cruiser *Portland*. But now he was back in Washington.

"Maybe a tad more dignified-looking," Joan said, moving back to her desk. "How do you like our new digs?"

Warren shrugged. "Impressive."

Joan grinned. "That's being diplomatic." Then, gesturing to the closed door, she said, "Go on in . . . the boss lady is waiting for you."

"That sounds almost ominous."

"It's been one of those days," she said. "Whatever could go wrong, has gone wrong."

"I know the kind," Warren responded as he went to the door, opened it, and walked into the room, immediately aware that Hilary was on the phone, engaged in what sounded like a very angry discussion.

She looked up, put her hand over the mouthpiece, and said, "Help yourself to a drink and bring me one too." Then she resumed speaking to the person on the other end of the line.

The brass bar cart, situated in one of the room's corners, resembled a turn-of-the-century street cart, complete with a slanted roof and handles for pushing or pulling it.

Warren helped himself to a club soda. He poured the same for Hilary, though he was certain she wanted something stronger. He put her drink down on a ceramic coaster she'd taken out of a drawer, and then he moved to the window.

It was one of those very clear early-summer days. From the thirty-second floor Warren had a panoramic view of the upper New York harbor, Governors Island close by, Staten Island in the distance, to the west; and looking toward the southeast, where the Narrows were located, the wonderful spiderweblike Verrazano Bridge spanning them.

Behind him, Hilary's voice rose and fell. He turned. This obviously wasn't the best time for them to talk things out. Two weeks ago, when they were together in Washington, he had asked her when she intended to leave the magazine and spend more time with him.

"About the same time you intend to leave the Navy and spend more time with me," she had said.

Her answer had precipitated one of the worst quarrels they ever had, and she had left the hotel early the following morning, telling him, in no uncertain terms, that their future together was open to discussion. . . .

Warren moved to one of the walls and examined the photographs on it. Some were of models and others were of screen and theater celebrities. The other wall had two large paintings illuminated by track lighting. One was a seascape with waves pounding against rocks, the other a reclining nude with small breasts and long blond hair. Both had been painted by Andrew, their son, who was now in his second year at the Academy and was planning to become a fighter pilot.

Warren examined the third wall, where there were

more photographs of famous people, including several in national politics. He heard the sudden clunk of the phone being dropped into its cradle, and turning around, he faced her.

Hilary was still a very beautiful woman, with a svelte body, lovely long auburn hair, which swirled around her shoulders whenever she moved her head, and an expression of mystery on her face and in her eyes.

She lifted her glass. "I hope this has some gin or vodka in it."

"Just soda water."

Hilary made a face and extended the glass to him. "Please put something stronger in it."

"You don't need something stronger," Warren said resolutely.

"With the kind of day I've had, I need—" She stopped. "All right, I'll drink it." She raised her glass. "Those who are about to die salute you." She drank, then made a face.

Warren settled into a chair next to the desk and unbuttoned his jacket. A chunkily built man, with a strong chin, almost sad gray eyes, and hair that was still blond, he was unmistakably a Troost.

Hilary leaned toward him and kissed him. "We have reservations for seven o'clock at the Russian Tea Room, unless you have some objection . . ."

"None."

"I spoke to Andrew last night," she said. "He's planning to divide his vacation time between London and Paris."

"His idea or yours?" Andrew's future was another area of disagreement between them. She wanted Andrew to "follow his own star," which would have meant going to some university or other as a fine-arts major—whatever the hell that was—instead of going to the Academy and becoming a career officer. If he wanted to paint, he could always do it as an avocation. But his real future was with the Navy.

"Both. He was thinking of going abroad and I happen to know two very fine artists, one in London and one in Paris, who are willing to teach him."

Warren looked for a place to set his glass down.

"Put it here," Hilary said, taking another coaster out of the top drawer. "I hoped you wouldn't have any objections to Andrew's plans."

"You knew I would, and I do. You're only making it harder for him to follow—"

"In your footsteps?" she challenged. "In the Troost naval tradition?"

Warren fished out his pipe. "He has a career. He can keep the painting as his avocation."

"Have you any idea how talented your son is?" she questioned. "For God's sake, Warren, there's much more to the world, to life, than the Navy. He's going to the Academy to satisfy you; he's even willing to become a fighter pilot for the same reason."

There was passion in her voice, and as Warren watched her face become flushed with it, he resisted the temptation to take her in his arms. Despite the several differences between them, he loved her very much. She still excited him. "Andrew has made his choice," he said quietly.

"He's made your choice," Hilary said, taking another sip of the club soda.

Warren didn't say anything. The pause in their discussion gave him the opportunity to finally fill and light his pipe.

Hilary sighed deeply, stood up, and as she walked to the window, Warren turned the chair to follow her. She moved gracefully, the curve of her buttocks and thighs sharply outlined under her white linen skirt.

"We have a real problem between us, Warren," she said, facing him. "We're two different people trying to be the same people we were when we met and fell in love a long time ago."

He took the pipe out of his mouth and stood up. A somewhat similar thought had occurred to him several times during the past two weeks.

She faced him. "I was going to wait until after dinner and we were alone in our apartment. But the conversation we just had about our son—well, there really isn't any reason for me to wait. What I'm trying to say with the least amount of fuss is that since we now live separate lives and have for several years, we might as well make the separation legal." She finished with a slight quaver in her voice.

A long silence followed.

Warren took several steps away from the chair, then moved back to it, "Separation or divorce?" he asked.

"I don't like doing things halfway," Hilary said as she moved back to the desk and sat down again. "What do you want, Warren?"

He tried to smoke the pipe, but it had gone out. "The truth?" he asked, remembering how they had made love only hours after they had met.

"Of course, the truth."

"Right now, I'd like very much to take you to bed. That's a howl, isn't it?"

She managed a smile. "Flattering, considering the fact that I just asked you for a divorce."

"You asked for the 'truth,' and that's what I gave you," he said, relighting his pipe and sitting down again.

"Be serious."

"I am."

"Do you want a divorce?" Hilary asked.

He stared at her for several moments and she met his gaze unflinchingly. There was so much that connected them and so much that separated them. "Yes," he finally responded with a nod, "a divorce is our only solution."

4

THREE MONTHS AFTER the fire, Jacob was host aboard the *Concord* to Senators William Chaffe from Delaware and Carl Hinze from Arizona. They had boarded the ship in Genoa for a two-day stay, during which they would observe flight operations and a display of the air wing's firepower capability. Both men were members of the powerful Senate Armed Services Committee. Jacob had met them two years before, when he testified before their committee on the Navy's need for an additional super aircraft carrier. Both men were conservative. Chaffe, a Democrat, usually voted with the conservative Republicans.

The second night at dinner in Jacob's sea cabin, Chaffe, the shorter of the two, offered Jacob a cigar and said, "Captain, we've heard a few things about you."

Jacob immediately thought about the board of inquiry's investigation into the cause of the fire aboard the *Concord* and the "letter of caution" he'd received, on the board's recommendation, from the commander of the Sixth Fleet. Had the letter been a reprimand, he would have never had the opportunity to make flag rank and would have had to give serious thought to resigning. But with his years of service and his excellent record, the "letter of caution" was nothing more than a bump, albeit an uncomfortable one for him. But now, with the senator possibly bringing the whole matter up again . . .

"The fact that you have managed to maintain the operational status of this carrier is much to your credit," Hinze said, speaking slowly and with a decided western drawl.

Greatly relieved, Jacob took a few moments to light the cigar before he responded. "That credit belongs to every member of the crew. They're the ones who never faltered."

Chaffe blew a cloud of bluish-white smoke toward the ceiling. "Neither did you, Captain. During the short time we've been aboard, we have learned that you run a tight ship and yet are popular with your men. Some of them think you're the best skipper they ever had."

Jacob felt the color rise in his cheeks.

"I did some checking on you before we came aboard," Hinze said. "You've had an illustrious career, Captain."

Jacob glanced at the steward. "Will you bring more coffee to the table?"

"Yes, sir," the steward responded with a grin.

"Our being here," Chaffe said, "is not fortuitous. We specifically requested this ship because we wanted to have the opportunity to present a possibility that might not have occurred to you."

The steward returned with the coffee and refilled the three empty cups.

"Myself," Hinze said, "Senator Chaffe, and several other senators hold the opinion that you should run for a seat in the Senate."

Jacob had put the cigar down in an ashtray and had started to lift the coffee cup to his lips, but immediately put it down.

"I see that you're surprised," Chaffe commented. He held the cigar between his thumb and second finger.

"Yes. The idea of running for political office never crossed my mind."

"But several times in your career you've had extensive dealings with various elected officials, and from the information we have, you managed very well, especially when you were before our committee to brief it on why the Navy needed another super aircraft carrier. Even the opponents to it admired the way you handled yourself."

"Gentlemen, I believed, and still do believe, in what I told the committee," Jacob said.

"That's probably why the Navy got that carrier," Chaffe said. "It was obvious to all of us that you were committed, and that is precisely why we're here. We, and others in the Senate, believe that you have the ability to win people over to your way of thinking, and that, for a politician, is a gift from God."

"But I'm not a politician . . . I'm just a sailor." Jacob's eyes went to the steward again. The grin on the man's face was even larger than before.

"You have a great many things in your favor that anyone opposing you would not. You're a war hero—"

"Gentlemen—"

"In two wars," Hinze added.

"You've served your country for more than twenty years," Chaffe added.

"And it's common knowledge that you're a multimillionaire many times over," Hinze said. "There would never be a question about venality."

The color was back in Jacob's cheeks and his eyes

went back to the steward. He had no idea how much the crew knew about him. But by the next morning he was sure they'd know he had millions.

"And there's another very important point," Hinze said, looking at Chaffe.

"What the senator means," Chaffe said, "is that you're a Jew . . . a Jew who has made it to the rank of captain in an otherwise gentile world. That and your record will make you an unbeatable candidate in your state."

Though he didn't move, Jacob could feel himself draw back.

"Your state has almost as many Jews as Israel," Chaffe said.

Jacob could feel his heart race. Though he was not a practicing Jew, he'd never denied that he was a Jew. His father had been a religious man and had wanted him to become a rabbi, in the tradition of his grandfather, great-grandfather, and several of his uncles and cousins. But he had heard a different voice, one that had called him toward the sky; he wanted to fly.

"You would probably win the liberal Jewish vote too," Chaffe commented.

Jacob wanted to tell them to fuck off, but he controlled himself, and looking at the clock mounted on the bulkhead, he calmly said, "Gentlemen, I am certainly honored by your . . . interest in my future. But as I told you a short while ago, I'm a sailor. Politics is a jumble to me. . . . Now, if you'll excuse me, I must go to the bridge." He was on his feet. "Please don't disturb yourselves on my behalf. . . . Gordon," he said, calling the steward by his given name, "bring some more of those wonderful pastries to the table for our guests." He crossed the cabin, opened the door, and was in the passageway before the man responded with, "Aye, aye, skipper."

Jacob hurried up to the flight deck and walked almost to the stern before he stopped; then he took several deep breaths. Men like Chaffe and Hinze were an insult to all of the people in the country, regardless of their religious persuasion, and an insult to him personally for thinking that he might be interested in their proposal. Someday he hoped to have the opportunity to tell them that. . . .

Andrew Troost squinted in the bright autumnal sunlight as he headed to the Mahan Library from Bancroft Hall. He had some reading to do for the exam in political science the following day. It was one of the few courses—the others were in the humanities, with the exception of free-handed mechanical drawing—in which he was an A student.

Troost resembled his mother more than his father. He was tall, lean, handsome, with expressive blue eyes and light brown hair. He walked with a determined stride, stepping on the balls of his feet.

The exam would be his last class before the Thanksgiving break. This year he wasn't sure what he'd do. Thanksgiving, Christmas, and Easter were the three holidays he always spent in New York with his parents and his grandmother, Gloria. Often his family would invite the Millers and the Trapassos out for dinner, or Mrs. Trapasso would have everyone over for dinner. There had been years when his father or Captain Miller couldn't be with them, but whether it was through his mother's or Mrs. Trapasso's efforts, it was a time when the three families always got together, making it seem as if all of them belonged to the same family. He had grown up almost believing that Simon Miller and

Michael and Ruth Trapasso were blood relations. Simon, Michael, and he had thought of themselves as the Three Musketeers. He and Simon, or Sy, as everyone called him, had entered the Academy the same year. Sy looked forward to a naval career, while Andrew intended to give the government not a moment more than the six years required by law after he graduated from the Academy; then he'd devote his energies to becoming an artist. Though there was this difference between the two young men, they were still best friends.

This year Thanksgiving dinner would be at the Trapasso house, but Andrew didn't have the same warm feeling about going there that he had in previous years. His mother wouldn't be there, and that made the difference. He'd said as much to Sy that morning on the way to the mess hall.

Sy had understood and in his characteristically soft voice he'd said, "If I were you, I'd feel the same way. But if you didn't show, your dad would be very upset and so would everyone else."

"I'll wind up going," Andrew said. "But this divorce has really gotten to me. I didn't think it would bother me, but it does. It really does. . . ."

He pursed his lips and resolutely strode up the steps of the library.

5

THE DAY AFTER Thanksgiving was gray and raw. Jacob was behind the wheel of a rented blue Caddy. Sy sat next to him, listening to the Sibelius violin concerto on the radio. They were driving out to visit Tara.

Jacob eased the car from the right to the left lane. To go from the Plaza Hotel, where he and Sy were staying, to the Shelter Rock Rest Home just outside of Northport on Long Island, usually took an hour, but depending on traffic on the Long Island Expressway, could run an hour and a half, sometimes more. Because many people took the day off to make it a four-day holiday, traffic was extremely light and Jacob maintained a steady sixty miles an hour.

"I deposited more money into your checking account," he said, and glanced over at his son, who bore a strong resemblance to him, though he had Tara's lovely gray eyes. "Aren't you even going to ask how much?"

Sy smiled, and opening his eyes, he said, "I already have more than I need. I had a five-thousand-dollar balance last month."

"Now you have fifteen thousand," Jacob told him.

"Enough to buy a car . . . I figured you might want and need one about now."

"You're something else!" Sy exclaimed.

"Is that supposed to be good or bad?" Jacob asked, glancing at Sy again.

"What do you think?"

"I think you must have been thinking about asking me for a car, that's what I think."

Sy laughed. "You have ESP."

"Any idea of what you want?" Jacob asked.

"None. Something that will take me from Annapolis to New York without any trouble. Nothing fancy, Dad. It could even be secondhand, if it's in good shape."

Jacob nodded approvingly and commented that they were making excellent time.

"Aunt Miriam outdid herself yesterday," Sy said. "It was great seeing everyone." Then he added, "I really wish that Mike was with us at the Academy. I know he had the grades to make it. You know, when he gets his commission he's going to apply for flight training. He wants to be a fighter pilot."

"I think Tony had hoped he'd go into the submarines," Jacob answered.

"Mike knows that. But he wants to fly."

Jacob suddenly realized he was evaluating each of the three young men with the objectivity of a professional. Mike seemed to possess that rare balance of control and aggressiveness that differentiated those men who were excellent officers from those who were good. His own son, so far as he could see, did not display these special characteristics. And Andy completely lacked them.

"You know I'm not going to fly," Sy said, his voice turning a tone lower.

Jacob nodded. "I figured if you had intended to become a pilot, you would have mentioned it to me by now."

"Maybe the surface force," Sy said, switching off the radio when the music stopped.

"It's your choice," Jacob told him.

"You're not disappointed?"

"No," Jacob answered. "I wouldn't be even if you chose not to remain in the Navy after you finish your obligation. You're entitled to your own life, Sy." He remembered the problems he had had with his father when he had told him that he did not want to be a rabbi. He could almost hear his father ask, "So what's better than being a rabbi in you head?"

And his own response: "I want to fly." All that had happened so long ago, and now his son was telling him that he saw something in his future better than flying. . . .

"Thanks, Dad. . . . I really mean it—thanks."

Jacob fished into his pocket for his pipe and tobacco pouch, and handing them to Sy, asked him to fill the pipe.

"Dad, I have a question I'd like to ask you."

"Ask," Jacob answered, and realizing he'd soon be exiting the highway, moved back into the right lane.

"Did you ever . . . I mean, I know it was before you met my mother . . . did you have a short-term relationship?"

"That's not the kind of question a son is supposed to ask his father." But then he said, "I was engaged to a woman who was killed when the *Shilo* went down. She was a newspaper reporter and was aboard to do a story about the kamikaze attacks."

"But didn't the *Shilo* take a torpedo?" Sy asked.

"She did, and Connie—that was her name—Connie

. . ." Jacob stopped, took the pipe out of his mouth, and said, "She knew that if she told me she couldn't swim, I would have jumped from the deck with her in my arms, or I never would have jumped at all. She never said a word, and I dropped her over the side. I went in after her, but she never came to the surface." He put the pipe back in his mouth and puffed hard on it; then he glanced at his son, whose face was turned toward the window.

"I often wonder what it would be like to have a real mother."

Jacob put his hand on Sy's shoulder and squeezed it, but didn't say anything. Ten minutes later, he drove through the huge wrought-iron gates of the Shelter Rock Rest Home, to a blacktop cul-de-sac bordered on each side by tall, bare-limbed maple trees.

"She's outside, waiting," Sy said as the large field-stone building came into view.

Tara wore a brown tweed three-quarter-length coat, a green tam-o'-shanter on her head, and a long green woolen scarf wrapped loosely around her neck. She looked almost girlish.

Jacob slowed, angled into a parking slot, cut the ignition, and left the car. He waited until Sy was alongside of him, and together they approached Tara.

"Hello, Tara," Jacob said softly, putting his arms around her and kissing her gently on the lips.

She nodded, but her eyes were on Sy.

Jacob stepped away.

"Hello, Mother." Sy took hold of Tara's hands and kissed her on the forehead.

She smiled.

"You're looking great, Mom," Sy commented, letting go of her right hand.

She remained silent.

Jacob took hold of her free hand. "Let's go inside. . . . I was told you'd started to paint again."

They went up the three broad slate steps and Sy opened the front door.

"Are you going to show us your work?" Jacob asked, unbuttoning his greatcoat and taking off his beaked cap.

"In my room," Tara said.

The three of them crossed the foyer and climbed a flight of blue-carpeted stairs to the second floor.

Tara separated her hand from Jacob's and opened the door to her room.

Jacob had been there many times over the years, and each time he was always surprised by its Spartan quality. White walls with no decorations on them. A light wood dresser. A small desk and chair. A picture of him, taken before she'd been raped, and a picture of Sy taken on his second birthday. And now an easel was placed close to the window, on it a canvas. Nearby, on top of a small table, were her palette, brushes, and tubes of paint.

Jacob slipped off his coat, folded it over his arm, and walked toward the easel.

"Dad!" Sy exclaimed, suddenly at his father's side.

The canvas looked as if it had been slashed with huge splashes of black and red paint.

Jacob stopped and bit his lower lip. A slight tremor passed through him. He squinched his eyes shut and told himself it was a beginning. . . . It had taken her years to put that paint there. Years!

"Dad, are you all right?" Sy questioned in a whisper.

"Yes," Jacob answered, and facing Tara, he managed to smile. "Good work. . . . Will you paint something for me? I still have the painting you gave me—"

A woman knocked softly and stepped through the

half-open doorway. "Excuse me, Tara, but there's a phone call for your husband," she said. "You can take it in the main office, Captain."

"I'll be right back," Jacob told them.

"Who'd call you here?" Sy asked.

Jacob shrugged and followed the woman out of the room, down the steps, and into the office, where he picked up the phone. "Captain Miller here," he said.

Tony was on the other end. "Jake . . ."

"What's wrong?"

"Your mother died a few minutes ago," Tony said.

Jacob gasped and clamped his jaws together. On the way back to the city, he'd intended to stop at the nursing home to see her. . . .

"Jake, Miriam wants to speak to you."

Jacob cleared his throat. "Yes, put her on."

"Jake, I called the same funeral home that buried Papa," Miriam said tearfully. "She died in the hospital, Jake. . . . She took a turn for the worse during the night . . . She died alone, Jake . . . Alone . . ."

Tony came back on the line. "Do you want me to do anything, Jake?"

"Nothing."

"How's Tara?"

"She's fine," Jacob said. "Tell Miriam I'll take care of the arrangements. . . . I'll see you in a couple of hours." He put the phone down in its cradle, wiped the tears from his eyes, and blew his nose. His mother was almost ninety years old and the last three years had been a nightmare of pain for her. "It was time," he whispered, and straightening his shoulders, he returned to Tara's room.

Sy looked at him questioningly.

Jacob shook his head. "Nothing that can't wait," he said, and gave his full attention to Tara, who was seated on the foot of the bed. She was still wearing her outdoor clothing.

"She's gone, Dad," Sy told him. "She's somewhere else."

"Let's get her coat and hat and scarf off," Jacob said, and when they finished, they left the room, closing the door softly behind them.

"Are you going to tell me who called?" Sy questioned as they moved through the open iron gates into the street.

Jacob rolled to a stop. "Your grandmother died," he said softly.

Sy tried to speak, but couldn't, and shaking his head, began to sob softly.

Jacob put his arm around his son's shoulders, and despite his effort to fight them back, tears rolled down his own cheeks.

"You know," Sy wept, "when I was a kid, I thought I was the only kid in the world with three mothers. Grandma and Aunt Miriam were the other two. They were, you know."

"I know," Jacob responded.

Sy eased himself away. "Do you want me to drive, Dad?"

Jacob shook his head.

6

THE WEEK BEFORE Christmas, Tony was summoned to Washington, where he was met at the airport by a tall, slow-speaking, cadaverous-looking man who introduced himself as Josh Cooper and then said, "We're due at a meeting in forty-five minutes. I have a car waiting."

"I hope it rides smoother than that plane," Tony commented as they headed for the parking area.

Cooper's thin lips drew back in a smile, but he didn't say anything.

The black limo was standard government issue. The two of them sat in the rear seat.

"Any idea what this is all about?" Tony asked as soon as they were moving.

Cooper took out a cigarette and offered one to Tony.

"No, thanks."

"I was only asked to escort you to the meeting," Cooper said, lighting up.

They reached Langley with twenty minutes to spare.

Cooper suggested they "make a pit stop at the commissary for coffee and."

Tony agreed and they wound up sitting opposite

each other at a small table against the wall under a photograph of President Eisenhower. There were a half-dozen other people there. Two women and four men. All of them looked like desk types.

Tony nursed a cup of coffee, but Cooper had coffee and a huge cherry-filled Danish.

He smiled at Tony. "It doesn't show, but I have an enormous appetite."

"I can't look at something like that Danish without putting on weight," Tony answered.

When they finally arrived at the room where the meeting was going to be held, Cooper said, "You go in there."

"Where do you go?"

Cooper gave him a toothy smile. "We part ways," he said, opening the door for Tony. Three other men were already there. One was an Army colonel, another a Navy captain. The third was a darkly tanned civilian. They were seated around a polished oak table.

Tony didn't know any of them.

"See you around," Cooper said, and walked away.

Tony entered the room, closed the door after him, and nodding to the three men, sat down next to the captain. "Who's running the show?" he asked.

"The DD for Central America," the captain said, filling his pipe and lighting it.

"The deputy director himself . . . I'm impressed," Tony commented, realizing that might be why the other nonuniformed man was there.

The captain's brow knit but he didn't say anything.

Tony looked around. The room was like so many other conference rooms he had been in. Pictures of the President and the Company's director were on the wall. Dark blue drapes were drawn across the window. The table was large, made of oak, and highly polished.

There was a metal tray on it with a pitcher of water and five clear plastic glasses. Stacked next to the tray were five yellow legal-size pads and five newly sharpened pencils. . . .

The door opened. A short man wearing a three-piece gray suit, a pearl stickpin stuck into a dark blue tie, and a white shirt with a starched collar entered the room and walked directly to the head of the table. "Gentlemen," he said in a nasal voice, "my name is Arthur Couch." His eyes went from man to man, and when they came to the dark civilian he added, "Good to see you again, Señor Ortega."

Ortega smiled. "The pleasure is mine."

Couch nodded and opened the manila folder he had placed in front of him. "Captain William James?" He looked up at the man.

"Yes, sir," James answered.

Couch looked down at the open folder again. "Colonel John Rice?"

"Yes, sir."

"And Mr. Tony Trapasso," Couch said.

Tony gave him the high sign.

"Well, gentlemen," Couch told them, "Mr. Ortega will explain why we're here today . . . Mr. Ortega, please."

In a matter of minutes Ortega told them that the Company was involved with anti-Castro elements and was recruiting and training hundreds of men who would invade Cuba and raise an army that would overthrow the Castro government. The sight chosen for invasion was a place called the Bay of Pigs.

"You men," Ortega said, his voice charged with emotion, "have been chosen to help my people regain their freedom." He then told them about the secret training base in Guatemala, the acquisition of WWII

B-26 bombers that would be used to destroy Castro's air force and the telephone communication system, which depended on microwave relay stations, and the ships already acquired that would transport the invasion force and its equipment to the beach.

"Colonel Rice," Ortega said, "will be in charge of landing operations . . . Captain James will command the invasion fleet, and Señor Trapasso will make a submarine attack in Havana harbor."

Tony almost started out of his seat.

Ortega smiled at him. "We know of your exploits when you commanded submarines during World War Two."

Captain James gave Tony a sideways glance.

"You're here because of that expertise," Couch said.

"I haven't been near a boat in almost ten years. Besides, I've been operating somewhere else for the Company. . . . This is way off my beat."

"Not to worry," Couch told him. "We've managed to get hold of the *Diablo*. You already know everything there is to know about her. The only thing she'll need is a new name."

"You're joking!"

"Certainly not."

Tony took a deep breath and slowly exhaled. "We don't have an experienced crew," he said, hoping to squelch what, to him, was a mad idea.

"We have enough of a crew to take the boat to Havana," Ortega answered.

"What about bringing it back?"

"You and your men will be picked up by one of our surface vessels and returned to the States."

More and more, Tony liked what he heard less and less. "You mean we're not expected to bring the boat back."

"After you expend your torpedoes on suitable targets, you will surface at the entrance to the harbor and scuttle the boat in the main shipping channel."

Tony looked at Captain James. "What's your opinion of this plan?"

"It might work."

"And it might not. From where I sit, there's more in favor of it not working than of it working."

Ortega looked at Couch. "The attack in the harbor must be made. It will throw Castro's defensive forces off balance." Then his eyes went to Tony. "This operation was carefully planned by the Joint Chiefs of Staff."

"Minutes after you leave the boat, you'll be picked up," Couch said. "There will be a high-speed boat standing by. You'll be in communication with it as soon as you surface."

Tony shook his head. "Once the shooting begins the Cubans will be all over us with everything they have. . . . And just suppose there are a few Russian cans there—just what do you think they'll be doing?"

"Mr. Trapasso, they will be your primary targets," Couch responded.

This time Tony did get to his feet, but before he could speak, Couch said, "If you sink or manage to severely damage the Russian destroyers, your escape will be much easier. The Cubans only have a few antiquated gunboats, none of which, according to our sources, are equipped with sonar."

Still on his feet, Tony reminded him that "sinking a Russian destroyer is an act of war."

Couch shrugged. "In the confusion—"

"Señor Trapasso, your attack will be coordinated with a bombing of the naval base and other attacks throughout the island. Once our forces have control, the Russians will never get the evidence needed to prove their ships were torpedoed."

Tony sat down. "How many men do you have for the crew?"

"Forty," Ortega answered. "Maybe forty-five."

"Can you operate with forty-five men?" Couch questioned.

"Eighty men constitute a full crew."

"You have a short run," Captain James said.

"It can be done," Tony said without enthusiasm.

"Mr. Kennedy, the President-elect, has been fully briefed on this operation and has given his approval," Couch told them. "And now, gentlemen, Señor Ortega will give you the operational specifics that have been set for each of your commands."

"D day is April 15, 1961," Ortega said. "That gives us four months to complete training before our men go into action. If everything goes according to our plans, it will be—what's that you say?—a piece . . ."

"A piece of cake," Colonel Rice said.

Ortega smiled broadly. "That's right, it will be 'a piece of cake'!"

7

TWO DAYS AFTER Christmas, Jacob drove out to the cemetery in Elmont, Long Island. He had declined Sy's offer to go with him. His father's plot was at the back end of the cemetery, close to the intersection of Roosevelt and Bethel avenues. Jacob parked the rented car off to one side and walked to where the graves were. Despite the bright sun and almost cloudless sky, there was a cold, cutting wind coming out of the northwest.

Jacob stood and looked at the two graves: his father's, now covered with neatly trimmed yews, and his mother's, still a mound of raw earth with a plastic marker bearing her name. Years before, when he first visited his father's grave, he'd met Yitzhok Grunveldt, a friend of his father who had tended the grave. Yitzhok had willed him a fortune in exchange for his promise to say kaddish for him and his wife. Through the years, Jacob had kept the promise.

But now, he was the only one at the grave, and other than the sound of his own voice as he softly intoned the kaddish for his parents and then Yitzhok and his wife, the wind sighed through the bare limbs and around the tombstones.

When finished, Jacob picked up a small rock and placed it on the tombstone; then he walked slowly back to the car. A few minutes later he drove out of the cemetery and headed toward the Cross Island Parkway.

Nothing significant had happened. He hadn't even wept, and yet, for some inexplicable reason, he felt considerably better than he had in several weeks. He reached over to the radio, switched it on, and found WQXR. He recognized Antoní Dvořák's Serenade in E for String Orchestra. Tara had introduced him to classical music, and through her he had come to appreciate and love the various colors of sound. . . .

Before Jacob realized it, he was on the Belt Parkway, going west past Kennedy Airport. The rest of the day was his until five in the evening, when he had promised to be at Tony's house. Tony and Miriam were going to have some friends over for drinks and dinner . . . "nothing formal," his sister had told him, "probably cold cuts. . . . There will be some very interesting people. . . ."

Changing lanes, Jacob smiled at his sister's euphemism for "eligible women." Her efforts were wasted. His choice of women was limited to those who were willing to be sexual partners without any long-term commitment on his part. Though he had had several intense love affairs since Tara had been institutionalized, he had never considered divorcing Tara and marrying someone else.

Suddenly Jacob saw the exit sign for Canarsie and made the instant decision to leave the Belt Parkway. The area held a host of memories for him. When he was a boy, his father brought the family to the Canarsie pier, an old wooden structure with green seaweed and clumps of black mussels clinging to the round, thick piles. The family rode the Reid Avenue trolley to the end of the line. The trolley line was more like a single-track railroad that ran past people's backyards, and its cars were more open than closed, with canvas-like shades that could be lowered when it rained or snowed. Then, most of the land on either side of the track was farmed by Italian immigrants. Some even raised goats, cows, and pigs. And all of them had chickens, even his father's friend, whom they sometimes visited. Now everything was either paved over or occupied by houses.

Jacob drove up Rockaway Avenue, where the trolley had traveled. Street after street was given over to auto-repair shops, junkyards, and factory buildings for small manufacturing operations. Some of the signs were in Spanish.

He stopped for a red light on the corner of Rockaway and Hegeman avenues. The trolley-car barn had been there, to his left, on the southwest corner, and a Silver Rod cigar store across the street. Now the site of the car barn was occupied by a multistory apartment house, part of a city housing project. There were graffiti all over the walls, and garbage in the street.

The light turned green.

Jacob drove one more block to Lot Avenue, turned left on it, and continued another block to Chester Street, where he made a right turn and stopped in front of the four-story red-brick house where he'd lived for so many years before going to Annapolis.

That the house and the empty lot next to it were still there amazed him. Only the billboards he'd once climbed were gone. Jacob got out of the car and stood in front of the house. This was the same house to which he'd come home on his first leave, shortly after the Battle of Midway. A few blocks up was the synagogue where he and his family had gone that first Saturday after his return. The neighbors . . .

All at once Jacob realized he was being watched by black people from several different windows. He managed to smile and at the same time decided that he was the "stranger in a strange land." He turned around and found himself facing four young men—punks, from the look of them, he decided. Two blacks and two Hispanics.

"What you doin' here?" the shorter of the blacks asked.

"He's goin' to buy the fuckin' buildin'," the other black answered.

"I used to live there," Jacob said, hoping that the explanation would satisfy them, but at the same time having the gut feeling that it wouldn't.

"No shit!" one of the Hispanics replied. "You come back to take a look? You gotta pay to look, ain't that right, guys?"

The four of them laughed.

"More than right, Louie," the other Hispanic said. "Now, listen, sailor man, ya give us your wallet an' ya watch an' we'll let ya get in ya car an' drive away without gettin' hurt and gettin' ya pritty uniform all full of shit-like."

Jacob could feel the color rise in his cheeks. "You're making a mistake," he answered, his voice flat with anger. He hadn't been involved in something like this since he had been a teenager and a couple of other teenagers had tried to take his bicycle away from him.

"No mistake, sailor man," Louie said. "You're the one makin' the fuckin' mistake, if ya think we're foolin' wid ya."

"Cut the shit," the taller of the two blacks demanded. "Let's take him!" And he lunged at Jacob.

Jacob threw a right cross that dropped the punk to his knees.

The remaining three rushed him.

Jacob caught one with an upper cut that knocked him back against the car.

The remaining two pulled back; then suddenly Louie was moving a spring-loaded switchblade knife between his hands. "Now ya goin' ta bleed, sailor man."

Breathing hard, Jacob looked at the blade and moved back toward the lot. He stumbled.

Louie stabbed at him.

Jacob regained his footing, and weaving to the right, escaped the knife thrust.

A window was suddenly thrown open and a woman started yelling in Spanish.

Jacob recognized the word for "police."

One of the punks looked up and answered.

Louie hesitated.

Jacob spotted the neck end of a broken bottle lying on the ground to his right. He scooped it up. "This evens it, doesn't it?" he said, looking straight at Louie. "This can cut you up pretty bad."

Again he heard the woman shout something in Spanish, but this time he was able to catch a glimpse of her out of the side of his right eye.

She had come downstairs and was standing on the stoop, wrapped in a quilted dark tan coat.

The punks looked at her, then at Jacob, and Louie said, "Dis be your lucky day, sailor man." He lowered his hand and closed the switchblade.

"Maybe it's your lucky day too," Jacob answered, aware now of how much he was perspiring and how fast his heart was beating. A man of fifty shouldn't tangle with four hoods, but unless he had given them what they had wanted, he hadn't any other option.

The boys grouped together and slowly crossed to the opposite side of the street.

Jacob waited a few moments before he dropped the broken bottle, and moving closer to the woman, he thanked her for helping him out of a very tight spot. "I grew up here and came back to look at it," he explained, removing his beaked cap and wiping his brow with a handkerchief. "I lived in apartment four C."

"Not much to look at," she answered, casting her eyes toward the lot. "Was it like this when you were here?" She spoke with a slight accent.

"Not much different," Jacob responded, aware of her sloe eyes and long black hair. "By the way, my name is Jacob Miller. And yours is . . . ?"

"Arlene Gomez. One of those boys is my brother Julio."

"I'm glad it wasn't the one named Louie," Jacob said.

She frowned.

"What I mean is that—"

"I warned my brother about Louie, but he won't listen," she complained. "I try to take care of him, but he thinks he's a tough guy."

Jacob glanced at the boys, who were still standing across the street. He'd seen tens of thousands like them come into the Navy and for the first time in their lives learn how to be responsible human beings. But the four he was looking at now weren't much more than a pack of wild dogs. Suddenly he realized just how close he'd come to being hurt . . . perhaps even killed. His eyes went back to Arlene.

"You're an officer, aren't you?" she asked.

"A captain," he answered.

"Well, Captain, I apologize for—"

"Those boys should be the ones who apologize," Jacob said.

"Never happen," she said; then with a smile she added, "I'm glad you weren't hurt."

"So am I . . . I'm too old to get involved in a street fight."

"I have to go now," she said, turning around toward the door.

Jacob moved closer to the stoop. "Miss Gomez, I'd . . ."

She stopped and looked back at him over her right shoulder.

"What I mean is, I'd like to have the opportunity to repay you. Would you have dinner with me?" He could hear the blood pounding in his ears as he waited for her answer.

She didn't answer.

Jacob thought about the cocktail party at his sister's house that evening and asked, "Will you, tonight?"

Arlene smiled. "Yes, I will."

"Good . . . very good. I'll call for you at four-thirty. My sister is giving a cocktail party . . . I promised her I'd be there."

"I'll be ready when you come," she answered, and opening the front door, she went into the vestibule of the house.

Jacob returned to the car, started it, and as he pulled away from the curb, he turned the radio back on. The orgasmic sound of the love music from Richard Wagner's *Tristan and Isolde* filled the confines of the car.

*   *   *

It was two A.M. when Jacob turned off the Belt Parkway and drove up Rockaway Avenue for the second time in less than twelve hours. Arlene was next to him. Her head rested against the back of the seat and her eyes were closed. She seemed to be completely at ease. He glanced at her. She had finely chiseled features, and when she smiled, there was just a hint of a dimple in her right cheek. He turned his eyes away from her just in time to stop for a red light.

"I think you surprised your sister by bringing me," Arlene said. "There were two unescorted women there, who looked daggers at me all night."

Jacob laughed. "I wasn't sure you noticed. Miriam has been trying for years to match me up with one of her friends."

"But you're a confirmed bachelor, right?" She lifted her head up and opened her eyes.

"I'm married," he said softly. He sensed her stiffening. "My wife, Tara, has been institutionalized for several years." He put the car in motion again. "She was raped and beaten—"

"Oh, my God," Arlene exclaimed, shaking her head.

"I was in Korea when it happened."

"I'm so sorry for you, for her. . . . I wondered about you—I mean, you somehow just didn't seem to be the contented-bachelor type."

"What did I seem to be?"

"Self-possessed," she answered. "But I assumed that went with the rank. And sad . . . at the same time you seemed sad. Contented bachelors aren't sad; they're too busy being contented to be sad about anything long enough for it to show."

"And you, what about you?"

She positioned herself catercorner on the seat before she said, "I'm thirty-five. I was married when I was twenty-three. It lasted a few years. But it never really worked. He's in the theater and you know how theater people are—they must be the center of attention all the time. After a while I felt myself being smothered, and rather than die of emotional suffocation, I left him."

"I heard you tell Tony that you teach Spanish literature at Brooklyn College. Is that what you want to do for the rest of your life?" Jacob asked.

"I'm also working on my PhD in the same field," she said. "Maybe I'll do some critical writing. . . . There are some very fine writers in South and Central America whose works haven't been translated into English. I might try my hand at that. But the answer to your question is yes . . . I love teaching."

Jacob took his pipe and tobacco pouch out and with one hand tried to fill the pipe bowl.

"Let me do that," Arlene said, taking the pipe and pouch from him. "You never told me whether you're stationed here."

"My ship is in Norfolk."

"Your ship?"

"I'm the captain of the aircraft carrier *Concord*," he said.

"My God, wasn't there a fire on board—"

"Yes, a bad one. We lost several men."

"How very sad. Such useless deaths."

Jacob stared straight ahead. "They died trying to save the ship. They were brave men, very brave men."

She handed him the pipe and pouch. "It's filled," she said. "Can you light it?"

"Yes," he answered, wondering if she blamed him for the deaths of the men.

"I'm almost home," Arlene commented. "Thank your sister and brother-in-law for their hospitality. I enjoyed meeting them and their friends."

Jacob nodded and turned into Lot Avenue, then Chester Street, and stopped in front of the house.

"Thank you for a lovely evening," Arlene said.

Jacob took the pipe out of his mouth. "Will I see you again?" he asked, suddenly feeling his heart race. He wanted to see her again, to get to know her better.

She hesitated. "Maybe it would be wiser to—"

"I wasn't responsible for the deaths of those men," Jacob said. "It was an accident, and I grieve for them."

"I know that."

"Tell me—"

"Our lives are so different," Arlene said. "What you see here is my world, at least until I can change it . . . and that's several years away."

He put the pipe down on the dashboard and took hold of her gloved hands. "I'm not interested in the differences between our worlds, or what would be the wise thing to do . . . I want to see you again. Tomorrow night?"

"Yes," she answered.

He squeezed her hands; then, letting go of them, he said, "I'll pick you up at seven."

She smiled at him, then let herself out of the car.

"Wait, I'll walk you to the door," Jacob told her. He left the car, and taking hold of her arm, escorted her up the steps.

"Good night," she said, facing him. "I really did have a wonderful time. Thank you."

"So did I," Jacob responded. He wanted very much to take her in his arms and kiss her, but didn't. Instead, he said, "Go inside."

A moment later she was on the other side of the door and disappeared into the dimly lit hallway.

Jacob returned to the car and lighted his pipe again before he began to drive.

8

IT WAS HILARY'S New Year's Eve party and the large apartment she now owned in the Dakota, a fashionable apartment house located on New York's West Side. Its rooms were filled with a variety of people from the worlds of high fashion, art, publishing, and film. It was decorated with hundreds of red, green, and orange balloons. Holiday trimmings and tinsel were everywhere.

Andrew was with his date for the evening, Ellie Erics, a twenty-year-old blond model whom he'd met two days before in offices of *The Complete Woman*. He'd spent Christmas Eve with his father at the Trapassos, and as much as he enjoyed being with them, he much preferred the exciting atmosphere where he now was and the excitement of being with a beautiful woman.

Andrew led Ellie to a hot buffet. "Allow me to have a plate fixed for you," he said. "Just tell me what you want."

"Everything looks so good," she said. "I'd love to have some fried rice, but it's loaded with calories."

"Tonight forget the calories," he answered, looking

directly at her breasts, which were bare almost to her nipples.

"Andrew, you're staring at me!" she chided.

He grinned wolfishly at her. "Pose for me," he said. On their first date he'd asked her to pose nude for him—he wanted to paint her and he desperately wanted to go to bed with her.

She fluttered her eyelashes at him. "I said I'd think about it."

He was about to tell her not to take too much time to think about it, because he had to be back at the Academy by the fifth of January, when he saw his mother moving toward him with a man in tow whom he did not recognize.

Hilary called his name, and when she came up to him, Andrew introduced Ellie to her. "Ah, yes, Miss Erics—I remember, you're one of the models in the spread we're doing in June on the latest in swimwear." And before Ellie could answer, Hilary said, "Andrew, this is Sean Devlin . . ."

Again there were introductions, but this time between Ellie and Mr. Devlin; then Andrew pointed a finger at Devlin. "I remember the name now—you're the author of the best-seller *All Hands, Now Hear This . . .*"

"And former shipmate of your father's," Devlin answered with a smile.

For a moment Andrew just looked at Devlin. There was nothing unusual about him. He was a man in his early fifties, with graying hair and a slight paunch. He wore tortoise-framed bifocals that gave him a professorial air.

"I saw some of your paintings," Devlin said. "I like them very much."

Andrew's eyes went to his mother. She'd set something up, or was trying to.

"Would you be interested in doing the cover jacket for my next book?" Devlin asked.

"Oh, Andrew, that would be wonderful!" Ellie exclaimed.

"That's very kind of you, Mr. Devlin—"

"Sean, please."

Andrew nodded. "It is very kind of you, Sean. But I'll be back at the Academy and my schedule will be hectic."

"Think about it," Hilary suggested.

Andrew didn't answer.

"I must see to my other guests," Hilary said, smiling at them. "I'll speak to you later, Sean." And she was gone.

There was something in the tone of Hilary's voice that made Andrew wonder whether she was sleeping with Devlin. Despite the fact that he knew it was none of his business, the possibility rankled him into pursing his lips.

"Is something wrong?" Ellie questioned.

"Nothing," he answered.

Devlin offered Ellie a cigarette, which she accepted. "You?" he asked, holding the gold cigarette case out to Andrew. "They're Egyptian. I order them from Dunhill."

Andrew hesitated. Ordinarily, he didn't smoke.

"They're very good," Devlin said. "They're slightly stronger than the ones we have here."

Andrew nodded and took one.

Devlin held the lighter for Ellie and Andrew. "What do you think?" he questioned, looking at Ellie.

"I like them," she responded with a smile.

"And you, Andrew?" Devlin asked.

"You're right . . . they are a bit stronger."

Devlin beamed; then he said, "I was your dad's XO on PTs—he saved my life, you know."

"I didn't know," Andrew answered.

"You didn't tell me your father was a hero," Ellie said.

Andrew gave her a quick glance. He'd told her almost nothing about his father. He didn't want her as a confidante; he wanted to play games with her in bed.

"When we first met, we weren't exactly the ideal team," Devlin reminisced. "But I soon learned he was one hell of a skipper, one hell of a man."

Andrew took a deep drag on the cigarette and let the smoke escape through his nostrils. He was so damn tired of being told how brave his father was, how . . . everything! Even his mother couldn't let go of the war hero. "If you'll excuse us, Mr. Devlin, I see some old friends."

"Will you think about doing the illustration for my book?" Devlin asked.

"I'll think about it, but I don't think I'll have the time. . . . It's been a pleasure to meet you."

Devlin offered his hand.

"A pleasure," Andrew said, shaking the older man's hand; then, taking Ellie by the arm, he steered her out of the living room and into another room, from whose windows they could look south toward the Empire State Building, whose top was illuminated for the holidays with red and white lights.

"You were rude to that man," Ellie said.

Andrew opened the window, crushed the remainder of the cigarette against the side of the building, and then let it fall.

"It's cold, Andrew!" Ellie complained, crossing her arms over her bare breasts.

Andrew faced her. "Let's go somewhere."

She looked confused.

"Somewhere where we could . . ." He put his arms around her.

"But the party is here," Ellie said, looking up at him. "And it's not even midnight yet."

He put his lips to hers and kissed her passionately, finding her tongue with his. He could forget about his father being a war hero for a little while if he could get her to go to bed with him. . . .

Dressed in a blue suit and wearing a silver party hat, Warren sat at the Circle in the Square, a singles bar on York Avenue and Seventy-eighth Street in Manhattan. He had had several invitations to see the new year in with friends, including Tony, who had told him that he and Miriam were having a few friends over for a quiet New Year's Eve. But Warren, through the years, had learned that Miriam's few friends could easily mean fifty to sixty people, and more recently, since he and Hilary had been divorced, Miriam always seemed to have several friends who were on the prowl for a second husband. He had honestly told Tony that he would be dull company and really didn't have any desire to meet any of Miriam's friends. Tony, of course, had understood. . . .

The place was dimly lit, smoky, and noisy. The small dance floor was crowded with couples . . . some of the dancers strained against each other, while others never touched, but gyrated wildly to the music.

Warren looked at the remaining Scotch in his glass. It was his second. Since the divorce, he drank more than he previously had. He was bored, more often than not frustrated, and drinking took the edge off both feelings. He signaled the barkeep to fill his glass;

then he looked at his watch. It was only eleven . . . another hour to go before midnight . . . and then what?

The barkeep filled Warren's glass and he nodded. The sum of fifty dollars covered an open bar and a smorgasbord, if he wanted something to eat. He remembered having had ham and eggs for breakfast, but he had forgotten to eat lunch.

He lifted his drink and was just about to drink, when he suddenly decided that he had had enough—enough Scotch, enough of the noise and smoke. He was going back to his apartment and go to sleep. Maybe, on the way there, he'd find an open luncheonette and stop off for coffee and a sandwich.

Warren stood up.

"You look as if you've had enough."

The woman was on the stool to his left. He hadn't even noticed her before she spoke.

"I feel the same way," she said. "I thought it would be a good idea to be out tonight . . . but it was dumb."

"I thought the same thing," Warren said, examining her more closely. He judged her to be in her late thirties . . . possibly early forties. She had long red hair, and the black cocktail dress she wore molded to a trim figure.

She smiled up at him. "My eyes are blue and I have freckles on my face, on the tops of my breasts, and in other places."

Warren colored. "I'm sorry . . . I didn't mean to be so obvious."

"Did I pass inspection?"

For a moment he hesitated; then to himself he said, *What the hell*, but to her he said, "Absolutely. My name is Warren Troost." He offered his hand.

She shook it. "Carol Langston."

"Well, Miss . . . or is it Mrs. Langston?" he asked, looking at her left hand and seeing a wedding band.

She held up her left hand. "I was Mrs. Langston until six months ago. It helps keep some of the wolves away." She lowered her hand. "Carol will do fine, if we're going to spend some time together. . . . Are we going to spend some time together, Warren?"

He liked her directness and decided to be as direct himself. "I would like to see those freckles on the tops of your breasts and in those other places you mentioned to me," he told her, expecting her to flinch. But when she didn't, he said, "My apartment is a few blocks from here."

She nodded, stood up, and took hold of his hand. "It's not going to be easy to get through this crowd."

"Just hold on," Warren answered, and with her in tow he threaded his way through crowds of revelers toward the door.

Outside, a light snow was falling.

"I have three grown children," Carol said.

Aware that she had entwined her arm with his, Warren told her, "One son—a midshipman at Annapolis."

She faced him. "You're in the Navy, aren't you?"

"I'm a captain."

"I knew there was something different about you."

"Not *that* different, I hope?"

"It was the way you held yourself . . . the way you sat," she explained.

"Stiff."

"Straight," Carol countered.

In a few minutes they were in Warren's apartment. "I stay here when I'm in New York," he said, "and when my son comes up, he uses it." He helped her off with the black seal coat and hung it in the hall closet; then he removed his own coat and did the same with it. "Would you care for a drink?"

"White wine?"

Warren led the way into the living room and went to the bar cart. "Just enough for a small glass," he said, picking up the bottle. "The glasses are in the kitchen."

She followed him.

Warren poured the wine into a long-stemmed glass and handed it to her.

"Aren't you having anything?" she asked.

"I had more than enough at the bar . . . but you go ahead and drink."

She raised the glass. "To the fates that brought us together."

Warren acknowledged the toast with a nod. "Would you like to listen to some music?" he asked, walking back into the living room.

"If you would like to," she answered, coming after him.

He shrugged. "No, not really." And moving close to her, he took the wineglass out of her hand. He put his arms around her. "I'm glad you spoke to me," he said.

She came close against him. "I would have sooner, but I couldn't think of an opening . . . but when I saw you getting ready to leave . . . well . . . " She smiled. "You know what happened." She leaned her head against his chest. "I wasn't going to let you get away without trying."

"How did you know I wasn't just going to the head—I mean, the bathroom?"

"You looked like I felt—bored and determined to do something about it."

Conscious of the floral scent of her perfume,

Warren gently put his lips to hers, and then, as he felt her respond, pressed with more ardor.

Her arms circled his neck. "Hold me tight," she whispered.

He delighted in the feel of her body against his. He hadn't been this close to a woman for several months; not that opportunities hadn't come his way, but rather that he hadn't had the interest or the emotional energy to enter into a meaningful relationship. And he was too old for one-night stands, especially with women young enough to be his daughters.

Warren moved his hand down the broad back and over her nates, while she slowly gyrated her hips.

"Maybe we'll really like each other," she said.

He nodded. "Maybe," he answered, and taking hold of her hand, he led her into the bedroom.

Mike and Sy were together, attending a New Year's Eve party given by Mike's frat brother Allen Sides, who lived in a huge corner house on Shore Road in Brooklyn and whose father owned a large medical advertising agency in Manhattan. Both young men were dressed casually in slacks and sport coats and blended in with the other men at the party.

Neither Mike nor Sy had a date. Allen had assured Mike, when he'd extended the invitation by phone the day after Christmas, that there'd be "plenty of women for you and your friend." There were, but most of them Mike pronounced to be dogs. And those who weren't had that I-want-to-get-married look, according to Mike.

Sy laughed at Mike's comments.

"Not funny," Mike said as the two of them advanced toward the bar. "The last thing either of us needs is to become seriously involved with a girl. Now it's just fun and games."

"But just suppose you met someone"—he looked around the crowded room, and spotting a beautiful dark-haired young woman dancing with a man, pointed —"someone like that girl over there with that tall guy. She's one of the best-looking girls here."

Mike studied her for a moment. "See the way she's dancing with him? Close enough for him to feel her belly against his."

"So?"

"That's one of the signs," Mike said. "Yeah, that's one of the signs that she's hearing wedding bells in her head, unless she's giving it to him without any strings attached. But she's certainly giving it to him." He took Sy by the arm, led him to the bar, and poured two neat Scotches. "*Salute!*" Mike toasted, giving the word an Italian pronunciation.

Sy repeated the word and the accent.

The two of them bolted the shot down.

"Again?" Mike asked, starting to pour another for himself.

Sy hesitated.

"C'mon, it's New Year's Eve!"

"What the hell, why not?"

Mike grinned, and this time he toasted, "To our futures, may they be brilliant and full of glory!"

They drank the second shot as quickly as the first.

"I think my father is seeing someone—a woman, I mean," Sy said.

Mike put the empty shot glass down on the bar.

"I hope she makes him happy," Sy said, placing his glass next to Mike's.

Mike nodded. "But doesn't it bother you?"

"He needs someone," Sy answered. "He has me

and the family, but he needs someone with whom he'd be able to share his life."

"I guess Andy's dad is in the same boat, so to speak."

"Worse, maybe, because of the divorce."

"I heard my dad tell my mother that Warren still loves Hilary. He says Hilary is into this women's-lib thing—Warren never wanted the divorce."

"I always liked Hilary," Sy said. "I'm sorry she's separated herself from the family."

Mike agreed, and putting his hand on Sy's shoulder, he commented, "You know, even though you're my cousin, I still like you."

Sy laughed. "The feeling is mutual, pal."

Mike looked around the room. "Well, we have to make a decision, Mr. Miller. Do we stay, or do we go?"

"If we go, where do we go?"

"Good question. But if we stay, what do we do?"

"Good question."

"Let chance make the decision?"

"Certainly," Sy responded, taking out a quarter. "Call." He thumbed the coin into the air.

"Tails we go!"

The coin turned over several times on the way up and on the way down before Sy caught it and put his hand over it. "Tails we go, right?"

Mike nodded.

Sy removed his hand from the coin. "Tails!"

"Okay, where do we go?" Mike asked.

Sy pocketed the coin. "I have a yen for some clams on the half-shell and maybe a couple of Nathan's hot dogs."

"Coney Island?" Mike questioned.

"Can you come up with a better place?"

"No, absolutely not. Coney Island, here we come!" Mike exclaimed.

"You're joking," Arlene said, looking at Jacob.

He smiled at her. "This is something special . . . much more exciting than any party could be." He was at the wheel of a rented car, guiding it through the Lincoln Tunnel.

"But tell me where we're going," she insisted.

"You'll see when we get there."

"How far away is it?"

"Not too far," Jacob answered. This was his seventh date with Arlene. He'd come up every weekend since he'd first met her, and though there had been a display of considerable passion on both their parts when he'd kiss her good night, Jacob had not attempted to caress her below the waist.

"I'm dressed for a party," Arlene reminded him.

"And you look beautiful," he told her. She was wearing a green dress with a slight décolleté neckline that allowed him to see part of the valley between her breasts.

"Jake, do you know where we are?"

He nodded. "Certainly. Even if there weren't road signs, I'd know—I'm with you in a car—"

"Your friends are going to be very angry with you," she told him.

He shook his head. "When they see you, they'll forget to be angry."

They drove for several minutes without speaking; then Jacob slowed and made a right turn.

"That last sign said Newark Airport," Arlene said.

"I told you I knew exactly where I was going," Jacob said, heading for a hangar. "Close your eyes and keep them closed until I tell you to open them."

"Is that an order, Captain?" she questioned with mock sarcasm.

"An order," he answered.

"Yes, sir." She saluted him. "Eyes closed, Captain."

"Keep them that way," Jacob said, slowing and turning into the space between two hangars before he brought the car to a halt. "Okay, open your eyes."

The light from the car's headlights illuminated a white twin-engine plane.

Arlene looked questioningly at him.

"It's mine," he said, smiling. "I bought it two days ago. It's a twin-engine Cessna. Now I can fly up here whenever I want, and I don't have to depend on the air shuttle or the train."

"But an airplane costs—"

He put his finger across her lips. "You must have guessed," he said softly, "that I have money."

"Yes. But—"

"I never before did anything like this," he said. "I guess I thought it was time for me to spend some of the several millions of dollars I have."

"Several millions of dollars?" She barely managed to get the words out.

"It's something of a long story," he told her. "I'll tell it to you, but first I'm going to take you for a ride in my new airplane."

"Now?"

"Yes, now."

"Aye, aye, Captain," Arlene responded, smiling broadly.

9

FILLED WITH ANXIETY, Tony boarded the submarine for the first time in the late afternoon of January 20. He hadn't been on a submarine for almost fifteen years, and yet in his mind he was able to visualize each and every one of its many controls; he was even able to remember its operating peculiarities.

The boat, painted gray without a flag on its jackstaff, was hidden under a corrugated-metal shed in a cove ten miles east of the town of Woodbine, Georgia, at the mouth of the Satilla River. The crew, a ragtag group of mercenaries, all of whom had previous submarine experience, lived aboard the boat. The area, for a distance of three hundred yards from the shed, was guarded by Company men and several attack-trained Doberman pinschers.

There were three men on the foredeck. Any one of them looked as if he could have stepped from the boat's steel deck onto the wooden deck of a pirate ship in a bygone age and been completely at ease.

None of them paid the slightest attention to Tony until he said, "One of you go below and get the XO."

"Who wants him?" the shortest of the three asked. He was unshaven, wore a dirty white beaked cap, faded blue jeans, and a gray sweatshirt. A sheathed, bone-handled knife hung from his belt. The other two were similarly dressed, but hatless.

Tony didn't like his tone. "The captain," he answered sharply. "Now, move it!"

The man hesitated.

"Sailor, get the XO topside now," Tony ordered. This was quickly promising to be an experience that neither he nor the men he was going to command would forget.

The man slid past Tony and disappeared down the open forward hatch.

The two remaining men eyed him with suspicion.

Suddenly a rangy figure of a man stepped through the conning-tower door and strode toward Tony, saluted, and said, "You weren't expected until the day after tomorrow, Captain." He spoke with a definite German accent.

Tony returned the salute, but didn't explain why he'd chosen to come aboard two days earlier. "My name is Trapasso, Tony Trapasso. What's yours?"

"Klaus Schmidt."

Tony nodded, half-expecting the man to click his heels. He figured Schmidt for a former Kriegsmarine officer. "Get the crew assembled topside," he said.

"Aye, aye, sir," Schmidt responded, saluting again.

Schmidt turned to the man Tony had spoken to and told him to call the men to the foredeck; then he explained to Tony that the boat's announcing system wasn't operating.

"Why?"

"It's being rewired," Schmidt answered. "It should be usable tomorrow."

The men began to come up on deck through the forward hatch and the conning-tower door.

Tony studied them and they were obviously doing the same thing with him. Most of them were dark-skinned Latin types. But a few, like Schmidt, were Nordic—Schmidt had wispy dark blond hair and blue eyes—and some looked Slavic. Tony counted thirty men.

"This all?" he asked, when it was obvious that no other men were going to appear.

"All present and accounted for," the XO answered.

Tony ran his hand across his jaw. The boat would have been hard enough to manage with half a crew, but with almost a third less than half, the task would be more difficult by a factor that could possibly cost them their lives.

"Form up into ranks," Tony ordered.

Grumbling, the men obeyed.

Tony walked down the length of the first rank and took a moment to look at each man. He did the same to the second rank; then he positioned himself in front of them and said, "My name is Tony Trapasso. I'm the captain of this boat. This isn't going to be a joy-ride. We have a mission to accomplish and we will do our very best to accomplish it successfully. To do that, all of us—"

"We don't need a pep talk," one of the men said.

He was one of the three men Tony had seen when he'd first come aboard.

"We know why we're here and what we gotta do," the man called out.

Tony immediately recognized the implicit challenge in what the man had said. And without bothering to ask the man's name, Tony said, "Pack your gear and get off this boat now."

"You can't do that. I have a contract—"

Tony turned to Schmidt. "Get him off the boat now," he ordered.

"Aye, aye, sir," Schmidt answered, and went over to where the man was standing.

As if nothing had happened, Tony picked up the thread of what he had been saying. "The first order of business is to make sure that you understand me. This submarine will be run just like every American submarine is. That means there is a chain of command. That means orders will be followed. That means that each of you is expected to do whatever must be done to ensure the success of the mission. Do any of you have any trouble understanding what I just said?" He waited a few moments before he continued. "No one. Good. . . . All right, Mr. Schmidt, why isn't that man off this boat?" Tony bellowed.

"He will not go."

Tony strode over to him. The man was a half-head taller than himself. "You have three seconds to move, mister," he growled, staring straight at him.

The man started to swing.

Reflexively Tony dropped into a crouch, rammed his shoulder into the man's chest, and gave him a quick hand chop across the bridge of his nose, smashing it.

With blood gushing from his nose, the man staggered backward.

"Get him off the boat," Tony snapped; then to the rest of the crew he said, "I want each of you to go below and report to your duty station now. I will make an inspection of who is where in the next five minutes. . . . Ship's company dismissed."

The men dropped through the forward hatch or went aft to the conning-tower door.

Tony waited until Schmidt had removed the man

from the boat and returned to the deck. "Come with me while I make my inspection," Tony said. "Make sure you have a pad and a pencil. I want a note made of any correction I order . . . and after the inspection, we'll run a diving drill."

Unable to control either the tone of his voice or the expression of surprise on his face, Schmidt asked, "A diving drill here, sir?"

"Here, Mr. Schmidt. Before we go anywhere where we can get ourselves killed."

"Aye, aye, Captain."

The weeks slipped by. Tony had succeeded in welding the ragtag group he had met the first day aboard into a disciplined crew.

He'd spend ten days on the boat and five days at home. The crew's schedule followed his. At the end of every ten-day work period they were taken by bus at night to Jacksonville, Florida, where at government expense they were permitted to fly anywhere in the United States.

During these five-day intervals the boat—nicknamed the *Gray Ghost* by the men—was completely sealed off, but it was still guarded by patrols of men and dogs.

The ten days that Tony spent aboard the boat, as far as Miriam or, for that matter, anyone else was concerned, took him to various capital cities in Europe, where he was in the process of negotiating very important business arrangements. Telephone calls between him and Miriam were arranged to pass through special Company circuits handled by operators who made them sound international.

The *Gray Ghost* was in excellent shape, and as the weeks passed, its condition was improved by the men, who quickly realized that Tony would not settle for anything less than excellence.

Practically all of the training was done at night, including the practice dives, which took place twenty miles offshore, at depths ranging from one hundred feet to three hundred and sixty, the boat's maximum diving depth. Because the training took place during the winter, the weather helped obscure the departure and arrival of the *Gray Ghost* from its protective shed, and because the ocean was particularly rough at that time of year, there were few pleasure craft around to see them when they surfaced, prior to coming into the cove.

On April 1, traditionally designated April Fool's Day, Tony received secret orders from Langley. They were delivered by chopper at four o'clock in the afternoon. He was to make his attack in coordination with the air strike against selected military targets in Havana on April 16, which meant that the *Gray Ghost* had to be in position, just outside the harbor, before dawn on that day.

Tony decided to divide the voyage south to Cuba into two parts. The first would be carried out at night, with the snorkel feeding air to the men and the diesels. During the second part, when he could see the lights of the city through the periscope, he'd switch to battery power and continue to use it until he was ready to surface and scuttle the boat.

Tony had no intention of revealing the date of the operation to any member of the crew. On the night before the scheduled operation, he'd order the boat out for what the crew would expect to be another practice dive. And only when they were under way and heading south would he make the announcement over the 1MC as to where they were actually going.

The operation was still fifteen days away. In that span of time, he'd have his five days home with Miriam.

10

ON SATURDAY AFTERNOON, April 8, Andrew met Ellie in the lobby of the Harbor View Motel in Annapolis. He greeted her with a hug and a kiss and then asked, "Did you have a good trip down?" It was only then that he realized that she looked less than her beautiful self.

Since New Year's Eve, when they had first slept together, Andrew had made the trip up to New York whenever he could, or Ellie had come down to Annapolis to be with him, even if it was for one night. During the time they spent together, Andrew had sketched her dozens of times, in dozens of different poses, some of them so erotic that they could have been considered pornographic. But this time she'd come down because he was ready to start a painting of her. The easel and paints were already in the room.

He stepped back and studied her for a moment. Her face was a tad puffier than usual. He wouldn't have noticed it, but just before he came down into the lobby, he'd been looking at drawings he'd made of her face.

"I wasn't feeling well on the bus," she said. "There was a man smoking a cigar a few seats in front of me."

Andrew put his arm over her shoulders. "A nap and you'll be okay," he said sympathetically. The word "nap" was a euphemism for sex in the afternoon. And he started to lead her down the corridor to the elevator. "I managed to get a room with a northern light."

Ellie answered, "I'm only staying tonight."

They were in the elevator before Andrew said, "I thought you were going to leave Monday morning." He hadn't seen her for two weeks and was looking forward not only to painting her but also to spending long hours in bed with her.

She shrugged but did not answer.

Andrew waited until they were in the room and the door was closed before he said, "I know something is wrong. Tell me what it is."

Ellie went to the window. The drapes were open and she looked out over the nearby marina, where a variety of small trim pleasure craft swayed gently on the sun-splashed water. "I have an appointment with a doctor on Monday morning at nine."

He gave her a questioning look and he began to perspire.

She faced him. "I'm going to have an abortion."

He repeated the word.

"It's no big deal," she said. "I must have forgotten to take the pill."

"How far gone are you?"

"Six weeks, maybe seven."

He took a deep breath and slowly exhaled.

"I wouldn't have told you until it was over," she said. "But I know I look awful and I do have to leave tomorrow."

Andrew wasn't sure of his own feelings about her having an abortion. He had never imagined himself in this kind of situation.

"After a few days' rest, I'll be fine," Ellie said. She left the window and went to where Andrew was standing. "It's nothing to get upset about. Once I have a real nap, we'll have the other kind and then—"

"Maybe we should talk about this," he suggested. "I mean, I'm kind of confused by what you're telling me. I am the father, aren't I?"

She took a step backward. "You mean, you think I've been sleeping with other men when I'm not with you."

"It's been known to happen," he responded sullenly.

"Well, I haven't," she shot back angrily. "I don't sleep around the way some of the models do."

"I'm sorry," Andrew apologized. "I never believed that you did."

"The baby is yours . . . don't ever doubt it."

Andrew suddenly was uncomfortable. All at once, his thoughts were flying off in several different directions. If he married her, he'd have to leave the Academy. That wouldn't be the worst thing that could happen to him, that was for sure. But then he'd have to face his father, and that damn well might be the worst experience of his life. For a moment he studied Ellie. When it got down to the bottom line, he liked her well enough to screw, but he didn't really love her. He began to feel physically awkward, and locking his hands behind his back, he said with little conviction in his voice, "Maybe you shouldn't have the abortion."

Ellie shook her head. "I don't want to have the baby," she told him. "I don't want to become a mother. I don't want to be tied down."

Andrew frowned. He had expected her to ask him to marry her, and that would have presented him with the problems he was already thinking about. But her attitude pulled the proverbial rug out from under him.

"Now, don't tell me that you're really the domestic type, because I know differently," Ellie chided. "Besides, I discussed this whole matter with your mother, and—"

"My mother? What does she have to do with this?" He unlocked his hands and color came into his cheeks. "You spoke to her before you came down here?"

"Believe me, she understands the situation."

Andrew began to pace, stopped, and in a voice edged with sarcasm asked, "You didn't happen to contact my father and discuss the 'situation,' as you call it, with him?"

She shook her finger at him. "Don't be nasty, Andrew. It doesn't become you. Your mother and I see eye-to-eye on this."

Andrew leaned against the wall. He was both ashamed and angry that Ellie had involved his mother in what, in his opinion, should have been their problem and their decision. After all, if he was man enough to get her pregnant, he should be man enough to . . . "God damn, Ellie," he railed, frustrated at not being able to finish his thought, "you didn't have any right to involve my mother. You didn't have any right until you spoke to me and I decided what to do. I mean, I'm the kid's father, right?"

"And I'm its mother," she answered in a hard brittle voice. "I'm its mother. But I'm not going to be its mother, understand. Your mother agrees that it would be a stupid thing to do, especially since I still have a brilliant career ahead."

"With my mother's help, no doubt?" he snapped.

"That's ugly," Ellie responded. "Ugly and not worthy of you. I went to her because . . . because she's a woman of the world and in the forefront of the women's-rights movement."

Andrew didn't answer.

"The choice is mine, Andrew," Ellie said, her voice now gentler than before. "It's my body."

"Naturally, my mother would agree with that," he responded. "But what about me? My feelings?"

"Be honest, Andrew, you don't want to marry me—since it would mean that you had to leave the Academy to do it."

Again color came into his face.

Ellie nodded. "I don't want to marry you either. What we had, we had, and it was good for me. You're a kind, gentle lover, but now, and for some years to come, you'd make a lousy husband." She smiled at him. "Don't be angry at me for saying that, Andrew—you know it's true. There are things that you want to do that you couldn't do if you were married." She paused for a few moments before she said, "I'd much rather be your friend than the woman you felt you were forced to marry, and I'd much rather bring a child into the world who would be wanted by me and its father, rather than one who would be only the cause of a marriage neither of its parents wanted."

Rubbing his chin, Andrew admitted to himself that he had never given much thought to the things Ellie had just said, even though he had heard his mother express similar sentiments many times. But so much of his life had been spent in "a man's world," it seemed that no matter what women did, they did it only because men allowed them to do it. But now, for the first time, he was seeing something from a woman's point of view and he realized that it was right. Right for the woman, for the man, and certainly for the unborn child.

"Are you still angry?" Ellie asked.

Andrew shook his head. "No," he said, going to her and taking hold of her hands.

She smiled up at him. "I'd like to take a real nap now, and afterward we could pretend-nap together."

"Before or after I start the painting?"

Ellie laughed. "I'll leave that to you."

11

WARREN ENTERED ADMIRAL George Hicks's Pentagon office and was surprised to find the admiral wearing a dark blue business suit and red-and-blue-striped tie. The previous afternoon Warren had received a phone call from the CNO's office, ordering him to report to Admiral Hicks at ten-thirty the following morning.

Hicks, a short, squarely built man, returned his salute and said, "It's a real pleasure to meet you, Captain. Please sit down."

Hicks placed his hand on a manila folder. "You've achieved an enviable record, Warren—I hope you don't mind my calling you Warren?" He raised his eyebrows slightly.

"No, sir."

Hicks smiled; then he said, "You seem to excel in what I like to term 'strange operations,' those that, more often than not, are one of a kind."

"Some of them were that," Warren responded.

"Your name and record were brought to my attention in a recent conversation with . . . well, who it was really doesn't matter. What does matter is that I need you to volunteer for another one of those "strange operations' that are your specialty."

Even as Warren listened to Hicks, he became aware of the austere atmosphere of the room. Nothing was on the walls. The desk and chairs were Navy issue. There were a phone and the manila folder on the desk, nothing else. It was, he realized, a temporary office set up . . .

"You can, of course, be ordered," Hicks continued. "But I'd prefer it if you volunteered."

"Can you tell me what I'd be volunteering for?"

Hicks fished out a pack of cigarettes from his jacket pocket and offered one to Warren.

"Thank you, but I prefer my pipe."

"By all means, then, smoke it," Hicks told him. "There's no need to maintain the usual formality between us."

"I'd like to know what I'm getting into," Warren said.

"For openers, I'm obviously involved with the Office of Naval Intelligence."

"I guessed that much."

"And I have connections to other government organizations," Hicks said, letting smoke flow out of his nostrils.

"Yes, I guessed that too."

"So you know that whatever I tell you has to do with a clandestine operation and, therefore, is considered top-secret information."

Warren nodded, and taking the pipe out of his mouth, used it to point around the room. "This is all temporary . . . for the meeting, only?"

Hicks nodded.

"What kind of an operation will it be?" Warren asked, smoking his pipe again.

"A landing."

"What?" The pipe almost fell out of his mouth.

"Not anything like the landings you previously . . . This is, by comparison, very small . . . almost minuscule."

Warren regained his composure. "Where?"

"Cuba, a place named the Bay of Pigs."

"You mean we're going to put troops ashore—"

Hicks held up his hand. "Nothing of the kind. Some of our people will go ashore with the invading force, but not in any numbers. No, the main force will consist of anti-Castro people, who have been training in special camps. Our job is to get them ashore. We have a commander for the invasion force and a commander for the land operations."

"Then what role would I have?" Warren asked.

"Backup . . . just in case something goes wrong and the men have to be taken off the beach."

"How many ships?"

"Two DEs—the *Pierce* and the *Nathan*."

"Air cover?"

"None."

"How far offshore will I be?" Warren asked.

"Five miles."

Warren puffed on his pipe. "How much time do I have?"

"Not much . . . a few days. This was a last-minute decision—I mean, to put a couple of DEs offshore. It's not our play, if you know what I mean."

"I think I do."

"Will you volunteer?" Hicks asked.

"I thought I had," Warren answered.

"I thought so too," Hicks responded with a grin, and extended his hand. "Welcome aboard, Warren."

Warren had chosen the *Nathan* for his command ship on April 13, when he had been flown from Washington to Guantánamo, where the *Nathan* and the *Pierce* had put in for a twenty-four-hour layover. Both ships were ostensibly on a routine "training cruise." At least half of each ship's complement were reservists on their annual "two-week training cruise."

But now Warren was on the bridge, worrying over the situation. Commander William Bryce, the ship's skipper, was on his right, and Lieutenant Steven Holt, the XO, was several paces behind him. He'd been told by Hicks at a second meeting that the attack would be "coordinated with air strikes." And the admiral broadly hinted that a submarine would attack ships in Havana's harbor.

He turned to look at the *Pierce*, running five hundred yards astern. It too was buttoned up—blacked out and its crew at battle stations.

Warren faced front. Bothered by the knowledge that half his crew was inexperienced, he was even more bothered by the fact that he was not permitted to be in communication with the attack force and that if his ships needed to cover a withdrawal, he would have to receive permission from Washington before he could take any action.

Suddenly the radar watch reported, "Bogeys . . . bearing eight five . . . range, twenty miles . . . altitude, twelve thousand . . . speed, two hundred knots."

Warren checked his watch. "On time," he said with satisfaction, and looked to the starboard, where some three miles away the three troop and supply ships hove to.

"We'll be reversing course in ten minutes, Captain," Commander William Bryce, the ship's skipper, said.

Warren acknowledged the information with a nod and focused his attention on the attack ships.

"Landing craft under way," the XO reported.

The strike aircraft flew directly overhead. There were a dozen planes.

Warren noted several twin-engine attack bombers and a few P-51s and P-47s. All of them were World War Two aircraft. The success or failure of the operation would in large measure depend upon whether or not those planes could knock out Castro's planes before they could take to the air.

"Gunfire, Captain," Bryce said, before the first low rumble coming from the direction of the beach died away.

Even before Warren could answer, a landing craft exploded into a mass of flames.

"The ships are moving away," Bryce said as a radio message was handed to Warren.

"We've been ordered to return immediately to Guantánamo," Warren told him.

"But the men—"

"Signal a change of course to the *Pierce*," Warren snapped. "These are not my orders, Commander; these orders come from Washington."

"Aye, aye, sir," Bryce responded. "Helmsman, come to one-five-zero."

"Coming to one-five-zero," the helmsman answered.

"Engine room, ahead full speed," Bryce said.

"Ahead full speed," the man at the engine-room telegraph repeated.

"God help those men," Warren whispered as the *Nathan* began to respond to the helm.

Running on her electric motor, Tony held the *Gray Ghost* at periscope depth and trailed a radio antenna on the surface. Draped over the periscope handles, he made a quick 360-degree sweep.

The entrance to Havana's harbor was two thousand yards dead ahead. The lights of the city were clearly visible. Though it was a moonless night, the light from the city touched the bottom of a few scattered clouds.

Tony snapped the handles up. "Down periscope," he ordered, stepping back.

"Down periscope," Schmidt repeated.

Tony looked at the bridge clock. It was 0530. The first assault wave of troops would be heading for the beach, and bombers would be coming in on the city lights. Their ETA was less than a half-hour away. He checked the chart table. According to the latest intelligence, two Kotlin-class destroyers, the *Krym* and the *Skoryy*, were tied up at a pier on the right side of the harbor, fifteen hundred yards from the entrance. He intended to put the *Gray Ghost* in position to fire a spread of four fish from the bow tubes and two from the stern, on the way out, if they were required.

Tony returned to the periscope, ordered it up, and made another quick sweep. Unlike the submarines he'd served on during World War Two, this one was equipped with a radar in its periscope and the azimuth and range of a target were instantly fed into the torpedo data computer, which in turn continuously fed the changing navigational parameters of the target into the torpedoes until the instant they were fired; then the fish's own sophisticated navigational system would keep it on its deadly course.

"Nothing," Tony said. "Not even a tug. Down periscope." They were coming very close to the harbor entrance. He'd hoped to enter the harbor either by trailing close behind a surface ship or by running directly under one. Either way would have provided a mask for the sounds made by the boat's electrically driven propeller.

He looked at the speed indicator. They were doing four knots. At flank the boat could manage six, but at that speed the batteries were drained very quickly.

"All ahead one-third," Tony ordered, reducing speed.

"All ahead one-third," the man at the engine-room telegraph answered.

"Up periscope," Tony ordered; then, to Schmidt, "You take a look."

Schmidt nodded and walked the periscope around. "Nothing," he said, and stepped away.

Tony stepped up to the periscope and placed the upper part of his face against the rubber eye piece. "You'd think there'd be something moving . . . a fishing boat, at least," he commented after a complete 360-degree sweep and ordering the periscope down with a quick hand motion.

"Something coming in, skipper," the radio operator called out.

Tony moved closer to the radio room.

"The bombers are on their way," the radio operator said. "They're encountering fighter opposition."

"What the hell—"

"Two have gone down . . . three more have been hit . . . the fucking Cubans are knocking them down!"

"Up periscope," Tony ordered. He snapped out the handles and rode it up. "The lights are gone."

"Targets, bearing three-five-eight . . . range, four thousand yards . . . speed, two-five knots," the sonar man reported.

Tony turned the periscope to 358 and switched on the radar. The targets would have been clearly silhouetted if the lights of the city had been on, but in the moonless night they were not visible.

"Destroyers," Schmidt announced, bending over the radar operator.

"Down periscope," Tony barked.

"Down periscope," Schmidt repeated.

"Skipper," the radioman shouted, "all attacking aircraft have been destroyed."

"Take in radio antenna," Tony ordered.

The radioman repeated the order.

"Helmsman, come to course two-seven-five," Tony said. "We're getting the fuck out of here."

"Coming to course two-seven-five," the helmsman answered.

The sonar operator reported the two targets on the same bearing, "closing fast."

"Diving officer, make two hundred feet," Tony ordered.

The DO repeated the depth.

"How much water do we have under us?"

"Twelve hundred feet."

"All engines stop," Tony ordered. His lips and throat were dry. He could hear the boom of his heart.

"All engines stop," the engine-room telegraph operator said.

As the *Gray Ghost* settled down, Tony's eyes were riveted to the depth gauge. The main ballast was flooded. They were passing through one hundred feet.

The swooshing sound made by the destroyer's propellers was much louder than it had previously been.

Tony glanced at Schmidt. The man's face was taut with tension and his shirt was blotched with sweat.

The sonar man was still calling out target readings.

"Two hundred feet," the diving officer reported.

The boat was trimmed.

"Rig for depth charges," Tony ordered.

Schmidt passed the order.

"They're echo-ranging on us, Captain," the sonar operator reported.

The destroyers were almost directly over them. The swooshing of their propellers filled the *Gray Ghost*. Tony had been counting on the fact that their captains wouldn't suspect that a submarine was outside the harbor.

Suddenly the pinging of the Russian sonar seemed to be inside the *Gray Ghost*.

"Four ash cans on the way down!" the sonar man called out.

"Dive to four hundred, now!"

"But that's below—" the diving officer started to complain.

"Get this boat down," Tony snapped. He knew damn well he'd ordered the boat fifty feet lower than its maximum diving depth.

The depth-gauge needle began to unwind.

The salvo of four depth charges exploded above them, driving them down with what felt like a single gigantic blow from a pile driver. The lights went out and the system immediately switched to emergency power. From stem to stern, the boat's plates groaned.

"Damage?" Tony questioned, his eyes still on the unwinding depth-gauge needle. They'd just made three hundred feet.

"No damage," Schmidt reported.

"Two more cans on the way down," the sonar man said.

Suddenly a man called out, "Taking water in the forward torpedo room." At the same instant the ash cans burst on the starboard of the boat's conning tower. The *Gray Ghost* heeled sharply to port. Cold seawater cascaded onto the bridge through the hatch's ruptured seal.

"Schmidt, any casualties?" Tony questioned.

"One man unconscious and another with a compound fracture."

"Trimming at four hundred feet," the diving officer reported.

With pistollike shots, rivets began to pop.

"Targets holding course," the sonar man reported.

"Breaking off," Schmidt exclaimed with disbelief.

Tony nodded and shrugged. His shirt was soaked with sweat. "All ahead one-third," he ordered.

The engine-room telegraph man repeated the order.

"We'll move back to the coastal waters of the United States," Tony said, "then we'll surface and head to our base."

"What do you think happened?" Schmidt asked.

Tony ran his fingers through his hair. "I think our guys fucked up," he said. "I think our planes were blown out of the sky by planes that weren't supposed to be there. . . . I think that those poor bastards who managed to get ashore in the Bay of Pigs have about as much chance of surviving as a snowball has in hell. And I think we—the guys on this boat—are lucky the Russkies were more anxious to run than hunt. If it had been the other way, all of us would have been sardines in a can."

12

TONY WAS BACK in the same conference room at Langley where he'd first met Arthur Couch, only this time they were alone. There were two new photographs on the wall: one of the President, the other of the Company's director.

Tony had requested the meeting the very same day he had brought the *Gray Ghost* back to its berth. But Couch had refused to speak to him. Tony had to wait a full two months—until the whole fiasco of the United States involvement with the Bay of Pigs adventure died down—before Couch had agreed to meet with him.

"All right, we're meeting," Couch said, leaning forward. "What do you want?" He had the haggard look of a man who found getting through each day a major accomplishment of willpower against the dark desire of throwing up his hands in surrender to those who would destroy him.

Tony stood up. "I want to know what the hell happened down there," he said. "I want—"

Couch took off his tortoise-frame glasses. "They had planes—"

"They weren't supposed to have any aircraft!" Tony shouted. "They weren't supposed to."

It was as if the shout knocked Couch back into the chair. His eyes glazed. "We were suckered in . . . I was suckered in . . . On paper the plan was great. You were lucky—Ortega, Rice, and James—all of them are dead."

"Dead," Tony repeated.

"Ortega was captured, tortured, and put to death by a firing squad. Rice and James were killed in the fighting."

"Christ!" Tony swore, turning away from Couch and forcing his fists into the sides of his back.

"We're lucky that nothing has been leaked about the submarine," Couch said, "or we'd have had a far bigger problem than we had—and still have. Because they weren't able to find any wreckage, we've been able to deny the Russky claim that we had several subs outside Havana's harbor."

Facing Couch, Tony said, "I dismissed one man. What about him?"

Couch shook his head.

"What is that supposed to mean?"

Couch put his glasses back on. "He was taken out."

"Taken out?"

"He was a security risk."

"He was a fucking loudmouth and that was—"

"He's water under the bridge now," Couch said. "There was nothing else to do. He was very angry about being thrown off the boat and having his nose broken by you."

Tony walked to the far end of the highly polished conference table. "Who gave the order to take him out?"

Couch shrugged.

"Did you?"

"I don't make that kind of decision," Couch answered.

Tony took a cigarette out of a gold case, lit it, and blowing smoke up toward the ceiling, said, "When I first walked in here and saw the way you looked, I actually felt sorry for you. I figured, here's a man who has been put through the wringer by circumstances not of his making. Maybe that's so—about the circumstances being out of your control—and maybe I still have some sympathy for you being caught between a rock and a hard place." He took another drag on the cigarette before he continued. "But deep down, Couch, you're a shit. That man was no more a security threat than I am."

"He was an angry man."

"He was angry at me. I could have handled it, if it came to that."

"I know all about you. I've read your file."

"Meaning?" Tony questioned. More and more, Couch irritated him.

"I know how you handled a certain Mr. Spilachi."

"He was garbage," Tony responded, stubbing out his cigarette in an ashtray on the table in front of him. "Garbage."

Couch stood up. "I have nothing more to say to you, Mr. Trapasso."

Tony left the far end of the table and walked to where Couch was standing. "Did he have any family?"

"Leave it alone, Trapasso!"

Grabbing hold of Couch's tie, Tony jerked the man's head down. "Listen," he said in a low, flat voice, "I want a fucking answer when I ask you a fucking question and if I don't fucking get it, I'm going to break your fucking neck now."

Couch screwed his eyes upward.

"Talk."

"A daughter, Barbara . . . she goes under her mother's maiden name, Grayson," Couch croaked. "She lives with her grandmother in Brooklyn."

"I never knew his name. What was it?"

"He had several."

"His fucking name!" Tony demanded, jerking hard on Couch's tie.

"Harvey Chase. The daughter's name is Barbara. She lives with her maternal grandmother, Sandra Grayson."

"Okay," Tony said, letting go of Couch's tie. "We'll go to your office and you'll give me the grandmother's address."

Couch rubbed his neck. "I won't forget this," he said.

"Don't. Maybe next time I ask you a question, you'll answer it," Tony responded. "Now, let's go to your office."

Late in the afternoon on a hot, muggy day two days before the Fourth of July weekend, Tony said to Mike, "Come on, let's take a ride."

"Where to, Dad?" Mike was home from college for a short stay before beginning eight weeks' training with the naval reserve in San Diego.

Both men were sitting in a screened-in porch at the back of the house that overlooked the bay from Todt Hill on Staten Island. Two years before, Tony had bought a three-acre parcel and had a house built to his and Miriam's specifications. It was a single-level brick structure with a finished basement and a raised mid-section, where Tony had his den, and an enclosed swimming pool to the left of the enclosed deck.

After a pause that allowed Tony to light a cigarette, he said, "I have to pay a visit to some people. I've been delaying it. But now . . . well, it just seemed like a good time to do it." He stood up. "Maybe we'll stop at Nathan's before we come back."

Mike grinned.

"Yeah, I thought you'd like that," Tony said. "Let's go."

"Go where?" Miriam questioned, poking her head into the porch area.

"Dad has some people he wants to see in Brooklyn," Mike answered, launching himself off the brightly cushioned chair.

Stepping out onto the deck, Miriam said, "I thought that later the three of us would go out to dinner, and I know if you go into Brooklyn"—she looked directly at Mike—"you'll somehow manage to wind up at Nathan's."

"*Moi*?" Tony asked, putting on an expression of innocence and adding to it by defensively holding up his hands, palms out.

Miriam nodded vigorously. "You're a Nathan's freak and you're making your son one too. Even your daughter talks about Nathan's to her friends as if it was a religious shrine."

"Maybe it is and we can't see it," Mike offered.

"I'm the only one in this family who was born and raised in Brooklyn, but you," she said, pointing to her husband, "have somehow convinced yourself that you're a Brooklynite."

"Just the way I made you an Italian by sexual injection, you made me a Brooklynite by sexual contact."

Mike laughed so hard tears came to his eyes.

"That's not funny," Miriam said.

"Maybe just a *little* bit funny?" Tony questioned, holding up his thumb and first finger with a small space between them for Miriam to see. "This much funny?"

"You're smiling, Mom," Mike said.

She shook her head.

"A hard case," Tony observed.

"Mom, are you really a hard case?" Mike asked.

"I can see that I'm not going to get anywhere with the two of you," Miriam said. "Just remember that whether or not you're stuffed to the gills with hot dogs and whatever else you eat, we're still going out for dinner."

"Yes, sir!" Tony saluted.

"Absolutely," Mike answered.

"Anything else?" Tony asked.

"The reason I came out here in the first place was to tell you that Ruth called to ask if she could bring someone home for the holiday."

"And what did you say?" Tony asked.

"I said she could."

Tony nodded. "Good, her friends are always—"

"It's a young man," Miriam said. "Ruth wants us to meet him, and the long weekend is a good opportunity."

Tony looked at her quizzically. This was the first time his daughter had asked permission to bring a young man home.

Miriam shrugged. "I don't know any more than you do. We'll find out what's going on when the two of them are here. She said he comes from a good family. His father is a lawyer. She didn't say anything else, except that we'd like him."

"I don't like to be told who I'll like," Tony responded.

"You're annoyed . . . I know you are."

With a wave of his hand Tony dismissed Miriam's observation, and looking at Mike, he said, "Let's get going." He led the way out of the screen door and around to the side of the house to the four-car garage.

"Remember what I said about dinner," Miriam called after them.

"Sure, Mom," Mike answered.

"You drive," Tony told Mike, handing him the car keys. "We'll take the Jag."

A short time later they rolled onto the green electric ferry that crossed from the St. George ferry terminal in Staten Island to Sixty-ninth Street in Brooklyn, and left the car to stand on the deck during the brief ride.

Tony was annoyed at the prospect of Ruth bringing a young man home with her for the weekend. Though she was almost nineteen and in her first year at Vassar, he hadn't given much thought to her becoming involved with a man. That word "involved" stuck in his craw. It conjured a host of images involving the two of them that made him very uneasy.

"Did you know anything about this young man of Ruth's?" Tony asked as the ferry got under way. Mike and Ruth were more than brother and sister; they were friends. They sometimes even went out on dates together. In many ways, their relationship was a lot like Miriam's with Jake.

"She kept him under wraps," Mike answered breezily.

"Must have," Tony responded, suddenly aware that Miriam hadn't mentioned the young man's name.

"He's going to have to bounce off the pilings to come into the slip," Mike said. "There's a hell of a tide running."

"What?" Tony asked, reaching the conclusion that Ruth had probably neglected to tell her mother the young man's name.

"The ferryboat captain . . ."

Tony looked toward the slip and immediately realized the situation.

"He'll have to go full back, then full ahead to make the slip, then cut to one-third ahead to hold his position, even with the lines out."

Tony grinned with satisfaction and put his arm around his son's shoulders. "Not bad for someone who's going to be a jet jockey."

"I learned good," Mike laughed.

The ferry made the bounce off the pilings that moved them to one side and then came into the slip.

Tony and Mike returned to the Jag and a short time later drove off the ferry and up Sixty-ninth Street.

"Are you going to tell me how to get to where we're going?" Mike asked.

"Make the first right . . . go up to Fort Hamilton Parkway and then make a left and just keep going. Eventually you'll connect with Caton Avenue, follow that to Flatbush, make a left—"

"Cue me in as we go along," Mike said, making a right turn; then he asked, "Who are we going to see?"

"Just some people," Tony answered evasively.

It took twenty-five minutes to go from the ferry to Flatbush Avenue, where Tony told Mike to turn left. "Now go up to Winthrop Street and make a left. It's just a few blocks from here."

Winthrop Street turned out to be a one-way street in the wrong direction.

"Go up to the next street and come around," Tony said. "On Winthrop we're looking for number forty-four."

When they came onto Winthrop Street, Mike said, "Forty-four has to be down close to the other end . . . we just passed a hundred and five."

"Park wherever you can," Tony said, aware that the houses on the street were a mixture of private homes and several large apartment houses.

Mike pulled into a space between two driveways that belonged to private houses. "Forty-four must be one of those buildings over there," he said, bobbing his head toward a grouping of six attached five-story walk-ups.

"It's the fourth one down," Tony said, opening the door to the car. "Better lock it and put the alarm on."

The two of them crossed the street and entered the small vestibule, where the bell for each apartment was located under the tenant's brass mailbox.

"What name?"

"Grayson," Tony answered.

"Top floor, apartment A."

Tony pressed the black bell button.

A few moments passed; then a disembodied woman's voice came over the speaker system. "Who is it?" she asked.

Tony gave his surname and gestured to Mike to go to the door that separated the vestibule from the hallway.

A moment later the buzzer sounded and Mike opened the door and held it open until his father was inside the hallway, which was badly lit and smelled of a variety of ethnic cooking styles. They started up the steps. There were two apartments on each floor.

A door opened above them and a woman called out, "Who are you?"

"Tony Trapasso and his son, Mike."

The woman didn't answer.

"I've never been in a house like this," Mike whispered.

"Is that a complaint?"

"No way," Mike replied. "No way."

By the time they reached the fifth landing, Tony could see the woman. She was bending over the railing looking down at them. He judged her to be in her early sixties, gray-haired and wearing a faded blue short-sleeved housedress.

"This is a climb," he said as he came within speaking distance of the woman.

She squinted suspiciously at him and Mike.

"Tony Trapasso and my son, Mike," he said, offering his hand.

She didn't take it. "What are you selling?"

Tony shook his head. "Nothing," he told her. "I came to see your granddaughter, Barbara . . . I hope she's in."

"Grandma, who is it?" a young woman called out from inside the apartment.

"A friend of your father's," Tony answered.

That brought her to the door. She was probably eighteen or nineteen. Twenty at the most. She was wearing a pair of blue denim shorts and a blue halter. Her long strawberry-blond hair was tied back with a white ribbon. She had green eyes. The bridge of her nose, her cheeks, and her arms were sprinkled with freckles. She didn't have on a bit of makeup and didn't need any.

"You're Barbara, aren't you?" Tony asked, and before she could answer, he said, "I'm Tony Trapasso and that's my son, Mike. I—"

"If you're looking for Harvey, he's not here," the grandmother said testily. "He finally got what was coming to him. He's dead. Killed in some stupid car accident."

Barbara winced. "It's all right, Grandma, I'll talk to Mr. Trapasso."

"Thank you," Tony said. "And please call me Tony."

To the obvious chagrin of her grandmother, Barbara invited Tony and Mike into the apartment and into the living room, which was immediately off a very small foyer. There were a couch and two club chairs in the living room. Two old lamp tables supported cheap lamps. Above the couch there was a large pastel drawing of a fox pretending to be asleep while an unsuspecting chicken approached.

Barbara and her grandmother sat on the couch.

Tony took the chair closest to the window. From where he was seated, he could see the bulge of the couch's broken springs. He glanced at Mike, who couldn't take his eyes off the girl.

For several moments no one spoke, then Tony said, "I had some business dealings with your father, Barbara . . . I hope you don't mind me calling you Barbara?"

Before the girl could answer, the grandmother said crossly, "If he owed you money, you can't collect from us. We have hardly enough to get by on as it is."

Tony, still looking at Barbara, said, "I owed your father money and since you're his next of kin I figured that I would give you what I would have had to repay to him."

Barbara frowned.

"Is anything wrong?" Tony questioned.

Suddenly Mike said in Italian, "She doesn't believe you and neither do I."

Tony shot his son a glance, forced himself to smile. "My son just reminded me that we have to be back home by five."

"Don't he speak English?" the grandmother asked.

"Yes, I do, ma'am, but some things are better said in another language," Mike responded.

"My father told you about me?" Barbara asked.

Tony nodded. "He even told me where I would be able to find you."

"Were you with him—"

Tony shook his head. "No, I wasn't."

"The police said he lost control of the car."

"Yes, I saw the police report."

"How much did you owe him?" the grandmother asked.

"I can't pay it all now," Tony said.

"How much?" the grandmother pressed.

"I'll write you a check for five thousand now," Tony answered, "and—"

Barbara leapt to her feet. "Five thousand dollars!" she cried. "My God, that's enough to see me through my senior year at college. My God, Grandma, we can buy something for the house. Five thousand dollars!"

"How much more after that?" the grandmother asked, still wary, but using a distinctly softer voice.

Tony shrugged. "My accountant has to come up with the figures . . . but I'm sure it will be substantial." He had already made up his mind to make it possible for Barbara to have the opportunity that her father would have never given her.

"When do we get that five thousand?"

"Now," Tony said, taking a checkbook out of his pocket.

Barbara sat down. "Make the check out to my grandmother," she directed.

Tony gave her a questioning look.

Putting her arm around her grandmother's shoulders, Barbara explained, "Everything I have I owe to her. She sews so I have money to buy books . . . she makes all my clothes, and—"

"All right, Grandma, I'll make the check out to you," Tony said, and when he finished writing it, he stood up, took two steps toward the couch, and handed it to the old woman. Their eyes locked, and before Tony could move back to the chair, she said softly, "God bless you." Then she bit her lower lip.

Tony looked at Mike. "Well, we should be on our way, shouldn't we, son?"

"Yes . . . but there's something you forgot to do."

Tony was taken aback.

"The party on the Fourth," Mike said. "You wanted to invite Barbara to our Fourth of July party. I'll pick her up and bring her back. . . . You remember now, don't you?"

Tony slapped his forehead. "I sometimes have a brain like Swiss cheese, full of holes. That's why I like to have my son with me. He plugs up the holes. Barbara, would you be our guest at a Fourth of July party?"

"Sure she will," her grandmother answered for her.

"Will you, Barbara?" Tony asked.

"I'd love to."

"Good. Mike, what time do you want to pick her up?" Tony asked, shifting his attention back to his son.

"Four o'clock?" Mike said, looking at Barbara.

Smiling, she nodded her acceptance of the time.

Tony and Mike shook hands with the grandmother and with Barbara, and the two women escorted them out to the landing.

"See you," Mike said to Barbara.

She repeated his words, smiled, and retreated into the apartment.

"Mr. Trapasso," the grandmother called as he started down the steps.

He stopped. "Mike, go down to the car. I'll join you in a couple of minutes." He waited until his son was out of earshot before he faced the elderly woman.

She waved the check. "Did you really owe that bastard money?" she asked.

"I owed him," Tony answered evasively.

"Who are you, really?"

"Someone who, from now on, will make a difference in your life and the life of your granddaughter."

"She's a good girl," the woman said proudly.

Tony nodded. "She's got a good grandmother," he answered, and taking her two gnarled, age-darkened hands in his, he kissed both. "You won't have to sew anymore." Then he turned, hurried down the steps and into the car.

"What was that all about?" Mike asked as he turned south on Flatbush Avenue.

"A game," Tony answered. "But this time the loser won, only he'll never know it."

"Sometimes I'm not even sure *I* know what the hell you're talking about."

Tony laughed, lit a cigarette, and said, "Speaking about not knowing what someone is talking about—that invite to the party you made came right out of left field."

"C'mon, Dad, she's gorgeous . . . I couldn't take my eyes off her."

"Yeah, I could see that."

"I'm a healthy male and—"

"And before you reveal any more secrets about yourself, let's go to Nathan's and have a couple of hot dogs," Tony told him as he suddenly remembered what his father had said to him about Miriam the first time he had met her, which had been on the afternoon of December 7, 1941. He and his father were mingling with the crowds on Broadway, who were watching the news about the bombing of Pearl Harbor flash across the Times Building. He bumped into a woman who was with her son and daughter. The daughter was Miriam and the son was Jake. Speaking in Italian, his father said, "She's like a ripe peach . . . ready for the picking." Then he added, "Some guys say there's nothing like a luscious Jewess. They can never get enough cock. . . ."

Tony smiled.

"What's funny?" Mike asked.

"Life," Tony answered, taking a deep drag on the cigarette. "Life is very funny."

"Nathan's, here we come!" Mike exclaimed, and then, looking at Tony, he said, "You know, Dad, you're something else, really something else!"

"I hope that's supposed to be a compliment."

"It sure as hell is."

Tony smiled, stubbed out the cigarette, and closed his eyes. He was a very lucky man. . . .

The night of the Fourth was clear and warm, with a slight on-shore breeze, which hardly ruffled the flag on the pole in front of Tony's house, but was just strong enough to make the red-white-and-blue Chinese lanterns, strung between the trees on the front and rear lawns, dance. To the south, the sky and ocean were seamed together in a continuous blackness in which there were millions of stars, while in the other three quadrants of the sky the lights from the city all but dimmed the brightest of the stars. Even the familiar configuration of the Big Dipper was almost washed away by the upward-reflected light from the city.

Sometime before people had started to arrive, Miriam had told him there'd be sixty guests. She had arranged for the affair to be catered. Two huge grills and bar were set up on the rear lawn, another grill was on the front lawn, and a bartender manned the bar in the recreation room.

Tony, standing at the bottom of the porch steps, looked at his watch. It was eight-forty. At nine the fireworks display would start in Coney Island and his guests would have "grandstand seats" on the lawn. He began to move among the guests again; sometimes he even stopped to chat with one or another of them. But most of the time he kept Ruth and her houseguest— whose name turned out to be Steven Cook—in sight. Steven, a sensitive-looking young man with bedroom eyes and long blond hair, usually had his arm around Ruth's waist or around her shoulders, with the tips of his long fingers resting just above her breast. Because Mike and Barbara were usually close to Ruth and Steve, Tony was also aware that Mike didn't seem to know what to do with his hands, other than use one of them to hold one of Barbara's. And when he looked at her, it was with spaniel eyes.

Tony pursed his lips. The previous night at dinner, Steve had said that he wanted "to be another Tennessee Williams." And later, Ruth tried to assure him and Miriam that Steve was "really very talented." Watching them again for a few moments, Tony was sure they were sleeping together; then, almost as if he'd suddenly experienced a sharp physical pain, Tony winced.

"Tony, are you all right?"

Blinking, he found himself looking at Jacob and Arlene.

"Tony?" Jacob called.

"Sure, sure, I'm fine," Tony said, embracing Jacob and then Arlene. "I was just thinking about something."

"You looked as if you'd just swallowed a toad," Jacob told his friend.

Completely composed, Tony laughed, waved Jacob's comment aside, and suggested the three of them have steak sandwiches. "I seldom have the opportunity to sample the food at these parties, and there aren't any two people I'd rather do it with than the two of you—if Warren was here, it would be three people."

At the grill Tony, knowing Jacob's and Arlene's preferences, ordered a medium-well steak for each of them and a very well-done one for himself. "Put all of them on toasted buns," he told the man working the grill.

"I'll get the drinks," Jacob offered.

"Beer for me," Tony said.

"Same," Arlene called out.

While Jacob was away from them, Tony said, "Since he's met you, he's been a new man."

"And I've been a new woman," Arlene responded. "Jacob has been good for me."

"You know that other than my own family, the two people I love most are Jake and Warren?"

"Yes, I know that. He feels the same way about you and Warren." She hesitated; then, in a lower voice, she added, "I think he feels that way about me too."

"I think so too," Tony responded, smiling.

"Thank you," she said.

Leaning toward her, Tony kissed her on the forehead.

"Three beers," Jacob announced, coming toward them.

"Steaks will be done in a couple of minutes," the man tending the grill said.

"To all of us," Tony toasted, lifting his paper cup of beer.

After the three of them touched each other's cups and drank, Tony said, "I'm really glad you came here tonight. I have some business to discuss with you."

"Tony handles my business affairs here," Jacob explained.

The man at the grill called out, "Steaks ready, Mr.

Trapasso . . . two medium-well and one very well-done . . . all on toasted buns."

"Good!" Arlene exclaimed after the first bite.

Jacob seconded her opinion.

"Jacob has me here in the West and his good friend Yashi handling his business interests in Asia," Tony explained.

"If you'd rather discuss this alone, I'll go and find Miriam," Arlene offered.

"Stay," Jacob told her. "There's nothing secret about any of my business arrangements . . . Yashi and I are old friends."

"You mean he's never told you about Yashi?" Tony shifted his eyes from Jacob to Arlene and back to Jacob.

"I just haven't gotten around to it," he said. "Besides, I was hoping she'd come to Japan with me and meet him in person."

"Japan?" Arlene questioned.

Jacob smiled. "I was thinking of going there for a visit."

"Wait a minute," Tony said. "I want to get this settled before you leave tonight."

"I'm listening," Jacob said.

"There are plans to build a bridge between Staten Island and Brooklyn."

"A tunnel would make more sense," Jacob commented as he finished the steak sandwich.

"A bridge will send the value of property skyrocketing and there's a construction company I know about that will do some of the roadwork on the approaches on both sides of the bridge."

"How much?"

"A mil for the property and another mil for the company. I'm going in for the same amount."

"All right," Jacob answered. "It sounds good. Set it up."

"Just like that?" Arlene asked. "No questions?"

Jacob nodded, then said, "You're right. I should have a question . . . I have a question."

"Shoot."

"When is the bridge supposed to be finished?"

"About 1965."

Jacob looked at Arlene. "That's a good date to finish building a bridge," he said.

"You're talking about four million dollars!" she exclaimed.

"Tony knows what he's doing . . . if he didn't, he wouldn't be doing it."

"The two of you are incredible men," Arlene said.

Laughing, Jacob asked, "Am I really 'incredible'?"

"If I am," Tony said, "you have to be."

Jacob took hold of Arlene's hand and kissed the back of it. "I'd trust Tony with my life."

Suddenly someone called out, "Look at that!"

High over Coney Island three rockets had exploded into red, white, and blue.

"The fireworks have started," Tony said. "Let's watch."

Jacob slipped his arm around Arlene's waist and she covered his hand with hers. "Will you go to Japan with me?" he asked, whispering the question into her ear.

Arlene squeezed his hand. "We'll talk about it," she answered.

Tony was already in bed when Miriam settled down next to him and turned out the light.

"It was a wonderful party," she said. "Everyone looked as if they were having a good time. . . . Mike seems really interested in the daughter of your friend."

"Too soon to really know," he answered, though from what he had seen of the two of them, he wouldn't doubt it.

"I'm sorry that Warren wasn't with us," Miriam commented. "He's been so distant lately. Do you think he's involved with someone?"

"I don't really know. He's closemouthed about most things."

Miriam sighed. "He should know that anyone he brings here would be welcome."

"I'm sure he does know that. But I'm also sure that he won't bring anyone here until . . . well, until he's ready."

"I suppose you're right," Miriam answered.

Suddenly Tony sat up. "Do you think Ruth and Steve sleep together?"

"Probably."

"Christ!" Tony swore, and leaving the bed, he went to the window.

"Tony—"

"I had hoped she'd have more sense than to get herself involved with someone like Steve . . . a would-be playwright, no less!"

"She's a woman, Tony," Miriam said gently. "She's not your little girl anymore."

He whirled around. "She is my daughter and I don't want her to come home with a belly. I don't want to be the father of the bride at a shotgun wedding."

"You have to trust her—"

"Trust!" he almost shouted. "Trust her, and she brings him home."

Miriam pulled herself up, and getting out of bed, she went to Tony. "Trust means that you have to let her make her own decisions, regardless of what you might think of them. Trust means that you know that we have provided her with the right values and that we trust those values."

"I don't want her to be hurt," Tony said softly.

"I know that," Miriam said, taking hold of his hand. "Neither do I." And she gently pulled him back to the bed.

13

AMONG THE HUNDREDS of people coming out of the customs area at Idlewild Airport, Warren immediately spotted Andrew. He was dragging a fold-up metal-wire cart filled with his luggage, several canvases, a folded easel, and a large wooden paintbox. The time abroad had changed him. He looked nothing like the midshipman he was. His hair was long. He wore blue jeans, a multicolored sport shirt, a blue kerchief around his neck, and a red one folded into a narrow band around his head.

Warren hesitated to move.

"Dad, over here!" Andrew called out. "I'm here!"

Warren waved and started toward him.

"Am I happy to see you," Andrew said, vigorously pumping his father's hand. He gestured back at the cart. "This was all I was allowed to carry. Everything else I had to ship home."

"How much more was there?" Warren asked as they started to walk to the exit leading to the parking lot.

"Ten more large canvases," Andrew said; then he asked, "Is Mom out in the car?"

"She couldn't make it," Warren answered.

Andrew's face clouded and the light in his eyes dimmed. "She's all right, isn't she?"

"She's fine. She's at some conference or other in L.A. She'll be back the day after tomorrow."

They stepped out into the parking area. Despite the fact it was September, the heat and humidity were oppressive.

"The car's this way," Warren said, moving to the right.

"You see Mom at all?" Andrew asked.

"Not much . . . but we manage to keep in touch," Warren answered. "We're not enemies, if that's what you're afraid of."

"No, I know you're not."

After they settled in the car and Warren guided it out of the parking area onto the roadway, he said, "I'll drop you off at the apartment and we'll meet for dinner."

"Where are you—"

"I'm at the Plaza—Jake has a three-room suite there and he's not in town now." Warren glanced at his son. "I have someone with me."

"Oh!"

Warren turned off the airport exit roadway and onto the Belt Parkway before he asked, "How was your summer?"

"Spectacular. The last time I spoke to Mom I told her that I produced enough for a showing . . . not a New York showing . . . but maybe in some small city or large town. I did some very good work, everyone said so. Mom said she knows a couple of places in Annapolis that might be interested."

"Annapolis?" Warren repeated incredulously. "Doesn't she realize—"

"That's just it," Andrew said, "she does realize it

and she thinks that it's time to set the administration on its ears."

Warren rubbed his hand across his chin. Nothing he'd say would stop Hilary from doing what she wanted to do, once she decided to do it.

"I'm not sure you'd be permitted to have anything to do with it. I don't know the rules and regulations that pertain to outside activities for midshipmen." He pulled his pipe out of a side pocket, and holding the wheel with one hand, he managed to fill and light it. "You could get yourself suspended."

"Never happen," Andrew answered. "Not the way Mom has it figured out. Besides, could you imagine what the press would do to the Academy if I was suspended? But it won't happen."

Warren puffed on his pipe.

"So when do I get to meet your lady friend?" Andrew asked.

The question didn't bother Warren as much as the tone used to ask it.

"Well, when do I meet her?"

"Tonight, at dinner," Warren responded, remembering the time, so long ago, when he'd met Kate, his father's mistress, for the first time. The meeting had taken place soon after he'd brought the *Dee*, a one-of-a-kind oiler and supply ship, back to Pearl after the Philippines had fallen to the Japanese. His father had arranged for the meeting to take place in a restaurant. Warren had liked Kate almost from the first hello, and later on he had come to love her. She had been good for his father, just as Carol was good for him. "Where would you like to have dinner?" he asked, glancing at Andrew, whose face was turned toward the side window.

"I don't have a preference," Andrew said, still looking out of the window.

Again it was Andrew's tone that bothered Warren, not what he said. "If you'd rather not meet—"

"It's okay," Andrew said.

For several minutes they continued to drive without speaking.

Warren was concerned that he'd been wrong to suggest that Andrew meet Carol, though he'd discussed it with her and she'd thought they should meet. And on top of his being troubled about how the events of the evening would go, he was equally disturbed about Hilary's plan to have a showing of Andrew's paintings in an Annapolis gallery. Uttering a weary sigh, he asked, "Would you want to bring a date along to dinner?"

"I wouldn't know who to call."

"What about that young lady you dated, the model who—"

"Ellie?"

"If that's her name, yes. She's certainly a lovely-looking young woman."

Andrew pouted. "I've been out of touch with her."

"Did you do a painting of her?"

"Several, and also several drawings . . . but that was before—" He stopped, looked at his father, and said, "I guess Mom didn't tell you about it."

"About what?" Warren asked, momentarily locking eyes with his son.

"Ellie became pregnant and had an abortion."

Warren bit down hard on the pipe stem and cracked it.

"Last I heard, Ellie was doing fine . . . but something happened between us." Andrew shrugged. "She didn't want to see me afterward."

"And your mother knew about the pregnancy?" Warren asked, taking the pipe out of his mouth. The tip of the stem was crushed.

"Did you just do that?" Andrew questioned.

Warren nodded. "Your mother knew about the pregnancy?" he repeated.

"She arranged for the abortion. Ellie went to her and the whole thing was settled between them. I'd have never known about it, but when Ellie came down to see me one weekend, she got sick on the bus, and when I saw her . . . well, she had to tell me.

"I offered to marry her," Andrew told him. "But she said I'd make a 'lousy husband.' Besides, she wasn't ready to marry."

Warren knocked the ashes out of the pipe bowl and into the dashboard ashtray. Then he put the pipe back into his pocket. "Your mother has seen to quite a few things for you," he commented.

"C'mon, Dad, she did the right thing with Ellie. If I had married her, I'd have had to keep the marriage secret until I finished my time at the Academy and at flight school . . . and that wouldn't be easy to do, especially with a baby. Anyway, it's not a problem and never really was one."

"She might have at least let me know what was going on," Warren said, not bothering to hide his anger. "After all, you are also my son."

"You know Mom—once she gets a handle on something, she takes charge."

Warren didn't respond. That he might have had a grandchild gave him a peculiar feeling of having lost something he had never had a chance to have, and almost immediately his thoughts switched to Irene Hacker, the Army nurse with whom he had fallen in love before she'd been killed by the Japanese during

World War Two. All he had ever had with her were a few brief intervals between his time at sea and her time in the hospital. He had never had the time to really love her.

"How about someplace American for dinner?" Andrew asked. "A steak house would be fine. That's something you don't get in either England or France, at least not the way we get steak here."

With some difficulty, Warren came out of his reverie. "There are several places near the hotel . . . but I was told to try the Homestead—it's on West Side, downtown. I'll make the reservation in my name for seven o'clock."

"I'll find it," Andrew answered.

Feeling that he had nothing more to talk about to his son, Warren reached over to the radio and switched it on. A woman's voice filled the car, but neither the song nor the voice was familiar to him.

Warren was at ease. He liked the restaurant's ambience and found the food excellent. Throughout dinner the conversation among the three of them had been lively. And as they waited for the table to be cleared and the waiter to take their orders for dessert, Andrew regaled them with stories about his adventures in London and Paris and did marvelous imitations of some of the people he'd met.

Though Warren had had some trepidation about the meeting between Carol and Andrew, he realized shortly after the three of them were seated at a table that Andrew had either done some thinking about the relationship in the intervening hours, or, having come face-to-face with Carol, decided he liked her. And she, looking radiantly beautiful, completely surprised Warren by displaying an amazing knowledge about art, and when he commented on it, she answered, "I used to work in a gallery and I read the reviews of the new exhibitions in the *Times*. I even go to see those that interest me."

"My mother—" Andrew stopped, his cheeks and ears suddenly turning red.

"It's all right," Carol said. "She'll always be your mother and there's no reason why you shouldn't speak about her, even to me."

"My mother is going to arrange a showing for me," he said.

"That's marvelous . . . really marvelous . . . don't you think so, Warren?"

Before he could answer, Andrew said, "My father is worried about how the authorities at the Academy will react to it."

"I can tell you they're not going to be pleased," Warren told them. "They're not going to be pleased at all."

"Will it jeopardize your standing there?" Carol asked.

With a shrug, Andrew said, "I doubt it."

Carol looked questioningly at Warren. "What do you think?"

"I don't really know what could happen, but I suggest before he and his mother go ahead with their plans, he should know the Academy's official position on the matter."

"You make it sound so . . . so formidable and so stuffy."

"It's certainly both," Andrew laughed.

"For a free spirit like yourself, I bet it is," Carol answered; then, looking at Warren, she asked, "Did you find it that way when you were there?"

Warren suddenly realized how hard Andrew was looking at him. "My circumstances were different," he

said, fingering the red-checkered tablecloth. He was
going to say, *My mother was an alcoholic and I was
glad to be away from home.* But instead he told him,
"I didn't have your unique talent, Andrew. I didn't
see any kind of future for me, unless it was a future
with the Navy." His eyes met his son's again.

"Didn't you ever want something different?" Andrew pressed.

"Maybe, when I got disgusted, I did . . . but the
war came and that changed everything. I felt I was in
the right place at the right time, doing the right thing,
and it was the most wonderful feeling in the world."

Andrew sighed. "I only feel that way when I'm
painting."

"Once you begin to fly, maybe you'll feel differently."

"Maybe," Andrew answered without conviction.

Suddenly Warren got to his feet and pushed his
chair back. "An old friend," he explained, and the
next instant a chunky redhead wearing service whites
came toward the table with a petite brown-haired
woman in tow.

"Captain"—the man saluted—"or is it Admiral Troost
now?" And shaking his head, he said, "There's no
way of knowing when a man is in civvies."

Warren returned the salute and then the two of
them shook hands. "Still going for the stars," Warren
answered, grinning. "And I see, Commander, you're
coming up the ladder too."

"My wife, Jenine," Sean said.

Warren shook her hand and said, "Commander Sean
Hacker, my son, Andrew, and Mrs. Carol Langston."

Sean shook both their hands.

"Have you dined yet?" Warren asked.

"We're on dessert," Jenine said in a pronounced
southern drawl.

"So are we," Warren responded. "Please join us."

"It would be a real pleasure," Jenine said.

Warren summoned the maître d' and arranged for two more chairs to be placed at the table.

The waiter came to take their dessert orders and suggested the deep-dish apple pie topped with vanilla ice cream.

Carol, Jenine, Andrew, and Sean ordered pie and ice cream, while Warren wanted only coffee.

"Where are you now, Sean?" Warren asked.

"I'm skipper of the AO-45, the fleet oiler, *Hudson*. She's tied up in Bayonne to have some work done on her. And where are you?"

"With the Office of Naval Intelligence," Warren answered. "I come here whenever I have the opportunity."

"Our home port is Mobile," Jenine said. "Coming up here is a real treat."

"It's a treat for me too," Warren said, "and I've even lived here for several years."

"Is this your hometown too, Mrs. Langston?" Jenine asked.

"Please call me Carol," she said, her eyes darting to Warren. "And yes, I was born and raised here . . . that makes me the only native New Yorker at the table."

Andrew suddenly pointed a finger at Sean. "Now I remember who you are. You saved my father's life, didn't you? You got him out of Hungnam after he was wounded."

Sean colored.

"He did," Warren said quietly. "He's the reason why I'm sitting here tonight."

Jenine drew slightly to one side of her chair and looked questioningly at her husband. "But you always told me he saved *your* life. We even named our boy Warren."

"He did," Sean responded. "He saved my life in a very different way. He gave me my name and my father."

The two men looked silently across the table at one another and then Warren gave a slight nod. "Thank you for naming your son after me."

"I swear, I don't understand what either of you is saying," Jenine exclaimed.

Sean laughed. "It's a joke between the two of us," he explained. "Somehow we managed to save one other, isn't that right, Captain?"

Warren nodded vigorously. "That's absolutely right."

Looking at Carol, Andrew asked, "Do you see what I'm up against?"

"What's that?"

"Having a father who was a hero," Andrew answered almost sullenly.

Sean looked at him. "Your father is more than a hero," he said, moving his eyes from Andrew to Warren. "He is a man other men respect and would follow into hell, if that's where he wants them to go—and some did do just that, Andrew." He nodded. "I did, and so did all of the other men who were under his command at Inchon and Hungnam."

Warren bowed his head. Those words coming from Sean Hacker meant more to him than he could ever explain to anyone. Sean, an excellent officer, had always been the one most distant from him until that day in the hospital, when Sean acknowledged that he was proud to be Lieutenant Commander Hacker's son. Hacker, his father and a mustang, had been the skipper of AKO-96, the *Dee*, in the early days of World War Two and had been killed by an officer who had gone berserk. He was also Irene's brother, the Army nurse with whom Warren had fallen in love before she had been raped, tortured, and killed by the Japanese.

Then in milder tone Sean told him, "I said it and it has taken me years, Warren, to say what I really wanted to say that day when I visited you in the hospital."

Warren raised his head. "All you said about me could also be said about your father. I was with him, so I know."

"I'd like to believe that."

"Believe it," Warren said. "Believe, Sean, because it's true. I was proud to have served with him."

At that moment the waiter returned to the table with the dessert.

"That looks simply scrumptious!" Jenine exclaimed as the waiter served her first.

Warren felt Carol's hand squeeze his knee. He looked at her and smiled.

Warren had always felt uncomfortable when he entered the offices of *The Complete Woman*. When he and Hilary had been married, he had the feeling that all of the women, from the fluff of a receptionist to Hilary's private secretary, looked at him as if he were a kept man, at best, or a sexual toy, at worst. And this time, as he waited for the receptionist to announce his arrival to Hilary, he felt the same feelings, even though he had purposely wore his tans rather than his service whites.

"Ms. Troost is expecting you," the receptionist said, looking up at him with an expression of open curiosity in her brown eyes.

Warren realized she was new, and to really give her something to think about, he said, "I'm the source of

the 'Troost' in 'Ms. Troost.' " Then he swung open
the glass door and entered the long hallway that led to
Hilary's office.

Greeted warmly by Joan Polk, Hilary's private secretary, he responded in kind. "Almost every time I
come here, I see a new face at the reception desk," he
commented.

"I don't doubt it," she said. "The girls find better
opportunities. After this Friday, you won't be seeing
me here."

"A better opportunity?" he questioned.

Joan shook her head. "I passed the age when that
kind of 'better opportunity' would be offered, and
even if one were, I doubt very much that I'd take it.
No, I have enough money, thanks to your . . . to
Hilary, to retire and enjoy myself."

"Good for you!"

She smiled and said, "I'll let the boss lady know
you're here." She announced him on the intercom.

"Send him in," Hilary responded.

Moments later, Warren was in Hilary's office and
she was in front of her desk to greet him with a
friendly hug and kiss. She smelled good and he couldn't
help being aware of the press of her breasts against his
chest.

Then, as they separated, she said, "Let's sit over
there . . . it's so much more comfortable than being at
the desk and so much more informal." She gestured to
the right, where there was an arrangement of a small,
comfortable-looking couch and two club chairs around
a square greenish-gray-marble-topped coffee table,
which had a silver platter with a carafe of coffee, two
mugs, a creamer, a sugar bowl, and a plate of small
sandwiches on it. "I hope you don't mind. At this time
of the afternoon I'm starved."

"I don't mind," Warren said, choosing one of the club chairs.

She sat down on the couch and began to pour the coffee. "Thank you for meeting Andrew," she said.

"He's my son too, remember," Warren responded, not without a touch of sarcasm in his voice.

She gave him a quick glance, finished pouring the coffee, and said, "The summer has done wonders for him. His work has gotten so much better." She leaned across the table, handed a mug of black coffee to Warren, and smiled. "You still do take it this way, don't you?"

Nodding, he found himself looking at the valley between her breasts, exposed by the two open buttons of the white blouse she wore.

"Have you seen Jake or Tony?" she asked.

"Not recently," he answered, drawing his eyes away from her breasts. "I speak to them on the phone. . . . Jake is seeing a woman."

"So are you, I was told by Andrew—Carol, that's her name, isn't it? I understand she's very nice and appears to be very fond of you."

Warren felt the color rising in his cheeks. "I'd prefer not to discuss her," he said.

Hilary picked up one of the sandwiches. "You really shouldn't be so sensitive, Warren, or maybe I should change that to 'stuffy.' I'd be perfectly willing to discuss any of my male friends with you. After all, we were married."

A vision of her reaching the height of orgasmic ecstasy with a faceless man ballooned in his brain for a moment and the very next instant exploded, leaving him staring at her.

"I never expected you to go without sex after we divorced," Hilary said.

"Obviously you don't," Warren responded, taking a sip of the coffee.

"My dear, I have the same needs that I had when we were married, and though I'm 'liberated,' I am very discreet about what I do."

"I didn't come here to discuss either of our sex lives," Warren said, hoping to gain back control of the situation, which he realized he had lost the moment she'd seen him look at her breasts.

"Obviously not . . . but it probably will prove to be more interesting than anything else we discuss."

Warren put his half-empty cup down on the tray. "You can't go through with the showing you're planning for Andrew," he said, getting to his feet.

"You're too late, darling," she said.

He squinted down at her. "What do you mean, 'too late'?"

"One of my friends spoke to Admiral George Pills, the Academy's commandant—"

"I know who he is," Warren snapped.

"I spoke to him this morning and he thinks it's a wonderful idea," Hilary said. "It's in line with his idea to broaden the scope of the educational experience at the Academy."

Warren was speechless.

"He plans to be at the opening ceremonies with one of the undersecretaries of the Navy, a few members from the Senate Armed Services Committee . . . The showing is scheduled for Saturday, October 20. Your old shipmate Sean Devlin has been most helpful getting to the right people."

Warren almost asked if she was sleeping with Devlin, but stopped himself. Who she wound up in the sack with was none of his business—not anymore.

"You haven't had any of the sandwiches yet," Hilary commented.

"You've covered all the bases, I guess," he said, sitting down again and starting to pour more coffee for himself.

"Let me do that," she said, taking the carafe from him. "I think I did cover all the bases. It's just a serendipitous situation."

"All the bases except one, Hilary, and that one has to do with the effect of this showing on your son."

"It will put him into the art world."

"It will separate him from the other men and it will do the same between him and his instructors. Now he's just another midshipman, but he'll be something else after the showing."

"He'll be recognized as the talented young man he is."

"He has another year to go at the Academy and then two at flight school."

"Maybe he should resign now," she said.

Warren was on his feet. "No," he shouted. "Absolutely not. You took care of his girlfriend's pregnancy—I can almost understand that, even if you didn't bother to discuss the matter with me . . . and I can, though I disagree with what you're doing, understand why you want to give him a showing . . . but when it comes to your meddling with him finishing his time at the Academy, that's where I draw the line. We've been over this many times in the past. He has to finish it and give himself a chance to be an officer. He'll see it through, if you don't get involved."

"He'll see it through because he doesn't want to disappoint you," she fired back at him.

"I don't give a damn why he does it, as long as he does it," Warren said, glaring at her.

She glared back. "You'd better go," she told him with controlled fury. "From now on, whatever we have to say to one another can be said on the phone."

Warren stood up, and without giving her the satisfaction of answering, he left the office. Once he was in the street, he walked rapidly toward Fifth Avenue. He was in a rage and he could do nothing but let it exhaust itself inside of him.

14

JACOB AND ARLENE left the Metropolitan Museum of Art and walked hand-in-hand into Central Park. The late–Tuesday-afternoon sky was clear and the light breeze that blew from the north had just a hint of the coming fall. Jacob had come to New York the previous day to take part in a symposium on "The Strike Capabilities of a Carrier Group" and he'd decided to stay in the city until Wednesday morning. Arlene had joined him Monday night, and though she had two late-morning classes to teach, they were able to spend the entire afternoon together.

She entwined her arm with Jacob's. "I have an early departmental meeting tomorrow morning," Arlene said, "and it's my turn to write up the minutes."

"Meaning that you want to be home tonight," he said. Usually she spent the night with him at the hotel and cabbed it to Brooklyn in the morning in time to make her nine-o'clock class.

"The meeting starts at eight. It would be easier—"

Jacob stopped, turned, and said, "You know, you really don't have to work. You don't have to live where you live. You can finish your doctorate in a year instead of two to three more years."

"Jacob"—she never called him Jake—"we've been through this before. I can't take those things from you. I can't let you support me."

They started to walk again.

"I need to know that I'm my own person," she told him. "It's one thing for me to be your mistress—"

"I love you," he said passionately.

She nodded. "I know that, and I love you."

"The money doesn't mean anything," Jacob said. "I'd never miss it. I want to give you everything I possibly can, and I know that whatever I give you is a poor substitute for giving you my name."

"I know that if you could marry me, you would. And I know that the money really does mean nothing to you. But I'd never want to feel beholden to you," she said, accentuating what she said by pressing his arm against her breast. "The love I give you, I give freely."

"It's just that I could make your life so much easier than it is," Jacob said.

"It's easier now that I know you."

"Mine too," Jacob responded; then he said, "Since you refused to go to Japan with me, I invited the Kurokachis here, as my guests, and Yashi agreed to come."

"When?"

"They'll be in New York a week from today, in time to go to Andrew's show, which is the following Saturday. I've made arrangements to take him on a guided tour of the Academy. Warren said he'd join us."

"Oh, how wonderful!"

"They'll stay at the Plaza when they're in New York, and I'd appreciate whatever time you could devote to Midori, Yashi's wife."

"Certainly I'll spend time with her."

"I'm really looking forward to their visit. Part of the time they'll stay with Tony and Miriam."

"You sound as excited as a little boy at his own birthday party."

"I am," he said. "I really am. Yashi . . . well, we have a kind of special relationship."

"You never did tell me how you met him," she said as they walked through the archway leading to the Children's Zoo.

Jacob spotted a chestnut vendor and immediately started Arlene toward the cart. "I love freshly roasted chestnuts . . . do you?"

"Obviously not as much as you do."

Jacob bought a bag of chestnuts, opened it, and handing a chestnut to Arlene, said, "They're hot, all right!" Then he took one for himself, broke open the shell, took out the white meat, and popped it into his mouth, commenting, "Damn good. I used to bring Sy and Tara here when Sy was a little boy. I'd buy him food to feed the animals, and sometimes, he'd eat it. He said the animals were sharing it with him."

"Are you going to tell me how you met Yashi, or—"

"Or he'll probably tell you," Jacob said.

"It had to be after the war," she ventured, "or maybe before?"

"Neither," he said, devouring another chestnut.

"Sometimes, Jacob, you can be infuriating."

"And sometimes," he responded, "like this very moment, a light comes into those black eyes of yours and a kind of blush comes into your cheeks and you're even more beautiful and more desirable than I thought possible. But you are." And wrapping his arm around her waist, he held her tightly against him for an instant, almost causing her to lose her footing.

"Jacob!" she cried.

"I've got you," he said, steadying her and bringing her around to face him; then he kissed her.

"That won't get you off the hook. I still want to know how you met Yashi."

They started to walk again.

"We met in the middle of the Pacific Ocean," he said, throwing the empty brown paper bag that had held the chestnuts into a trashcan. "I was shot down—"

"Shot down!" she exclaimed in alarm. "He shot you down?"

Jacob shook his head. "He was in the drink before me. Both of us were in the Battle of Midway. Anyway, I went down and managed to get into my life raft, when I realized that someone was swimming toward me. It was Yashi."

"There has to be more to it than that," Arlene insisted.

"He clung to the raft and we were rescued by an American destroyer."

"You make it sound so ordinary," she told him.

Jacob shrugged. "It wasn't ordinary, but—"

"He might have tried to kill you. After all, you were enemies."

"He was unarmed. I had the revolver."

"Then why didn't you kill him?" Arlene asked. "You would have done it if you were in the air; then both of you would have tried to kill the other."

Jacob filled his pipe and lit it.

"You couldn't kill him, could you?" Arlene questioned.

Quietly Jacob answered, "I couldn't kill a defenseless man. I couldn't do that and still think of myself as a human being."

"You're . . . you're . . ." Her voice broke and she uttered a wordless sob.

"Besides," Jacob said, "before I left, my father—may he rest in peace—said, 'Jacob, never do anything that you would be ashamed to tell your son about.' "

She lifted his hand and kissed the back of it.

"So now you know how Yashi and I met," Jacob said.

"I know, and I also know why he's made you his business partner, why he has named his son after you, and why I love you more than I can ever tell you. Oh, Jacob, take me back to the hotel and make love to me!"

Resting against the bed's headboard, Jacob was only halfheartedly watching the seven-o'clock news, while Arlene, still nude, stood in front of the mirror and began to dress. From where he was, he could also see her reflection. She was beautiful to look at. Her breasts were firm and her nipples were dark pink. Her body was supple and the convexity of her buttocks was as lovely to him as the thrust of her breasts.

She smiled. "I thought you were watching TV, but you're devouring me."

"I already did that," he answered, remembering how, just a short time before, his mouth was pressed against her sex. "You're delicious."

"So are you," she said, and began to dab perfume on her breasts and behind her ears.

"I love watching you dress."

"You just like looking at me naked."

"That too," he said. "I look at you standing there and I know I'm a lucky man . . . I know that you belong to me. Yes, I mean it that way, even if it is childishly possessive. I know that you've given me a second chance to be loved and give love—and that, for a man my age, is a precious gift to receive from a woman."

She made a half-turn. "The way you look at me, Jacob, makes me feel special . . . makes me feel wanted, loved."

He moved down the length of the bed until he reached her; then he buried his face in the hollow of her stomach and cupped each of her nates with his hands. "I can never get enough of you," he passionately told her, and was about to kiss her vagina again, when suddenly the phone rang.

"Who—"

"Probably a wrong number," Jacob said, still holding her buttocks.

The phone continued to ring.

"Does Julio know you're here?"

She nodded. "But he wouldn't call unless it's an emergency. Maybe it's Tony?"

"He's in Hong Kong," Jacob answered, realizing that he'd given the hotel's phone number and Tony's to the department's security officer so that he could be reached in an emergency.

"Better answer it," she said.

Jacob let go of her buttocks, and launching himself up the length of the bed, he reached over to the phone on the night table. "Captain Miller, here," he said.

The man on the other end said, "This is Captain Clark Houser."

"Yes, Captain," Jacob answered. He and Houser worked for Admiral Bench, who was chief of planning.

"We're on a Yellow Alert," Houser said. "You're to report back here as soon as possible. A government vehicle is on its way to the hotel and you'll be flown back by chopper."

"I have my own plane—"

"The admiral wants you here, Jake. The chopper will be waiting for you at Floyd Bennett Field Coast

Guard Station in Brooklyn. See you soon." The line went dead.

Jacob put the phone down, and looking at the TV, he wondered if he'd missed something.

"What's wrong?" Arlene asked.

He shook his head. "I don't know. I've been ordered back to Washington."

She came to the bed and rested her knees on it.

Suddenly the TV commentator said, "This just in from Washington, D.C. There are unofficial reports from our nation's capital that the Russians have installed ICBMs on the island of Cuba—"

"Oh, my God!" Arlene exclaimed, suddenly crossing her arms over her bare breasts.

"We repeat," the commentator said, "there are unconfirmed reports that the Russians have installed ICBMs on the island of Cuba. We will keep you informed as the situation develops. And now, back to our regular scheduled news. . . ."

"Oh, Jacob, I—" Her voice broke.

He took her in his arms. "I don't have much time," he said. "A car is on its way to pick me up."

She kissed him, her face wet with tears.

"I have to dress," he said, forcing himself away from her.

She nodded and stood. "I'll go down with you."

They dressed without exchanging a word. The TV commentator repeated the initial announcement two more times before Jacob turned off the set and said, "I'm ready to go."

Arlene moved close to him. "Do you think this means war?" she asked in a whisper.

"It could," he reluctantly admitted.

Simultaneously they embraced each other.

Jacob kissed her passionately on the lips. "I love you, Arlene," he told her in a husky voice.

"You're my life," she answered, stifling sobs.

He took hold of her hand, opened the door to the hallway, and gently led her out of the room. "I'll be in touch with you as soon as I can," he said, aware that she might be in more danger than he was. There was no doubt in his mind that at least one of those missiles was targeted on New York.

When the elevator came, there were several people already in it, and because Jacob was in uniform, he was the center of attention.

"Excuse me, sir," one of the women said, "but I just heard that the Russians put missiles in Cuba. Do you know anything about it?"

"No ma'am," Jacob answered. "I heard the same thing."

"I have a nineteen-year-old grandson who's in college," she said. "If something happened to him, it would kill my daughter."

"I have a son too," Jacob said quietly.

"How could we let this happen?" she questioned.

To Jacob's relief, the elevator car reached the lobby, the doors opened, and he didn't have to answer the woman. But to Arlene he said, "I don't understand people like that. Doesn't she realize that my son is as precious to me as her grandson is to her daughter? When all is said and done, our children are the only reality we leave behind." He shook his head.

"She's frightened," Arlene responded.

"So am I—I'm frightened because I've been there . . . I saw what a nuclear bomb did to Hiroshima."

Hand-in-hand they walked toward the entrance and went through the door, held open by the doorman.

As soon as they stepped out into the street, a black

limo pulled up, the driver got out, and said, "Your car, Captain Miller."

Jacob nodded and turned to the doorman. "Cab, please, for the lady."

"Yes, sir." The doorman blew a whistle.

A cab drove up and stopped behind the limo. The doorman opened the vehicle's rear door and stepped aside.

"I'll call you as soon as I can," Jacob assured her, kissing her again.

"Take care of yourself," she whispered.

Jacob nodded and helped her into the rear seat. "See you soon," he said, backed away, and nodded to the doorman to close the door. Moments later the cab began to move away. He saw Arlene looking back at him out of the rear window. He waved, blew a kiss to her, and then went to the waiting car.

15

BY THE SIXTH day of the Cuban missile crisis, as it was called by the newspaper and TV reporters, Warren had been reassigned from the Office of Advance Planning back to the Office of Naval Intelligence, where he coordinated the evaluation of updated intelligence data on the position of Russian warships and missile-carrying freighters that were in violation of President Kennedy's quarantine, and recommended to Admiral Charles Wiggs, the director of ONI, points of intercept by American naval vessels.

He was well aware of the fact that Jacob had been given command of the carrier *Trenton*, and at 1600 he had received a copy of the radio message from the *Trenton* stating that one of her reconnaissance aircraft had spotted two missile-carrying freighters forty miles from her present position.

"We don't have anything closer than the *Trenton*," Warren commented aloud to Lieutenant Norman Tragel as the two of them scanned a huge map of Cuba and the surrounding waters in a radius of five hundred miles.

"They're making fifteen knots at the most," the lieutenant offered.

Warren looked at his watch. "Even with the *Trenton* going at flank, they'll make the intercept about fifteen minutes before sundown," he said, looking toward Tragel.

He moved from the wall map to a desk, and picking up a phone, dialed the admiral's number. "Sir," he said as soon as he had identified himself to Burns, "the *Trenton* reports two missile-carrying freighters forty miles northeast of her present position of twenty-four degrees north, seventy-five degrees east, which puts them, on their present course and speed, within three hours of our quarantine line."

"You're certain of that?" Burns questioned.

"Yes, sir . . . Captain Miller would not have permitted the information to be radioed unless he was absolutely certain."

"Miller is a steady man, from what I hear," Burns commented.

Despite the seriousness of the situation, Warren almost smiled. "Yes, sir, that's the reputation he has."

"Advise the CNO of the situation," Burns said, "and suggest that Captain Miller proceed at flank speed toward the Soviet ships, but he is not to fire unless fired upon."

"Aye, aye, sir," Warren answered.

"As soon as he has visual contact with the ships, he is to radio for further instructions. Those instructions will come directly from the President."

Warren was too surprised to respond.

"He has assumed his constitutional right to become the commander in chief. No attack against any Soviet ship will be made unless he personally orders it."

Warren couldn't help hearing the disgust in the admiral's tone.

"It's the President's show," Burns said.

"Yes, sir, I understand," Warren responded. He put the phone down, only to pick up another that gave him a direct line to the office of the CNO, and he made his report to the watch officer.

"I wouldn't want to be in Miller's shoes," the man commented. "It's a damn tight fit when you can't act on your own and have to wait for someone else, who isn't even there and doesn't really know what your situation is, to make up his mind about what you should do."

"Captain Miller can handle it," Warren answered. "He's been in some tight fits before." Then he put the phone down, and as he went back to look at the map, he filled and lit his pipe. He wasn't exactly sure how he felt about President Kennedy *taking command*, so to speak. The situation was sufficiently fraught with danger for every precaution to be taken to avoid an accidental firing by either a very nervous officer or a trigger-happy one—and unhappily, there was that kind in all of the services, especially when it involved their thinking about the Russians. Although, as a professional, he felt that civilian interference in military matters almost always resulted in a disaster, this time, in his opinion, the stakes were too high to allow the military to act on its own. He had heard that some Air Force brass has pushed for and still were pushing for bombing the missile sites, but could not guarantee that all of them would be knocked out. And certain Army generals wanted to invade Cuba, while some of the admirals were intent on launching air strikes from carriers, which would be followed up by a Marine assault. All of these suggestions made a larger and certainly more destructive conflagration with the Soviets an absolute certainty. . . . Warren puffed hard on his pipe. He could understand why Kennedy wasn't taking any chances. In his place, he would have taken the same route.

Seated calmly in the captain's chair on the *Trenton's* bridge, Jacob maintained direct radio communication with the chopper pilot who was in visual contact with the two Russian ships that by now had been ID'd as the *Gagarin* and the *Komiles*. After having received his orders directly from the CNO, he immediately had implemented them. Now, as it always had been in the past, there was the period of waiting before sighting the enemy.

Jacob knew that he and the other captains in command of the patrolling ships shouldered an awesome responsibility. And though the actual command to fire would be made by the President, one or another of them would relay that order to his men.

"Blue Base, this Blue Bird One, I have you in sight," the chopper pilot radioed.

"Are the ships proceeding?" Jacob asked.

"Roger, sir. They're proceeding on course and maintaining their previous speed."

"We'll be sending up another chopper," Jacob advised. "Hold your position until he arrives."

"Aye, aye, sir," the pilot answered.

Jacob put down the phone, made a slight turn, and in a normal voice he said to the OOD, "Launch Blue Bird Two and make preparations to recover Blue Bird One."

"Aye, aye, sir," the OOD replied.

Jacob resumed his original position, aware that twilight was already beginning to darken the sea and sky in front of the *Trenton*.

"Blue Bird Two launched," the OOD advised, even

as the chopper whirled over the carrier's deck, gained altitude, and headed out in front of it.

"Let's put our attack bombers on deck, ready to launch . . . just to give them something to look at," Jacob told the OOD, without turning to look at him.

As soon as the order went out over the 1MC, the elevators began to deliver the aircraft to the deck, and the yellow jerseys—the plane handlers—moved them into position along the ship's port side, while the ordnance handlers, in red jerseys, armed them, and the men wearing purple jerseys fueled them.

In a matter of minutes the OOD reported that "Attack bombing squadron four is ready to be launched."

Jacob acknowledged the information with a nod.

"Sir, we have radar contact with the two ships," the OOD said.

Jacob left the chair and went directly to the radarscope. "Not long before we make visual contact," he commented.

"Fifteen minutes at the very most," the OOD responded.

The 1MC bawled, "Deck crew, stand by to recover chopper. . . . Stand by to recover chopper."

"Skipper," the OOD said, "Blue Bird Two reports the two ships have reduced speed . . . and communications reports heavy radio traffic."

Jacob saw the change of speed on the radar display scope. "They probably have us on their radar," he said, walking back toward his chair.

"Targets, bearing nine-zero," another officer on the bridge reported, looking through a pair of field glasses.

Jacob saw the twin smudges of black smoke against the rapidly graying twilight sky.

"Notify Washington that we have made visual contact," he said, picking up his own pair of binoculars and training them first on the smudge of smoke, then lowering them until he had the two ships in focus. "Stand by to reduce speed. All engines ahead one-third."

"All engines ahead one-third," the engine-room telegraph operator repeated.

Putting the binoculars down, Jacob said, "Signal our escort to reduce speed one-third ahead."

"Aye, aye, sir," the OOD answered.

"Illuminate the flight deck," Jacob ordered, aware of the rapidly diminishing light.

"Escorts reducing speed," an officer of the watch reported.

"General quarters," Jacob told the OOD. Up until that moment the *Trenton* and her escorts were at a Condition Two of readiness.

The 1MC gave a long shriek; then the OOD announced, "All hands, battle stations . . . All hands, battle stations . . . All hands, battle stations."

Moments after the voice on the 1MC stopped, a bridge phone rang and the officer answering it said, "Sonar reports a target bearing eight-five degrees . . . range, twelve miles . . . speed, twenty knots . . . depth, three hundred feet . . . closing."

The next instant the two lead escorts reported making contact with a submarine.

"One of theirs," the OOD commented in a low voice.

"Radio Washington and—"

The phone next to the captain's chair rang. Jacob picked it up and identified himself.

"This is the President," the voice on the other end said. "Give me an exact description of what you have out there, Captain Miller."

"Mr. President, in the few minutes that have elapsed since our radio transmission to headquarters, we have picked up a submarine between us and the two Russian ships."

After a momentary pause President Kennedy asked, "Are you absolutely certain that it is a submarine and that it is a Russian submarine?"

"Yes, Mr. President," Jacob answered.

"Stand by," President Kennedy said. "This is a development that we hoped would not occur. . . . I will be in contact with you again as quickly as possible."

"Standing by," Jacob responded, and putting down the phone, he left the captain's chair and positioned himself to its right, facing the ship's bow. From the sonar report, he knew the submarine was now within ten thousand yards of the *Trenton*, moving at the same speed and depth and still closing. There wasn't any doubt in his mind that her torpedo tubes were armed and ready. . . . "Signal our escorts to reduce speed to ahead one-third," he told the OOD.

"Aye, aye, sir," the OOD replied.

Then Jacob ordered the same speed reduction for the *Trenton*. He stood in an at-ease position, though he was as far from being at ease as a man could possibly be. Should the order come to attack and destroy the submarine, he'd have to risk taking a torpedo or having one or more of the escorts take one. That would be his immediate concern. Beyond that, there was the real possibility that missiles targeted on New York and other American cities would be launched from Cuban bases. There were his sister and Arlene—

The sonar report put the submarine on the same bearing, speed, and depth . . . only now it was a thousand yards closer and still closing.

The sudden ring of the phone on the silent bridge startled Jacob. He turned toward the chair, took a step closer to it, and picked up the phone.

"Captain," the President said, "use your sonar to signal the submarine to surface. If it does not obey your order, attack it. If it still refuses to surface, destroy it."

Jacob swallowed hard and finally managed to answer, "Yes, Mr. President."

"This line will remain open," the President said. "I want to be informed of events as they occur."

"Yes, Mr. President," Jacob answered; then, turning to the OOD, he said, "Have sonar order the submarine to surface."

The OOD hesitated.

Jacob repeated his command, but this time there was a snap to his voice.

"Aye, aye, sir," the OOD answered, his face suddenly flushing.

Jacob nodded, and turning away, looked out over the flight deck. He wanted to pace, but would not permit himself the luxury of showing just how anxious he was.

"Sonar is sending the message, using the international Morse code," the OOD said.

"Stand by to launch squadron four," Jacob said.

The OOD phoned the order to the air boss, who immediately came on the 1MC and ordered, "Pilots, man your planes."

"Make sure Blue Bird Two has a fix on the sub," Jacob said.

"It has. I already checked on that. We'll be able to lay down a pattern of bombs all around it."

"Captain Miller?" President Kennedy called.

"Captain Miller, here," Jacob responded into the mouthpiece of the phone.

"Any response?"

"Not yet, Mr. President," Jacob answered.

"Try again. How close is that submarine to you?" the President asked.

"Nine thousand yards."

"That's well within the range of her torpedoes, isn't it?"

"Yes, Mr. President, it is," Jacob said. He could hear the President take two deep breaths, and just as it seemed he was about to speak, the OOD said, "Sonar reports the submarine heading toward the surface."

"The submarine is on her way up, Mr. President," Jacob said.

The President uttered a deep sigh of relief. "Thank God!" he exclaimed. "Thank God!"

"Blue Bird Two reports the freighters are dead in the water," the OOD said.

Jacob relayed the information to the President.

"Heave to," the President said, "and see what the Russians do before you order the ships to turn back."

"Yes, Mr. President," Jacob answered. But his intuition told him that for him, at this place and time, the crisis was over. Those freighters would not challenge the quarantine.

"Submarine surfacing two points off the starboard bow," an officer on the bridge called out.

"Mr. President," Jacob said, "the submarine is on the surface." Then he ordered his escorts and the carrier to "hold steerage way."

One of the bridge phones rang and the officer nearest to it picked it up. "Sir, the Russian submarine captain has signaled that neither he nor the two cargo ships will attempt to cross our line of quarantine."

Jacob grinned and gave the information to the President.

"Well, now," Kennedy said, laughter in his voice,

"we might have just given the human race another chance."

"I hope so, Mr. President," Jacob answered. "I hope so."

16

THE CUBAN CRISIS was over, and Andrew's first show, which had been postponed because of it, was held, though not in Annapolis, as Hilary had initially envisioned, but—in the interim, she had been able to use her considerable influence—in a small, highly regarded gallery on Madison Avenue in New York.

The opening of the show took place on the first Friday night in November.

The time specified on the invitation was seven P.M., but Warren and Carol didn't arrive until seven-thirty, and by then the gallery was crowded with people and the air already filled with cigarette smoke. Waiters dressed in tuxedos and white gloves moved among the guests offering champagne in tulip glasses and various hors d'oeuvres.

Though Andrew had already met Carol, this would be the first time Warren would introduce her to his friends and former wife, Hilary. Since he'd started his relationship with Carol, he hadn't made any effort to have her meet either Jacob or Tony.

Dressed in a dark gray business suit, Warren, except for his posture, looked like many of the other men there. And Carol, in a lovely dark green cocktail dress, was certainly an attractive, if not beautiful, woman.

The moment he took the tag from the coat-check girl and headed for the other guests, he saw Andrew coming toward him.

Andrew shifted the glass of champagne from his right hand to his left and with a big boyish smile offered his right hand, exclaiming, "This is really something, isn't it!"

Warren shook his son's hand and answered, "Looks that way, doesn't it?" Show or no show, he still considered Andrew a naval officer, nothing more and certainly nothing less.

Andrew shook Carol's hand. "If I remember nothing else in my life," he commented, looking back over his shoulder, "I'll remember this. It's a lot like being born again."

"Hopefully not as traumatic," Carol responded.

Even as the exchange took place between Andrew and Carol, Warren saw Jacob, and seeing a woman very close to him, knew that Jacob had brought her. "I see Jacob, but no one else," Warren commented.

"Uncle Tony and Aunt Miriam are here too, and so are the Kurokachis," Andrew answered.

"Anyone come up from school for this event?" Warren asked. He hadn't remembered that Yashi and his wife would be in New York at this time, though he did recall being told by Jacob during one of their phone conversations that they were coming for a visit.

"Sy couldn't make it," Andrew said.

"I think I'll go over to Jacob and introduce Carol to him," Warren said. "Then I'll take a look at your work." Though he'd known exactly where Jacob was during the crisis, he doubted if Jacob had any idea how closely they had been linked.

Andrew nodded; then to Carol he said, "It's a pleasure to see you again," and went off in the direction of his friends.

"You should be very proud of him," Carol whispered as they moved across the room.

Warren didn't answer. His feelings were mixed. He knew that without Hilary's help none of it would be taking place, but he also knew, though admittedly from a nonprofessional viewpoint, that Andrew was an extremely talented artist.

"I saw you the moment you came in," Jacob said, breaking into a smile as soon as Warren was close. "But I didn't want to interrupt a father-son confab."

The two men shook hands.

Warren introduced Carol to Jacob, and Jacob said, "Arlene Gomez, Captain Warren Troost and Carol Langston."

"We're going to have to go through this all over," Warren told them.

"Worse things could happen," Carol said.

"Word is out that you're a 'cool cat,' " Warren said, looking at Jacob.

"Never believe that kind of word," Jacob replied. "I sweated off ten pounds in ten minutes out there, until that Russian captain got the word to turn around and go home."

Warren nodded sympathetically. "I would have much preferred to be out there doing something than where I was."

"Where were you?"

"ONI."

"Then you knew—"

"Minute by minute, ol' buddy," Warren laughed.

"Just before I left Norfolk to come up here, I received an invitation from the President to visit him at the White House and then be his guest for a long weekend at Hyannis."

"He must have been impressed," Warren commented. "That just about guarantees you two stars when the time comes, or maybe even before it."

Jacob flushed. "I guess it could happen that way, but it probably won't. I'm told he thinks of himself as one of us. After all, during the war he was a PT skipper, just the way you were."

"And now he's the President, the commander in chief—our boss."

With a shrug, Jacob said, "The wheel of fortune . . . we all have one, only his really had a fortune."

"Here comes Tony and Miriam!" Arlene exclaimed.

"You know them?" Warren questioned, surprised at the obvious familiarity.

"They've met several times," Jacob said.

Warren's eyebrows raised slightly, but then he quickly masked his surprise and gave his attention to Tony and Miriam, who were almost in front of them.

"Well, you should certainly be the proud father," Miriam commented, looking at Warren.

"*I* certainly would be," Tony said.

"You know Warren," Jacob laughed. "He doesn't ever say a hell of a lot."

All of them laughed.

"I haven't even seen most of the paintings," Warren said. "I'll give you my inexpert opinion after I've looked at them."

"How about the eight of us getting together after?" Tony asked. "Yashi and his wife are somewhere in this crowd."

Jacob looked questioningly at Arlene.

"I'd like that," she said.

"Warren?"

"I'll have to stay to the end," he answered.

"We'll stay too," Tony offered.

"No, tell me where you'll be, and Carol and I will meet you there," Warren said.

"Good. Let's make it easy. . . . The Pierre's cock-tail lounge."

"That's fine," Warren answered, and taking Carol's hand, he said, "I better start looking at the paintings—Andrew has been glancing over here with a—"

"Go!" Jacob exclaimed. "There's no need to explain."

Warren took hold of Carol's hand and led her off to look at his son's paintings. He started at the beginning, near the gallery's door. The first painting was an acrylic titled *A London Street.*

"It's almost like a photograph," Carol said.

Warren agreed.

The next three were done in the same medium and style: there was another London scene from the East India Dock section; a beautifully executed painting of the Cutty Sark, in Greenwich; and the third was of an old woman sitting on a park bench feeding pigeons small pieces of bread.

"You never said Andrew was this good," Carol commented.

Warren turned and moved to the fourth of Andrew's canvases, a nude reclining on a bed. It was an oil painting.

There were seven more of the same model, and all of them were nudes. The next painting was a nude also, but the model and the medium were different. Andrew returned to acrylic paints, and again the style was almost photographic.

"You can see every hair in her crotch," Warren

remarked. "Even the droplets of . . ." He stopped and looked at the title of the painting. *"After an Orgasm,"* he read aloud, and immediately felt the color rise in his cheeks. "Why the hell would he paint something like that?" he asked in a low, tight voice.

"Captain Troost?" a man called from behind.

Warren turned. He didn't recognize him.

"Michael Lipner," the man said. "Art critic for the magazine *New Perspectives*."

Warren looked at him questioningly. "I'm sorry," he said. "I don't know—"

Lipner gave a squeaky laugh that was oddly in keeping with his small, slight build and thin black mustache. "The competition for your wife's . . . I mean your ex-wife's magazine."

"I wasn't aware that *The Complete Woman* had any competition," Warren answered. Though only a few moments had passed, he already intensely disliked the man.

"We're the more conservative of the two," Lipner said, and gesturing toward the painting, he commented, "Your son certainly has an eye for detail."

Before Warren could answer, Lipner asked, "Tell me, Captain Troost, what do you think of your son's paintings?"

"Ah, Warren, there you are!"

Warren saw Sean Devlin coming toward him.

"I see Mr. Lipner has cornered you, and I have come to rescue you from him," Devlin said, extending his hand to Warren.

They shook hands.

"I had no idea that you knew Captain Troost," Lipner said.

"Captain Troost was my CO during the war," Devlin

said; then, putting his hand on Warren's shoulder, he said, "We're old friends."

Lipner nodded and with a thin smile took two steps back. His smile to Warren was almost a leer, a knowing leer at that.

"Perhaps you'd care to answer the question another time, Captain?" Lipner asked.

"I'll answer it now. I think my son is very talented."

"Then you fully support him—"

"I answered your question, Mr. Lipner," Warren said. "Now, if you'll excuse me, I'd like to view the rest of the paintings without being disturbed."

"To put it more bluntly," Devlin said, "get lost!"

As soon as the three of them were alone, Devlin said, "I'm really glad to see you, Warren."

Again the two of them shook hands.

Warren introduced him to Carol and said, "Sean saved my life." And was about to add, *He was and probably still is my ex-wife's lover,* but didn't. Instead he added, "Now he has saved me again—from the 'competition.'"

Smiling, Carol said, "Thank you for saving him twice."

"He's worth it," Devlin responded, returning her smile; then he said, "I'll let the two of you see the rest of the show. It was a pleasure to meet you, Mrs. Langston."

"Please, call me Carol," she said.

"Carol. I'll catch the two of you later." Devlin turned and quickly melded with the crowd.

"What a charming man!" Carol exclaimed.

"He certainly is that."

"The name Devlin . . ." Carol began as they came to the next painting.

"Yes, he's the famous writer," Warren answered.

The painting showed two nudes: a woman and a man embracing.

Warren said nothing about the subject matter. The paintings that followed were either street scenes in Paris or portraits, and there was one wonderful pastel of Sy—just his head and shoulders. "Looks like his father," Warren commented; then wistfully he added, "But those gentle eyes belong to Tara, his mother."

"Did Jacob divorce her?" Carol asked hesitantly.

Warren shook his head, and wrapping her arm around his, he said, "No . . . he's still married to her. But she's in an institution . . . It's too long a story and too sad . . ." He saw Hilary. She was halfway across the room. She was wearing a metallic blue gown cut so low the bare tops and sides of her breasts were clearly visible. She held a white cigarette holder in her left hand and a drink in her left. "That's my ex-wife," he told Carol, his voice just above a whisper.

"She's very beautiful," Carol answered.

Silently Warren nodded. Suddenly he realized why he hadn't introduced Carol to his friends: he didn't want them to compare her to Hilary. Carol, though attractive, was nowhere near as sophisticated as Hilary, either in her choice of clothes or in her attitude. Hilary was a worldly woman, while Carol was a secretary in a large insurance-brokerage house.

"She's seen us," Carol said.

Hilary smiled, nodded, but made no movement toward them.

Warren returned the nod, but not the smile. Their last meeting had ended with both of them angry. He steered Carol to where Jacob and Arlene, Tony and Miriam, and now, Yashi and Midori were standing.

Jacob introduced Carol to the Kurokachis, and Yashi

said to Warren, "I have had the honor of buying several of your son's paintings."

"And I bought the pastel of Sy," Jacob added.

"I bought the painting of the Cutty Sark for my den," Tony said, "and a Paris street scene for the foyer."

Warren was too overwhelmed to respond with anything more than, "Thank you."

"They will prove to be valuable investments," Yashi said. "I have been buying the work of promising young artists for some time now, and in my humble opinion, your son has a brilliant future ahead of him."

"You're very kind," Warren answered, looking quickly to where he'd seen Hilary. She was still there, and this time their eyes locked, and though only for an instant, it was long enough for Warren to catch the glint in her eyes and see the hard lines around her chin. She was either angry or had had too much to drink. Perhaps both.

"All right," Tony said, "I think it's time for us to head for the Pierre. The crowd here has thinned out, and according to the invitation, the gallery will close at nine-thirty." He looked at his watch. "In another few minutes it will be closing time."

"We'll join you as soon as we can break away," Warren replied.

When they were alone again, Carol asked, "How did Yashi manage to become part of your group of friends?"

"That too is a story," Warren answered, taking two more glasses of champagne off the tray of a passing waiter.

"This is the first time I've been to the opening of an art show," Carol said. "What about you?" she asked as she lifted the glass to her lips and drank.

"Many," Warren said, also drinking, and as he drank, he looked around. There were fewer than twenty people left, and all of them were standing around Andrew. Then suddenly he saw Hilary coming toward them and felt Carol stiffen.

"Well, well, well," Hilary began, looking hard at Carol. "Not bad, Warren . . . not bad."

Warren attempted to introduce Carol.

"I'm not interested in knowing her name," Hilary said, "but I am interested in knowing if she's as good in bed as I am."

"You're drunk, Hilary," Warren said harshly. Suddenly he remembered the many times he'd seen his mother in the same state and his father trying to smooth over an ugly situation, just as he was now attempting to do. Filled with fury, he hated Hilary for doing this to him and to Carol . . . and to herself.

She uttered a shriek of laughter. "C'mon, Warren, don't be such a stiff . . . I want to know if she's a good lay."

Aware that the three of them were now the center of attention, Warren said, "Hilary, why don't we go somewhere and talk?" He took hold of her arm.

She pulled herself free. "Does she or does she not fuck . . . No, let me put it to you this way: on a scale of one to ten, how does she rate?"

"Warren, I'm leaving," Carol said, starting to walk.

"Carol?" he called.

"Let her go," Hilary said. "I'll—"

Warren saw Lipner grinning at him.

"Carol?" Hilary shouted. "Carol?"

"Andrew," Warren called. "Andrew, take care of your mother." And he went after Carol, finally catching up when she was forced to stop for a red light.

"I don't want to talk," Carol sobbed. "I don't want to do anything but go home."

"I'll take you," Warren said.

The light changed and Carol dashed across the street.

"Please come to the Pierre with me, then," Warren said, trying to take hold of her arm.

"I don't want to go," she said. "I want to go home alone."

"I'll call you tomorrow," Warren said.

Carol didn't answer.

Warren stopped, turned around and, full of sadness, started to walk slowly in the direction of the Pierre.

The next morning Warren tried to decide what to do. He sat on the edge of the bed. The way he saw it, he had only two options: to call Carol or to return to Washington without phoning her. He was almost as angry with her for running home as he was with Hilary for the way she had behaved.

He stood up and began to pace, still trying to make a decision. He certainly could understand Carol's humiliation—he himself felt humiliated not only by Hilary's words but also because she demeaned herself by saying what she said. That she should even think about his sex life was beyond his comprehension, especially when she'd on several different occasions let him know she had various lovers, including Devlin. . . .

"There was no way she could be jealous!" he exclaimed, and then he questioned whether he was jealous of her.

"Not anymore," Warren answered. "Maybe when we were first separated . . . but not now."

The phone rang.

He looked at it.

It rang again.

"Captain Troost, here," Warren said, picking up the phone and speaking into the mouthpiece.

"Warren, I want to see you," Carol said. "Can we meet somewhere?"

"Yes, I'd like that," he answered. "I'd like that a lot."

"Where?" she asked.

He thought for a moment. He really wanted to be either in her apartment or in his hotel room . . . someplace where he could make love to her, but he realized that she would not agree to either place. "How about Rumpelmayer's?" he asked. "I can be there in fifteen minutes."

"I'll need a bit more time."

"I'll wait," Warren answered, and then, just before the line went dead, he said, "I love you, Carol."

Rumpelmayer's decor was Victorian, complete with the multicolored Tiffany glass shades for the various ceiling chandeliers and small wall lamps. There were lit candles in pewter holders on the table.

Carol arrived ten minutes after Warren. He already had a table for two against a wall. They sat facing one another without speaking, except for the necessary exchange that allowed Warren to give the waitress the order.

"I'm glad you called," he finally said, and reached across the table to enclose her hands in his. "You're absolutely ice!" And he began to rub her hands.

"If I hadn't phoned, would you have?" Carol asked.

"I was thinking about doing it," he answered, still rubbing her hands.

She insisted on a direct answer.

"I was angry with you when you walked away," he

said. "I wanted you to be with me . . . I wanted to be with you last night . . . I want to make love to you now." He saw the waitress approach the table with a tray holding two cups of coffee and a basket of sweet rolls.

"I was too hurt to be with you," Carol responded.

He withdrew his hands from hers before the waitress placed a cup of coffee in front of each one of them and the basket of sweet rolls in the center of the table.

When they were alone again, Carol looked straight at him. "I'm not a whore," she said in a choked whisper. "The night you met me—picked me up—I was there, in that place, for the first time."

"You don't have to explain anything to me."

She shook her head. "I needed to be held, to be . . . no, to be fucked. Yes, just the way you needed to be laid. . . . But . . ." She paused, took a tissue out of her bag, used it wipe the tears off her cheeks, then blew her nose into it before she returned it to her bag. "I was with one other man before I met you—a man I met through a friend, and that was only once. I never saw him again."

The waitress brought their breakfast order. Warren had sausages and eggs, flipped over and well done, while Carol had two eggs and bacon.

As soon as the waitress left them, Warren said, "I didn't expect Hilary to act that way."

Bending her head toward the plate in front of her, Carol said softly, "She still loves you, Warren."

He was too stunned to answer.

Carol looked up at him. "She does, even though she may not even know it. Believe me, I'm right." And she began to cut the eggs.

"I love you, Carol," Warren told her. "I wouldn't be here if I didn't love you."

She put her knife and fork down. "I love you too . . . but I can't . . ." She took a deep breath, and after exhaling said, "I don't want to be your girlfriend—'mistress' would be a more accurate description."

Warren swallowed the piece of sausage in his mouth before he asked, "Are you presenting me with some kind of ultimatum?"

"No. I know better than to do that. I'm the one who is going to make the choice," she said. "I can't be your mistress any longer and still respect myself. I know that sounds crazy. But after last night . . . well, I just couldn't bear to have that happen again. I was hurt, and you were too . . . I know that. I saw it in your face."

Warren cast his eyes down; then, looking straight at her, he said, "It brought back a host of ugly memories. My mother was an alcoholic."

"Oh, my God!"

"Last night cast me in a role that I had seen my father take so many times," Warren said sadly. "And until last night I never fully understood the anguish he felt. I hated Hilary . . . I truly hated her."

"Do you hate her now?"

"If you're asking, and I think you are, whether or not I love her, the answer is, I don't love her, Carol. I love you. I don't want you to be my mistress either. I want you to be my wife."

Carol hesitated before she asked, "Are you sure, Warren, that's what you want?"

Nodding, he answered, "I'm sure . . . I'm absolutely sure I want to marry you."

She smiled, and tears began to flow out of her eyes.

Warren handed her his handkerchief.

For a moment Carol held on to his hand. "You're a good man, Warren, a very good man."

Janet's three-room apartment was in an apartment house on Waverly Place in Greenwich Village. Andrew cabbed back there from his mother's place, and when he arrived, Janet, a strawberry blond with a svelte body and firm, high breasts, was sitting cross-legged in bed with only a red silk kimono on that was parted on the bottom, revealing what in the vernacular was called "the hungry eye."

Andrew sat down on the bed and slowly moved his hand over one of her bare legs.

"How did it go with your mother?" Janet asked.

"We wound up in an argument," he said. "She won't admit that she was wrong."

"Even if she did, what difference would it make now?"

Andrew uttered a deep sigh. "None," he admitted. "But it's just that . . . well, neither my father nor Carol deserved that." He reached her knee and was beginning to want her. They had made love last night when they came back to the apartment after the gallery closed, and again in the early hours of the morning.

He opened the kimono, and laying bare the entire front of her body, he caressed the inside of her thighs.

"We can't have a meaningful conversation if you're going to play with me," Janet told him.

Andrew shook his head. "I don't want a meaningful conversation about my mother and father. Whatever I have to work out, I will."

"My advice, for what it's worth, is to stick with your mother," Janet said. "You yourself told me that your father only sees the world in navy blue. At least you can't ever accuse your mother of being that narrow."

Her skin felt delightfully warm to him.

"I guess you don't want to have a conversation, meaningful or otherwise," she said.

Andrew shook his head and stroked the moist lips of her vagina.

"Your tune," Janet said huskily, as she eased herself down on the bed and splayed her naked thighs.

17

JACOB SPENT THE second weekend of December as a guest of President Kennedy at the famed Kennedy Compound in Hyannis, Massachusetts. During his stay, he was given complete freedom of the house and met not only members of the President's family but also several people on the President's staff who were guests at the compound that week.

Because the President had been the skipper of a PT-109 in the Pacific during the war, Jacob enjoyed talking to him about the various actions in which they had participated.

On Sunday afternoon, immediately after lunch, the President asked Jacob to walk with him along the beach. The day was clear, cold, and so blustery that the sea gulls had difficulty flying. A high sea was running and the waves crashed with a roar against the sand beach. Behind them and to their side walked a protective screen of Secret Service and FBI agents.

Puffing on a huge cigar, Kennedy said, "I don't have to tell you how much I admired your performance a few weeks back. It took a special kind of courage not to react to that submarine."

"I was following orders," Jacob answered. "That's what I was supposed to do."

The President took the cigar out of his mouth and laughed. "I'm glad you did, or maybe—no, for sure—we wouldn't be walking along this beach now." He replaced the cigar and took a long drag on it, letting the smoke escape through his nose, before he said, "I was told you're a very wealthy man."

"Yes, Mr. President, that's true."

Kennedy stopped. "Tell me why you chose to stay in the Navy."

"After the war—World War Two—I still wanted to fly, and the Navy offered me the opportunity."

"You could have flown for an airline," the President countered, beginning to walk again.

"Not likely for a Jew to be able to do it, not at that time."

Kennedy squinted at him but didn't say anything.

Smiling, Jacob said, "I couldn't see myself doing anything else then, or, for that matter, now. Besides, now I'm too far along to try my hand at something else."

"Just how much money do you have?" Kennedy asked.

"In available cash, or cash and assets."

"Combined."

"I'm told in excess of fifteen million," Jacob answered quietly.

"Then you're definitely not staying in for your pension," the President said with a smile.

"Hardly," Jacob responded, shaking his head. "I'm in for the ride, Mr. President . . . I'd like to see how far I can go."

The President said, "I can understand that. After I finish this job—hopefully, I'll have a second term in which to do it—there are a few things I'd like to try to

see how far I can go with them." Again he stopped.
"Sometime ago I understand you were approached by
two senators to run for office, isn't that so?"

"How did—"

"There's not much I don't know about you, Captain. I know you kept the *Concord* in the Med. and
operational after the fire in her number two main . . .
I know about how you met your good friend Mr.
Kurokachi and what that relationship has led to . . . I
know that your wife, Tara, is in an institution and that
your present companion is Hispanic."

Jacob flushed.

"Would you tell me why you refused their offer?"
Kennedy asked.

"Two reasons, mainly. At least one of them was
from the wrong party. Like yourself, Mr. President,
I'm a Democrat. And the other votes with the wrong
party."

Yanking the cigar out of his mouth, Kennedy guffawed. "What's that old saw about the man leaving
the Marine Corps, but the Corps never leaves the
man!" He pointed the cigar at Jacob and said, "I'd be
willing to bet your father was a union man."

"ILGU," Jacob answered; then he added, "He came
to this country from Germany after World War One
and placed a high value on the political freedom he
found here."

"A liberal—"

"No, Mr. President, he was far from being a liberal. He was totally orthodox in his faith. But when it
came to politics . . . well, he'd come from a country
where the privileged class 'walked, as he said, 'on the
backs of the people.' "

Kennedy began smoking again. "Now tell me, what
was your second reason for turning the senators down?"

"They would have had me trade on my war record,"

Jacob said, knowing full well Kennedy had done exactly that, even to the point of having written a book about his wartime experiences aboard the PT-109 and having the book turned into a film.

The President nodded but said nothing, and for a while they walked side by side in silence.

Certain that he had offended the President, Jacob chided himself for not being more diplomatic. He didn't fault the President for capitalizing on his war record, or anyone else who did it. But he couldn't do it.

Kennedy broke the silence. "We'll soon be entering a new year, a year that's going to see profound changes in the United States. The millions of black Americans are going to demand and get changes. The civil-rights movement will change the southern states forever."

"Yes, I believe it will," Jacob answered, wondering what point the President was trying to get at. It seemed unlikely that he wanted to talk about the civil-rights movement with a career naval officer.

"I don't want to become too deeply involved in the problems of Vietnam. We already have a few thousand advisers there, and the Diem government is always asking for more men and matériel. To answer your question, even before you ask it: yes, we don't want it to fall to the Communists, but we don't want to become involved in a war the way the French did to hold the north and wound up at Dienbienphu."

Jacob understood the President's implication: if France, a modern Western nation, lost the war in the jungles of North Vietnam, we ran the risk of losing the jungles of South Vietnam, and he did not want to take that risk.

Glancing at Jacob, the President said, "I want you to go to Saigon for me and give me . . . not a report— God knows, I get enough of them. I want your personal impressions of what's happening there. I have the feeling that more is happening, much more, than I know about."

Jacob missed a step and almost lost his footing. "I'm honored, Mr. President," he answered.

Kennedy stopped. "I'll have you transferred to the White House. Your orders will be cut as soon as we return to Washington."

"When do you want me to leave?" Jacob asked.

"Early next year," Kennedy answered. "Will that be convenient for you?"

"Yes, Mr. President."

Turning toward the sea, Kennedy waved the cigar in front of him and said, "Looks like we're going to get some weather."

"It does," Jacob replied, knowing the President was referring to gray clouds forming over the churning ocean.

Kennedy put the cigar back in his mouth and started to walk back toward the compound. "You know," he said wistfully, "I wish I could be sure that I'd have the time to finish 'the ride,' as you called it." Then with a rueful smile he added, "But hell, we can't be sure of the next moment, let alone anything beyond it."

"The best we can do, Mr. President, is make the moment count, and hope."

"Not pray?"

"That, if it makes you feel better," Jacob responded.

Kennedy gave him a quick sideward glance.

"I'm not much of a believer, Mr. President," Jacob confessed.

Kennedy didn't answer.

18

WEARING CAMOUFLAGE FATIGUES, a broad-brimmed bush hat, dark amber-colored sunglasses, and carrying an M-14, Tony walked alongside First Lieutenant Paul Doza, a tall, broad-shouldered Marine officer serving with the Special Forces in South Vietnam.

"We got Charlie sighted in," Doza said. "He's got his camp five clicks south of the border. My guys have been watching them two, three weeks." Doza, a former grade adviser at Wagner High School in Staten Island, had volunteered for the Corps in 1960, and after basic, he applied for and was accepted into the Corps Officer Training Program. After a tour of duty in the Mediterranean, he was recruited by a special agent for duty with the Special Forces, and now his first tour of thirteen months in Indian Country, the slang designation for those areas the Vietcong controlled, was two weeks shy of coming to an end.

Tony accepted Doza's information without comment. He'd worked with this Spike Team a half-dozen times before and he'd learned to trust Doza. Besides, it was too fucking hot to comment. His shit-colored go-to-hell rag, the khaki-colored towel around his neck, was soaking wet with sweat.

Suddenly Doza's radio came to life. His right hand immediately shot up to halt the dozen LLDB, men belonging to the South Vietnamese Special Forces, who were behind him.

"Big D, this is Robin Hood." The voice belonged to Sergeant Fine.

Doza spoke into the hand-held radio. "What do you have?"

"Looks good . . . ten hostiles visible . . . more goodies than we saw last time."

"Copy," Doza answered. "Hold where you are."

"Wilco," Fine answered.

"If we go in now," Doza said, "we'll have trouble regrouping in the darkness."

Tony glanced at his watch: it was four-thirty. Then he looked up into the trees, through which, even in the fullness of the afternoon, scant light penetrated. But now, at the beginning of twilight, the jungle, always filled with a gray dimness, was quickly filling with long dark shadows that would soon join to create a heavy, almost palpable blackness.

"We've got twenty, maybe thirty minutes more before we lose the light," Doza commented. "If it's over quickly, we could regroup and be away before the real darkness settles in."

"Let's move," Tony said.

Doza signaled his men to move forward; then he called Robin Hood. "We're coming in."

"Roger," Fine said.

"Stay where you are," Doza told him. "Maintain radio silence."

"Wilco."

"Out."

Using the go-to-hell rag, Tony wiped the sweat from his face and from the front of his neck. This mission, like the others he organized, was clandestine. All of them were CIA operations from inception to execution. Neither the military nor the diplomatic personnel at the embassy in Saigon knew about them. The fewer people who knew just what he did, the more chance he had of succeeding. There wasn't any doubt in his mind—or anyone else's who understood what was happening in Nam—that Charlie was wired into just about everything that happened in the embassy. Through his own sources Tony had learned that Jacob had already made three trips to Saigon for Kennedy and was due to arrive the day after tomorrow, the twentieth of October. According to the information he had, Jacob was not exactly the most popular emissary from the United States. He asked too many questions about why the ARVN forces couldn't handle the VC, and never gave any indication what he intended to tell the President about the situation. Jacob's present itinerary called for him to spend several days in the Mekong Delta region with a VNN—South Vietnamese Navy—riverboat unit before going back to the world, as the American troops in Nam called the United States. Tony's movements in Nam were known only to the Company station chief and men like Doza. As far as any of the records showed, he'd never been in Nam, though he'd be on his way back to Hong Kong the day before Jacob would leave Saigon.

To signal a quickening of pace, Doza clenched his fist and pumped his right hand up and down.

Tony was silently telling himself that he was "too fucking old to be running along a jungle path—"

The first burst came from behind the column.

"Hit the deck!" Doza yelled in Vietnamese.

Tony dropped to the jungle floor and rolled into the growth alongside the trail.

Two more bursts came from the right.

Doza went down. The left side of his face was gone and blood poured down his fatigues.

Automatic fire raked the trail. Several of the men screamed.

"Walked into it," Doza croaked.

Someone in the column fired an M-70. The grenade tore up a patch of jungle on the other side of the trail.

Working his M-14 back and forth, Tony emptied a clip, pulled it out, and slamming a fresh one in, continued to fire.

Another M-70 round crashed into the jungle.

A searing pain ripped across Tony's left shoulder. "Christ!" he exclaimed, knowing he'd been hit. One of the LLDBs crawled up to him. In the now deep twilight he couldn't tell who it was.

"Many men hit," the man said. "Most dead." He looked at Doza and clicked his tongue.

Tony suddenly realized the firing had stopped and he was looking at Kim Tu, a lieutenant in the LLDB and the only other English-speaking man in the Spike Team.

"Too dark to shoot now," Kim Tu said.

Tony took hold of Doza's right hand and felt for a pulse. There wasn't any. "Dead," he told the man.

"Get the fuck out of here," Kim Tu responded.

Though he was less than a yard away, Tony could just about see his face. "Charlie will be on the trail. Can't go that way."

"Into the jungle on the other side of the trail. Move back onto trail in the morning."

Tony took the radio from Doza and tried without success to make contact with Fine. The sergeant and the two men with him had been either killed or captured. If they were captured, they'd soon probably wish they were dead. The VC didn't follow the Geneva Convention; they didn't know it existed, and if they did, they pretended not to know, which came to the same thing: brutal treatment for men they captured.

"Pass the word to the men to move out," Tony ordered. In the jungle on the other side of the trail, they'd be safe. The darkness would shield them from Charlie, and Charlie from them. With the coming of first light, they'd move parallel to the trail, and only when they were sure Charlie wasn't either in front of or behind them, they'd go back on the trail.

Tony bellied his way into the heavy jungle growth on the other side of the trail. His left shoulder was already beginning to feel sore and stiff.

There were movement and voices on the trail.

"Don't fire," he ordered in a loud whisper. "Don't fire. . . . Pass the word."

The sounds coming from the trail stopped.

Tony sucked in his breath and slowly let it out. He tried not to breathe too hard, afraid that Charlie might hear him. The rest of the night would be very long compared to the firefight, which had probably lasted no more than five minutes and more likely closer to three. But the rest of the night . . . well, that might easily be as long as a lifetime. Time enough to come up with a good cover story to explain the bullet wound in his shoulder.

"Charlie still on trail," Kim Tu whispered. "Six, seven maybe."

"How many do we have left?" Tony asked.

"Ten okay. Three wounded."

"Use Willie Pete in the M-79," Tony said. "Two quick rounds . . . everyone throws a grenade and we go back on the trail."

"Okay . . . wilco," Kim Tu answered. "Charlie still on trail."

Tony heard him move away. He took a grenade off his bandoleer, pulled the pin, and holding the plunger, took another deep breath. By the time he was finished exhaling, a loud bam broke the jungle silence and a white phosphorus grenade exploded on the trail.

Then another bam and the fire from another grenade poured flames into the night.

"Now!" Tony shouted, heaving his grenade onto the trail.

Explosion after explosion followed; some merged and some came within moments of each other.

Leaping to his feet, Tony ran onto the trail.

Charlie was screaming. Some were on fire and several had been torn apart by the grenades and were dying.

Holding the M-14 at the hip, Tony squeezed the trigger.

Two of the men on fire dropped to the side of the trail.

"Run," Tony shouted, starting down the trail. "Run." He ran until his chest ached and his vision was blurred with sweat. The darkness swallowed him up and he continued to run until he had to stop in order to breathe; then, looking back over his shoulder, he didn't see anything. "Safe," he gasped. "Safe. . . ."

19

IN THE PREDAWN grayness of Monday, October 28, Jacob was driven out to Hotel Three, the nickname for the helicopter landing area at Saigon's Tan Son Nhut Airport. The car sped through the city's dark, quiet streets that retained so much of the Gallic touch that they were almost Parisian in character. Even most of their names were still in French, as was the Splendide, the name of the hotel in which he was living during his stay in Saigon. This was his fourth visit in-country and his third to Indian Country. During these visits he'd learned that though many of the government and military people were corrupt, there were just as many who were not. His Vietnamese counterpart, Captain Chu Be was an honest navel officer who not only hated the Communists but also was truly fearful of what they would do if they won.

The car turned into the airport and stopped at a security gate. After he ID'd himself to the Marine guard, he was allowed to proceed. Several minutes later the car stopped at Hotel Three, and just as Jacob left it, Captain Be's car pulled up.

The two men exchanged salutes.

Be, a short man with a ready smile and bright black eyes, said, "You're here early."

"I was up earlier than usual," Jacob answered as they moved toward the Huey, which was on loan from the United States, like so much of the equipment they used, including the cars that had brought them to the airport.

Be nodded sympathetically, then said, "Maybe twenty minutes in the air."

That was about the flying time Jacob had estimated, looking at a map of the Delta region the previous evening. RAG-27, one of the River Assault Group of the VNN in the Delta, was located at My Tho.

The pilot came out of the chopper and saluted them.

They returned the courtesy and Be introduced Jacob to Lieutenant Dang Duc Khoi. "He was trained at Pensacola," he said.

"So was I, a long time ago," Jacob responded.

The three of them boarded the helicopter and the pilot moved forward to the cockpit.

Jacob strapped himself into the seat.

The sun, glowing red in the east, already had a portion of its circle above the horizon and had pinked the distant clouds.

A man came out to the pad and with two cones of light guided the pilot into a huge white square.

The rotors spun faster and faster, making the whole craft vibrate. Then the tail end of the chopper rose and the rest of it seemed to follow. Within a matter of moments they were above the airport and Jacob was able to watch the lights of Saigon wink out in the ever-increasing light of dawn.

The helicopter banked to the right and headed south. Below, Jacob watched the patterns of rice-field squares and rectangles emerge from the earth in brightening light. Already, straw-hatted people were at work in the shallow water.

"Look there!" Be shouted above the roar of the chopper's engine. He pointed to a small boat on one of hundreds of now glistening tendrils of the Mekong River. "Charlie going home." Then he picked up the intercom mike and headset. "We'll go down and take a closer look."

The chopper made a sharp left bank and rapidly dropped down, making a pass over the boat at no more than a hundred feet.

The two black-pajamaed individuals were firing AK-47s at them.

Be took down an M-14 from the rack behind him and told the pilot to make another pass at the boat.

The chopper climbed, then banked around in a tight right turn before it roared down at the boat, this time coming in at just a few feet above the water.

Be chambered a round, pointed the rifle out of the chopper's port-side open bay, and when the chopper was parallel to the boat, he squeezed the trigger, just long enough to rake it from stem to stern.

One of the pajama-clad figures went over the side and the other slumped toward the bow. Its starboard side badly holed, the boat began quickly to list to the right.

Be spoke to the pilot again.

The chopper rose and resumed its former course.

"We caught them by surprise," Be said, clearing the M-14's chamber, removing the clip, and putting the safety on before returning the weapon to the rack behind him.

Jacob nodded.

"They were probably taking supplies inland from a junk on the coast to a base camp," Be explained.

"Maybe it was their last trip." Then as an afterthought he said, "It *was* their last trip, wasn't it?"

Almost as soon as the base at My Tho came into view, the chopper was making a vertical landing on a large white circle painted on the surface of a wooden platform built out into the water and connected to the shore by a causeway of earth held between two wooden bulkheads. Anchored in midstream were two landing craft, LCMs, left by the French and refitted to be command vessels. Tied up alongside each of them were five RPCs, river patrol craft, capable of fourteen knots, according to the information Be had previously given Jacob, and mounting a combination of .30- and .50-caliber machine guns.

As soon as the Huey's rotors stopped, Jacob and Be left the chopper and a half-dozen NNV sailors and two NNV officers ran toward them along the causeway.

"The chopper must be guarded while it is here," Be said, explaining the reason for the sailors. "The officer on the right is Commander Dong Lam Chu, the base commander; the other man is Lieutenant Commander Ho Quac Lien, the base executive officer."

In the remaining moments before Jacob would meet the base CO, he took another look at the boats. The hulls of the LCMs were splotched with scabrous rust spots and in the after section on both craft, lines of laundry hung limply in the already steaming air. The exteriors of the RPCs were less than shipshape, by Jacob's standards. None of them looked as if they were ready for action.

Jacob suddenly realized that Be must have sensed that his attention was focused elsewhere, because he loudly cleared his throat when the base CO and his XO were practically in front of them.

The salutes and introductions were over quickly, and as they left the causeway, the six NNV sailors, all armed with M-14s, surrounded the Huey.

Commander Chu, a chunky man with a moon face, spoke English, and on the way to a small building situated close to the causeway, but hidden from sight by skillful camouflage, he said that he'd learned English in a mission school run by Catholic sisters from the United States and he himself was a Catholic.

The base XO, Lien, a dour-looking man, didn't given any indication that he either understood or spoke English.

The building was made of wood and topped by a corrugated iron roof. Inside, there were a wooden table and chairs with wicker backs.

"We will have breakfast," Chu said as the four of them sat down at the table. "Then we will go on a tour." He clapped his hands and spoke in Vietnamese.

Moments later two young women wearing traditional white *ao dais* brought trays of food into the hut. Neither, Jacob judged, could be more than sixteen.

"In your honor, Captain Miller, we have an American-style breakfast," Chu said smiling.

Jacob nodded politely, but he wasn't sure how the watery-looking eggs and the greasy bacon would sit on his stomach. He would have preferred to eat native fruit, as long as it had been washed, and drink native tea rather than the bitter coffee in his cup.

"By tomorrow evening, before you leave," Chu said, "you will have a list of the equipment we need."

Jacob glanced questioningly at Be, whose face was expressionless. "I am not sure I understand, Commander," Jacob said. "What is it that you expect me to do with the list of equipment you need?"

"To give it to your chief supply officer," Chu answered ingenuously.

Jacob said, "That's not why I'm here, Commander. I have nothing to do with the chief supply officer."

Chu spoke in Vietnamese.

Be responded.

Lien joined the conversation, which, from the sound of their voices, was quickly becoming a heated exchange between Be and the two base officers.

Jacob considered interrupting, but immediately realized it would be the wrong thing to do.

Suddenly the argument stopped and Be said in English, "They were told you were a supply officer."

Jacob looked at Chu; then at Lien; then back to Chu. "I am here only as an observer for President Kennedy."

Lien looked even more dour than before.

"Then perhaps you will tell him of our great need," Chu said.

"I will tell the President what I have seen," Jacob replied; then, after a pause that neither Chu nor Lien could misinterpret, he added, "He trusts me to be his eyes and ears."

"That is certainly a great honor," Chu commented.

Jacob nodded. "It is, and therefore must be responded to with great honor," Jacob said, sure that his point would not be lost.

Chu nodded.

As soon as breakfast was over, Jacob was escorted out to the end of the causeway. The Huey was still there.

"I thought it would be back at Hotel Three by now," Jacob said, gesturing toward the chopper as the group passed it on their way to the small boat that would take them to one of the LCMs.

"It will leave before sundown," Chu said. "If we have any casualties during the day, it is available for a dust-off."

Several minutes later Jacob climbed aboard the LCM nearest the helicopter pad.

"This is where we live," Chu said.

"And the other LCM, what is that used for?" Jacob asked.

"For the same thing," Chu replied.

The deck was littered with debris of all sorts, including pails of human feces that would no doubt be used to fertilize the nearby rice fields.

Chu showed Jacob the radio room, the area where the men lived, and then crossed over to the second LCM. "You will stay on board this one tonight," he said to Jacob, and led them to a small cabin in a wooden superstructure that had been built on the craft's forward deck.

Jacob was sure the cabin belonged to Chu, or was kept ready for "important visitors," not that it really mattered which was the case. Along one bulkhead there was a cot with a clean white sheet on it, a window opposite it. A small table, a chair near the window, and a place for clothing were along another bulkhead.

"Toilet is outside, midships," Chu said.

Jacob thanked him, put his shoulder bag on the table, and asked to be shown the RPCs.

Even though they were relatively new, the thirty-five-foot power boats were in deplorable condition. Two out of the ten at the base were operational. The other eight were down because of specific mechanical problems or, in three instances, for causes that neither Chu nor Lien could explain. On all of the eight boats at least one of the machine guns was inoperative.

Jacob was appalled by the situation, but managed to smile, nod, and say nothing.

By noon the heat and humidity were almost unendurable. Most of the men slept. But because many of them smoked marijuana, the air around the two LCMs had a cloying sweet scent.

For the next three hours, except for the intermittent shuttling of the small boat between the helicopter pad and the LCM closest to it, nothing moved. Even Be was sleeping in the cabin he shared with the dour-looking Lien.

Jacob lay stretched out on the cot. The cabin was hot and airless, despite the whirring effort of a small electric fan. In a few days he'd be back in Washington, and though November was usually dreary, it was, with the coming of Thanksgiving near its end, the beginning of a pleasant season. He hoped he'd be able to see the President within a day or two of his return and then go up to New York and spend a few days with Arlene. Now that Julio was in boot camp, Jacob sometimes spent the night at the apartment, though he much preferred her to stay with him at the Plaza. He longed for her—to be near her, to touch her, to smell her, to love her . . . His eyelids became too heavy to hold open. He let them close and slept.

In midafternoon Jacob awoke. He was drenched with sweat and left the cabin to wash his face. Moving aft, he saw the small boat pull away from the LCM. There were two women in it. One sat on the thwart amidship and the other on the one close to the bow. From the glimpse he caught of them, they didn't seem to be the same girls who had served breakfast. He was aware that in certain situations, when a base was close to a village, men were permitted to have their wives and sweethearts visit them. Though such a condition put less emotional strain on a couple, it certainly could have a profound effect on the man's military obligation if it came to a choice between protecting his wife or sweetheart and leaving her to fight where he was ordered.

Suddenly Jacob felt a slight breeze move across his sweaty face and the LMC moved ever so slightly. He looked toward the east, where the sky was boiling with clouds varying in color from gray to black, and as he watched the rush of clouds, rain swept in huge sheets from the sea and for the next hour everything was caught under the monsoon deluge. Then as quickly as it had begun, it was over. The sun came out and the land began to steam again.

At 1600 Jacob was invited by Chu to take part in a raid on a North Vietnamese supply junk. The operational RPCs cast off, revved up, and with Jacob, Chu, and Be in one and Lien in the other, they roared down the estuary toward the sea. Chu held the helm. Slicing through the placid, almost stagnant water, the boat's bow created a huge curtain of spray that refracted the sun's light into the colors of the spectrum.

The distance between the banks widened as they approached the sea, and the boat began to bounce at it met the ocean's swell. They cleared the land, and as they raced out to sea, they slammed into waves with such force that Jacob had difficulty keeping on his feet. The spray now flew over the boat, drenching all of them.

Chu had intermittent radio contact with Lien, whose boat followed behind and to the starboard, about twenty yards away. Several times, Chu changed course.

It didn't take Jacob long to realize that they were doing nothing more than weaving back and forth, always in sight of land, and just as he came to the conclusion that the operation had been staged to impress him, Chu shouted above the roaring of the boat's engine, "The junk has gone . . . we are returning to our base." And he turned the small helm hard over to the right.

To Jacob, the return trip took less time than the trip out. By the time they came in sight of the two LCMs, the sun was low in the west. The Huey was still sitting on the pad.

Dinner was served ashore in the cabin by the same two young women who had been there in the morning. The food was again their version of American cooking. This time it consisted of underdone pork, rice, and cake and coffee.

Very little conversation took place during dinner. Jacob had no appetite, and only out of politeness did he manage to eat part of what had been put on his plate.

"You see, Captain Miller," Chu said, stirring sugar into his coffee, "The Vietcong are hard to find. They are someplace one minute, and you go looking for them there, and they are gone."

Jacob nodded and waved away an attacking mosquito. "Yes, I understand that." He fished out his pipe, and as he filled it, he said, "Perhaps, Commander, if you could find a way to verify the information you receive about where a junk is, then you might not make as many false runs." He'd chosen his words carefully.

Several moments of silence followed before Chu, continuing to stir his coffee, answered, "Yes, I agree."

Using a Zippo lighter, Jacob lit his pipe, puffed some smoke out of it, and then, claiming he was tired, excused himself from the table. Outside, the blackness seemed weighted. From where he was standing, the

Huey was almost invisible. But the stars were extraordinarily bright. Later, Jacob knew, the moon would rise, but since it would be a thin, waning crescent, it would not dull too many stars.

Jacob heard someone behind him, and as he turned and saw Be, there was an enormous explosion.

Wrecked, the Huey burned fiercely. The orange flames cast a wavering light over the causeway and the nearby LCM.

Chu and Lien dashed out of the cabin.

The firelight silhouetted the LCMs and the ten smaller craft moored to them.

The NNV sailors shouted to each other.

Chu and Lien ran along the causeway, now turned a garish mixture of yellow and orange by the flames.

The chopper pad began to burn.

The next instant two rocket rounds slammed into the LCM nearest the pad. It began to burn. Men leapt over its side into the water. Then a powerful explosion tore the craft apart and sent flames shooting out over the RPC moored to it.

A mad minute followed. Those VNN who could, fired their small arms in the directions of a dike that ran along the side of the bank. A rice field was below.

Somehow, some of the sailors managed to get to the machine guns on the two RPCs that were operational and raked the bank with light and heavy machine-gun fire for at least two full minutes without stopping.

Chu and Lien shouted orders, and a dozen men armed with M-14s, grenades, and carrying two bandoleers of ammunition crisscrossed over their chests started toward the dike.

The machine-gun chatter stopped.

The Huey, the stern section of the LCM, and three of the fire RPCs were still burning.

Chu came back to where Jacob and Be were. He shook his head but didn't say anything.

Some of the sailors had rigged up a hose to a pump and were pumping water from the estuary to fight the fire on the helicopter pad.

Though none of the NNV had been killed, many suffered third-degree burns.

Suddenly the men on the dike began shouting.

"They caught two of them," Be translated.

Within minutes, Jacob saw the captives. There were two of them. They had their hands tied behind them; they had ropes around their neck and long leaders were used to pull them. One was a woman—perhaps, Jacob thought, one of the two he'd seen in the boat. A short while ago she might have been pretty, perhaps beautiful. But now her long black hair was disheveled and streaked with mud. Her face was already bruised, and blood was caked on her left cheek. The *ao dai* she wore was torn and smeared with mud. Stumbling, the two were brought face-to-face with Chu.

He barked something in Vietnamese.

Be translated. "He said they will die."

By this time Chu, the two prisoners, Jacob, and Be were ringed by the entire complement from the base.

Chu went up to the man and smashed his fist into the man's face. Blood spurted from his nose. Then Chu tore away the top of the *ao dai*, exposing the woman's small but beautifully shaped breasts.

Her olive skin glowed in the shifting firelight.

Chu fondled one breast, then the other.

Her nipples budded and became stalks.

Then Chu squeezed her right breast until the woman screamed.

He spoke again. " 'You're a whore,' " Be translated in a whisper. " 'I'm going to make an example of you.' " He went to one of the men and took his *ka bar*, a trench knife used in hand-to-hand combat. He returned to where the woman was kneeling and stood directly in front of her. With one quick stroke he severed her right breast from her body.

She screamed in agony.

"My God!" Jacob exclaimed, fighting down the urge to vomit.

Chu cut the woman's other breast off, and as he shouted, Be said, " 'Tomorrow we will nail them up in the village for all the other *co cong* to see.' "

Bleeding to death, the woman was facedown on the ground.

Chu grabbed hold of the man's hair, yanked his head back, and using the bloody knife, slashed the man's throat. Then, looking at Jacob, he said, "Go back and tell your President what we do to the Vietcong!" He dropped the knife, turned, and walked toward the causeway, where the fire was still raging.

Late the next day, Jacob and Be were choppered back to Hotel Three and were able to get a jeep and driver to take them back to Saigon. They parted outside the Splendide, shook hands, and Be said, his face suddenly turning serious, "Don't judge Commander Chu too harshly. Worse was done by the VC to his wife and his thirteen-year-old daughter."

"It would be hard for me to imagine anything much worse," Jacob answered honestly.

"Daughter and mother were given to the men to be used by them; then they were drugged and dragged naked from one VC camp to another and in each place the men used them. When they were finally too exhausted to be of any more use, they were decapitated and their heads were sent to Chu."

Jacob nodded. Even after so many years had passed, the image of Tara being raped flooded his mind. . . . He managed to nod.

"I hope to see you again before you return to the United States," Be said.

"Yes, I would like that," Jacob responded, knowing they would not, but nonetheless acting the role in which he'd been placed by the situation.

Be saluted.

Jacob returned the salute, lifted his shoulder bag out of the jeep, and with a nod and a smile turned toward the entrance to the hotel.

As soon as he was in his room, Jacob stripped off his clothes and enjoyed the wonderful revivifying effect of a hot bath. Then with a towel wrapped around his midsection he picked up the phone, dialed the embassy number, and spoke to the woman responsible for making the travel arrangements for embassy personnel and for those individuals like himself, who were in Saigon for special reasons.

"The earliest flight we can get you on would be tomorrow evening at seventeen hundred," the woman said.

"Direct—"

"No, Captain, it makes a stop in Manila."

"How long a stop?"

"Two hours, sir."

"I guess that will have to be it," Jacob said.

The woman gave him the flight information and told him he could pick up his ticket at the embassy.

He thanked her and put down the phone. A few minutes later he was dressed and on his way to the Chanticleer, a restaurant near the hotel whose French-Vietnamese food and subdued atmosphere he enjoyed.

As Jacob started across the lobby, he heard his rank

and surname called. He stopped, turned, and found himself facing a rear admiral.

"Sir," Jacob responded, saluting and at the same time wondering how the man knew him.

"Name is Mosely," the admiral told him, returning the salute. "Casper Mosely." Then he said, "I'm here with a Senate fact-finding group."

Jacob nodded. "Sir, how did you know—"

Mosely, a portly man with red cheeks and nose, smiled. "Just information I happen to have, Captain." He touched the right side of his nose with his forefinger. Then he invited Jacob to join him and several of the committee members for a drink at the bar.

"A pleasure," Jacob answered, interpreting the request as an order.

There were a half-dozen senators at the table.

"What's your pleasure, Captain?" Mosely asked, making it seem as if he and Mosely had more in common than the uniform they wore.

"Bourbon on the rocks," Jacob answered, aware that the bar was crowded, noisy, and filled with smoke.

"The admiral informed us that yesterday you were involved in action against the VC," one of the senators said. "We'd appreciate it if you told us what took place."

Jacob was somewhat surprised that Mosely knew about it. But on second thought, he wasn't—the man obviously had a very good source of information in the embassy.

"We're here to find out how we can best help these people to fight the Communists and prevent them from taking over the country," another senator said.

The waitress put Jacob's drink down in front of him.

"It's always best to get information about what's happening in a place from one of our own people," the senator who had spoken first said. "That way we know we're getting the truth, if you know what I mean."

Jacob raised his glass. "To the truth, gentlemen, no matter what it is," he toasted.

Mosely did a double-take, but he raised his glass.

The senators followed suit.

"Well, what happened?" Mosely asked.

"I'm afraid I'm not at liberty to tell you," Jacob said. "What I have to say is for the President only. I'm sorry, gentlemen, but those are my orders." He looked at each of the senators and then at Mosely. "You understand, sir, that those orders come from the commander in chief."

"We will see the official report," Mosely said, obviously trying hard not to let his anger show, even though there was a definite edge to his words.

Jacob shook his head. "I didn't file one, sir . . . I didn't participate in any action . . . I'm here as an observer for the President. But I'm sure there will be an NNV report on the action."

"What's NNV?" one of the senators asked.

"The acronym for the Vietnamese Navy," Jacob answered, and standing, said, "Gentlemen, thank you for the drink. And if you will excuse me, I have something—"

Mosely stood up. "Captain, I'd like to have a word with you."

"Certainly, sir," Jacob responded.

"There," Mosely said, gesturing toward the end of the bar.

Jacob led the way, and when they reached the bar, Mosely said, "Pulling that shit about the commander in chief does not impress me, Captain."

"With all due respect," Jacob answered, "it wasn't meant to impress you, or the senators."

"Then what was it supposed to do?" Mosely demanded in a harsh but low tone. "What was it supposed to do, suppose you tell me?"

"To remind everyone at the table that I was sent here by the President to do something for him and only for him."

Mosely uttered a disdainful snort.

"I will not violate his trust," Jacob said.

Mosely squinted at him. "I heard about you, Captain Miller . . . I heard all about you."

"What is that supposed to mean, sir?"

Mosely nodded, and pointed to the two stars on his collar. "These say I outrank you. . . . Just remember that."

Angry, Jacob said, "I hardly think you'll let me forget it, sir."

"When payback time comes, you better believe I won't," Mosely growled, and he left the bar.

Shaken, Jacob summoned the barkeep. "A double shot of bourbon on the rocks," he said. There was no doubt in his mind that when payback time came, as Mosely referred to it, the man would pay back in spades.

Jacob knew he was dreaming. He and Arlene were together. They were out-of-doors, somewhere near the sea. Though he could hear the sounds of the breaking surf, he couldn't see it. Then he was kissing the soft, warm inside of her naked thighs, and at the same time caressing her dark pink vaginal lips. The boom of the surf became sharper, more like a sequence of sudden cracks. . . . He opened his eyes. The room was swathed in blackness. Just as he reached over to the night table for his watch, the sharp sputter of rifle fire came from the street. Instantly the fire was returned.

Jacob, fully awake now, attempted to switch on the small night-table lamp. It wouldn't light.

Someone knocked at the door. "Captain Miller, report to the lobby," the voice said.

"What the hell is going on?" Jacob called out.

"Don't know," the voice answered.

Intermittently lighting his Zippo lighter, Jacob managed to find his trousers, a shirt, and wearing his shoes without socks, he went into the hallway, where there were already a dozen officers gathered.

"Elevator is out," an Air Force captain with a flashlight announced. "I'll lead the way downstairs."

The group moved quickly down to the lobby, where a small table was illuminated by half a dozen candles. Admiral Mosely was behind the table.

"Switchboard is dead, sir," an Army major reported.

Suddenly there were the unmistakable flat blams of exploding mortar rounds coming from the direction of the Presidential Palace, two blocks up the street from the Splendide.

"Christ, there are fucking troops all over the street," a man called from the doorway.

"Pete, get your dumb ass away from there," another officer yelled.

Jacob went up to the table. "Captain Miller, reporting as ordered, sir," he said, saluting.

Mosely looked up at him. "Captain, you're the second-ranking officer."

"Yes, sir," Jacob responded, knowing that Mosely had probably checked that out.

"In another few minutes there'll be enough light outside for you and a few of the other men to make your way to the embassy and inform the ambassador of our situation," Mosely said and, almost as an afterthought, added, "We are completely cut off here and are in great danger of being killed or captured by attacking VC."

The rattle of machine-gun fire came from the street.

"Pick your men, Captain," Mosely said.

A mortar round exploded in front of the hotel door, shattering it and sending huge splinters of glass hurtling into the lobby.

"Anyone hit?" Mosely called out.

After a few moments an officer answered, "Seems like we're all okay."

The gray light of dawn filled the open doorway.

"Get your men, Captain, and get moving," Mosely said.

Before Jacob could answered, four ARVN soldiers entered the lobby. All of them looked like teenagers. All wore two bandoleers of ammunition crisscrossed over their chests. One of them was a lieutenant. He came directly up to Mosely and leveled his M-14 in front of the admiral's chest. "Order men to stay here," he said. "Order now."

Steely-eyed, Mosely looked up at him. "I will report—"

The crack of a single shot exploded.

Mosely's chest turned red and he fell forward on the table, knocking over two of the candles.

"You," the ARVN lieutenant said, waving his M-14 at Jacob, "you officer?"

"Yes."

"Order all men to stay here. Order now."

"You men heard him," Jacob said, looking around at the startled faces now clearly visible in the early-morning light. The senators he'd met the previous evening were gathered in a small knot against the wall.

"Order!" the lieutenant said, waving his rifle in front of Jacob.

"Every man stays here . . . that's an order," Jacob responded.

"Good. Soon shooting is over can leave," the ARVN officer told him; then, speaking to his men in Vietnamese, he led them out the door.

Jacob was about to go to Mosely when a mortar round slammed into the street, cutting down the lieutenant and his men.

"That fucking gook has no legs," one of the men yelled from the doorway.

Jacob pulled Mosely back. "Get him onto the couch," he said, pointing to two of the officers. Then, turning to the rest of the men, he said, "Looks like we're caught in the middle of another kind of war. There's nothing we can do but sit tight and wait until our people come for us. As soon as we have some more daylight, three men at a time will go up and dress." Then he asked, "Do any of you have any weapons?"

A few said they had revolvers or GI .45s.

"Don't bring them down," Jacob said. "I repeat, don't bring them down. We don't want anyone else killed by a trigger-happy Marvin Arvin. Okay, where's the manager of the hotel?"

A heavyset man came forward.

"Get your kitchen people to prepare breakfast," Jacob said.

"But—"

"Do it," Jacob ordered. Then, looking at the senators, he said, "Gentlemen, you are free to go to your rooms and dress, but please return here as quickly as possible."

The firing coming from the direction of the Presidential Palace increased. Suddenly there was the throbbing sound of propeller-driven airplanes overhead, followed by the scream of falling bombs, and within moments the sound of a half-dozen explosions burst over the upper end of the street.

"The palace is being bombed!" someone shouted from the doorway.

"Stay the hell away from there," Jacob called out.

The droning of plane engines faded away.

"I want the switchboard operator at the board," Jacob said.

There were several bursts of machine-gun fire, then the rumble of tanks from the street.

Suddenly the lights came on in the lobby and the switchboard began to ring and light up.

Jacob immediately picked up a phone.

The ambassador was on the other end.

Jacob identified himself and quickly explained what had happened to Admiral Mosely and what the situation was.

"Stay put, Captain Miller," the ambassador said. "We're in the midst of a coup. We're certain that Diem has been killed and that General Minh has taken over. As soon as its feasible, we'll send a detachment of marines to escort you to the embassy."

"Yes, Mr. Ambassador," Jacob answered.

"Do you have any wouned?"

"No, sir," Jacob answered, aware that his flight back to the States would be delayed for several days.

"Sit tight," the ambassador said, and clicked off.

Putting the phone down, Jacob called out, "Everyone, gather round." He waited until he faced a semicircle of men before he said, "That was the ambassador. Diem has been killed—"

"Holy shit, we're in the midst of a fucking coup!" a lieutenant exclaimed.

"I couldn't have stated that any better," Jacob said. The men laughed.

"As soon as the situation permits, we'll be escorted to the embassy by a detachment of marines," Jacob told them. "But until that time, we'll just sit tight. No one goes near the door unless he has my permission. No one carries any weapons. . . . Everyone understand that? . . . Good. Okay, all staff and field-grade officers work up a roster of the men in your respective services. I want to have every man's name on a roster by branch of service. . . . Dismissed."

Jacob moved to the table that had been used by Mosely. It was stained with the admiral's blood. "One of you men," Jacob called, "get a couple of people from the hotel staff to clean this up." He stepped up to the couch where Mosely's body had been placed. The admiral's eyes were still open.

"Seemed like a pretty good guy," another officer said, looking at Mosely.

Reaching down to close the admiral's eyes, Jacob said, "He probably was a real good guy."

The next instant two jeeps loaded with fully armed marines and three empty deuce-and-a-half trucks pulled up in front of the hotel.

"Looks like the Marines have landed," Jacob commented, and headed toward the door to greet the Marine officer.

20

IT WAS LATE Friday morning, November 22. A cold, raw wind was blowing off the Chesapeake, bringing with it gray clouds and, according to the National Weather Bureau, the promise of light snow later in the day.

Warren was at home, with the flu, which gave him a temperature of 101 and made him feel, as he had told Carol earlier in the morning, "like a soggy noodle." He was hoping to be well by Thanksgiving, which was going to be celebrated this year at his house. Despite Tony's shoulder wound, which he'd gotten in a scuffle with a mugger in Hong Kong, he and Miriam were going to fly down to Washington and then rent a car. Jacob and Arlene would come. Even the boys were coming: Andrew, Sy, and Mike. It would be a full happy house.

Pushing himself up into a sitting position, Warren reached over to the night table for the remaining orange juice that Carol had given him earlier. He drank it, and leaning back on the pillow, closed his eyes.

He was happier now than he had been in a long time, except for his deep concern about Andrew's future—he was slowly coming to accept the fact, though it was extremely difficult for him, that once Andrew completed his obligatory service, after his graduation from the Academy, he would leave the Navy, and the Troost tradition would come to an end. Warren hadn't realized just how much that tradition had come to mean to him over the years until he was confronted with it ending. He had, since the night of Andrew's show, given that tradition a great deal of thought and found himself almost, as it were, trying to explain to his father what his grandson was set on doing. His father, for whom Andrew had been named, would not have understood it. The Navy, except for his love affair with Kate Hasse, had been his entire life. Strange as it was, over these many years, Warren had come to understand the man and love him. One of his more formidable regrets was that he and his father had never had the opportunity to share their love. Yet Warren was certain his father had loved him and respected him, after he had earned that respect.

"He was a good man," Warren whispered to himself, and once again he thought about his son. A couple of days after Jacob had returned from Nam, they'd had a conversation about the boys. They agreed that though all of them would make good officers, Tony's son, Mike, was the only one who possessed that unique combination of toughness and humanity which can help make a man a superior officer. He and Jacob had recognized that they had it and agreed that Tony possessed it too.

Warren pulled himself away from the pillow and laid it flat before he moved down on the bed again. Though Jacob didn't speak about his trip to Nam—and Warren would not ask him any questions—he knew Jacob well enough to know that he had been displeased by whatever he had seen there, and—

Suddenly Warren heard Carol running up the steps.

"Warren," she called. "Warren?"

Raising himself, he rested on his forearms.

Carol was in the doorway. "Oh, Warren . . . Warren," she cried.

"What is it? What's wrong?"

She shook her head. "It came over the radio . . . the President has been shot . . . in Dallas."

"Oh, my God!"

"He's being rushed to the hospital now," she cried, going to the TV and turning it on. Instantly the screen was filled with a commentator who was saying, ". . . it's believed that the bullets that struck President Kennedy were fired from the building directly behind me, a warehouse for the storage of textbooks. . . . At this moment an intensive search is under way for the person or persons responsible for firing those shots. . . ."

Warren eased himself back against the headboard, while Carol placed the pillow behind him, and sitting down on the bed, she took hold of his hand. Too stunned to speak, they watched the TV screen.

That same evening Tony and Miriam sat on the couch in the rec room and watched, along with millions of other Americans, Lee Harvey Oswald on the TV, the man arrested and charged with assassinating the President, being moved from a police precinct to a more secure location, when suddenly a man darted forward and fired several shots at Oswald, who fell to the ground. In an instant the police had the gunman in custody.

"I don't believe it!" Tony exclaimed, leaping to his feet. "I don't believe it." He'd moved more violently than he should have and a sudden knifelike pain in his left shoulder made him wince.

The TV commentator said, "It appears that Lee Harvey Oswald, the alleged triggerman in the assassination of President Kennedy, has been himself shot to death."

Suddenly the phone began to ring.

Tony answered it. "Jacob," he called over to Miriam. "He can't believe what we just saw happen either."

"Johnson has already taken the oath of office," Jacob said.

The TV commentator said, "The man who shot and killed Lee Harvey Oswald has been identified as Jack Ruby, a nightclub owner here in Dallas."

"Did you get that—about Jack Ruby?" Tony asked.

"Yes," Jacob answered.

"I know that guy," Tony said.

"Are you sure?"

"I'm sure," Tony answered, suddenly realizing that he should not have said anything about knowing Ruby.

"How?"

"Just forget you heard me say it, okay?"

"Okay, sure," Jacob answered. "Things are going to be in a turmoil for a while . . . until Johnson puts his men into place and the government begins to function again."

Tony agreed.

"See you and Miriam at Warren's next week," Jacob said.

"Are you coming to New York tomorrow?" Tony asked.

"Probably not. Everyone on the President's staff has been asked to remain on standby," Jacob answered. "But I've arranged for Arlene to fly down, though I don't know how much time I'll be able to spend with her."

"Did you ever make your report to Kennedy?"

"No, it was postponed until after he returned from this trip," Jacob replied.

"Have you any idea what Johnson's view of the situation out there might be?" Tony asked.

"Only rumors," Jacob said, "which have already begun on his views on Vietnam and just about everything else."

"Right now the only one that interests me is about Nam," Tony said.

"A more active role," Jacob answered. "More arms, advisers, and, now that Diem is gone, if needed, our actual military presence."

"Interesting," Tony commented.

For several moments neither one spoke; then Tony asked if Jacob was going to be involved in funeral ceremonies.

"No . . . I haven't been asked to, and I don't want to be."

"Understandable," Tony replied, now anxious to end the conversation and put through a call to the Company.

"I'm sure there will be a great number of changes," Jacob commented. "Johnson's style is very different from Kennedy's."

Tony could hear the wistfulness in his brother-in-law's voice. "All we can do is wait and see what happens," he said.

"Though I really didn't know him, except in an official capacity," Jacob said, "I still liked the man. The first time I was with him in Hyannis, I remember him saying that he hoped he'd have the opportunity to finish a second term in order to bring to fruition some of his programs. Hell, he didn't have the chance to complete his first term."

"I guess it's the idea that the President could be

taken out so easily that disturbs me more than anything else," Tony commented. "If he's not safe, who the hell is?"

"Well, I guess you're right: there's nothing we can do but wait. You know, in some strange way, it's almost as if our father was killed."

"C'mon, Jacob, that's really weird, especially coming from you."

"Freud claimed that a dissident group had murdered Moses, and the guilt for that crime has been with Jews ever since."

"I don't buy that—not about Moses and certainly not about Kennedy," Tony answered. "Okay, he was killed . . . but that won't change the country. As soon as Johnson takes hold, things will be on track again. Kennedy's death will go down in the history books and that will be the end of it."

"Maybe, maybe not. I hope you're right."

"I know I am. Nothing, absolutely nothing, remains in the minds of the people very long."

Jacob uttered a deep sigh before he said, "I'll see you and Miriam for Thanksgiving."

"You want to speak to her?" Tony asked.

"No . . . not now. Give her my love," he said, and clicked off.

Tony put the phone down. "Jacob is very upset," he told Miriam.

"Aren't you? I know I am."

"I'm upset . . . but I can live with it," Tony said as he started to leave the room.

"Aren't you going to watch TV with me?"

"I'll be back in a few minutes. I want to get something cold to drink."

"Want me to—"

"I'll be back in a few minutes," Tony said, interrupting her. He left the room, went straight to his study, and put through a call to his Company contact.

Because of Kennedy's death, Sy felt the deep need for what he interpreted as spiritual solace. He had a long telephone conversation with his father and sensed that he too was agonizing over it. Though Sy did not follow any particular faith and considered himself an agnostic, if not an atheist, he asked for and received special permission to attend the Saturday services in Annapolis' only synagogue.

He drove there with two other midshipmen: Keith Williams, from Rapid City, South Dakota, and Harold Orinsky, from South Bend, Indiana. Keith had a Jewish mother, and Orinsky, like himself, had a Jewish father and had been raised in the faith, even barmitzvahed.

Out of respect, Sy parked two blocks away from the synagogue, which turned out to be an old building with a Greek-style portico and a stained-glass Star of David above it.

Inside, the synagogue was surprisingly full. Sy and his companions sat together in the rear of the temple.

The services included the reading of the Torah by various male members of the congregation, all of whom kissed the fringes of their tallithim and with them touched the Holy Scroll before they began to read; then a bar-mitzvah ceremony of a thirteen-year-old kinky-haired boy followed, whose speech, after reading his portion of the Torah, was about the brotherhood that should exist between all men.

Finally it was the rabbi's turn to deliver the sermon.

Though all of this was somewhat familiar to Sy, because on various occasions involving the Miller side of the family he'd accompanied his father to the synagogue—sometimes he was even with him when he went to say kiddish for his parents and for Mr. and Mrs. Grunfeldt, an obligation his father had never forgotten—nonetheless he now felt oddly out of place.

The rabbi, a tall, dignified man, slowly approached the lectern. His face was full of pain, and gripping the sides of the lectern, he nodded, bit his lip, and then in an unsteady voice that still retained the accent of his Polish origins, he said, "What can I tell you that all of you already know?

"One of Aristotle's definitions for tragedy was that the king must fall, and that this fall, by its very nature, would have an enormous impact on his subjects. Well, our President has fallen and the effect on us and upon those generations yet to come will be profound. In this we have prided ourselves upon a democratic system that transfers the stewardship in an orderly manner, according to the will of the people. Not only did an assassin's bullets deny all of us our President, those same bullets denied us our constitutional right."

Then, holding up his left forearm, he pushed up his jacket sleeve, and peeling back his shirt sleeve, he revealed the tattooed numbers. "Auschwitz," he said. "These numbers on my arm and on the millions of other arms are grim reminders of what happens when bullets speak and not the will of the people. Here and now in this country one assassin had killed another. Here and now, we must hold fast to the rule by law and not by guns. As I look out over the congregation, I see three young men from the Naval Academy, who have come here, as no doubt many of you have— there are many unfamiliar faces in front of me this morning—because they too have felt the need for solace in this time of deep national sorrow."

Several people turned toward Sy and his companions.

"I welcome the young gentlemen from the Academy because they will be the protectors of our way of life, a way of life that exalts the civilian over the military and yet asks of those in the military service that they be ready to give up their lives should the situation demand it. Rather that way than the reverse—where the civilian cower in fear of the military, lest their lives be taken by soldiers with guns.

"Ladies and gentlemen, I cannot give platitudes to satisfy your need for solace. I cannot even assuage my own grief . . . but perhaps the very fact that those of us here this morning share a common sorrow for our dead President is enough to make each individual aware that he is not alone and that as our bar-mitzvah boy said so wisely, 'We are all brothers—brothers in the way we come into the world and brothers when we come to our final end.' I have nothing else to say, except to repeat our people's ancient cry in duress and in happiness, 'Hear O Israel, the Lord our God, the Lord is one . . .' and to add, may God bless and keep all of you safe."

Then he said, "On behalf of Mr. and Mrs. Fields, everyone here is invited to the kiddush, the traditional offering of wine and food to the members of the community by the parents of the bar-mitzvah boy. And I personally extend that invitation to the three midshipmen from the Academy. Come and help us celebrate Nathan's bar mitzvah."

Sy had expected a different kind of sermon, but what he'd heard moved him, and turning to the other midshipmen, he asked, "Are you going?"

They were undecided.

"If we don't show, even for a few minutes, it will be discourteous," Sy said.

The other men agreed he was right, and the three of

them found their way to where the refreshments were
being served.

The rabbi saw them, smiled, and beckoned to them.
They approached him.

"I'm Rabbi Stikosky," he said, "and you gentlemen
are . . . ?"

Sy and each of the other men gave their names and
shook the rabbi's hand.

"Miller . . . Miller," the rabbi said. "I once knew a
Jacob Miller." He smiled. "I didn't know him as Jacob
Miller then. I found that out later, when I saw a
photograph of him when he was the captain of the
aircraft carrier *Concord*."

"That's my father," Sy said, feeling a combination
of surprise and embarrassment.

The rabbi's brown eyes appraised Sy and then with
just a hint of a smile he said, "The next time you see
him, ask him about the *Pelican*, a ship of Liberian
registry."

Sy nodded. "I will," he answered, now more confused than anything else.

"Uncle?" a woman called.

The rabbi's head turned slightly to the right, and
smiling broadly, he said, "My niece, Heather Gershon."

Sy found himself looking at a petite woman with a
finely chiseled face, alert green eyes, and light brown
hair that cascaded down to her shoulders.

"Before I answer whatever question you have," the
rabbi told his niece, "let me introduce you to these
three midshipmen." And he took a moment to do
that.

She shook hands with the three of them; then she
said, "Please, call me Heather—'Miss Gershon' is so
. . . so formal."

She had a deep, throaty voice that made Sy wonder

what she'd be like in bed. Then, suddenly aware of what he was thinking, he felt his cheeks burn.

"Now, your question?" the rabbi asked.

"Would you mind if I had dinner with Mr. and Mrs. Herman tonight?" Heather asked.

The rabbi smiled. "Not to mention Ralph, who just happens to be down from—"

"Oh, Uncle!" she exclaimed, her cheeks and neck suddenly a deep pink.

The rabbi wagged his finger at her. "At least wait until Ralph begins his residency," he teased.

The pink blush became deeper.

"Yes, certainly you may go," the rabbi said.

Heather flung her arms around him, gave him a kiss on the cheek, and turning to Sy and his two friends, said, "It was a pleasure to meet you." And leaving them, she hurried across the room.

Sy's eyes followed her to where she joined three people, a woman in her late forties and two men. One of them was a tall good-looking young man, who was obviously Ralph.

"Heather and Ralph have known each other since they were in their early teens," the rabbi explained. "I'm looking forward to the time when I marry them."

Deep inside of him, Sy felt a sudden twist. "She couldn't be more than seventeen or eighteen," he mumbled.

"She will be twenty-one on December 9," the rabbi responded; then with a note of pride in his voice he added, "She's been more like a daughter to me than a niece. That young lady is a biochemist, and by next June will have her doctorate. She's doing cancer research at the Sloan-Kettering Institute in New York."

Sy nodded appreciatively.

"Gentlemen," the rabbi said, "I've kept you from

the refreshments. Please, go to the tables and enjoy. Mr. Miller, don't forget to ask your father about the *Pelican*."

"I won't," Sy replied.

The rabbi smiled.

Moments later Sy and his friends were at one of the tables, where there were trays of honey cake, cookies, and miniature Danish pastries. Though Sy pretended to be interested in what he chose to put on his plate, his eyes constantly sought Heather.

"All right," Keith laughed, "you've made it very obvious that you've fallen in love on first sight."

"Never!" Sy lied.

Harold rolled his eyes. "If it ain't love, it sure as hell is lust," he said; then, growling wolfishly, he bit into a piece of honey cake.

The three of them moved away from the table and off to one side.

"What was all that about your father?" Keith asked.

Sy shrugged. "I have absolutely no idea."

"Do you think the rabbi actually knows your dad?" Harold asked.

Again Sy shrugged.

"It would really be a coincidence if he does," Keith said; then with a lascivious laugh he added, "Even more of a coincidence now that his son has the hots for the rabbi's niece."

"That's not funny," Sy responded with defensive anger. The more he looked at her, the more he wondered what she would be like in bed.

Keith nodded. "I agree. I'd say it was damn serious . . . wouldn't you say it was 'damn serious,' Harold?"

"Absolutely serious."

"Okay, guys, knock it off," Sy responded. "Leave it alone."

"Sure, Sy," Keith responded.

"Not another word," Harold answered.

"Good," Sy said. "Now, let's get some coffee and leave." Before either of his friends could speak, he started to move to where the coffee urn was located, and at the same time his eyes went to where Heather had been standing. She was no longer there. He quickly scanned the room and caught sight of her just as she was leaving with Ralph. In that instant he decided that regardless of her relationship with Ralph, he was going to try to make her fall in love with him. Though he had been sexually intimate with various women, he'd never had the instantaneous reaction that he had just had to Heather. It was a new—and totally exciting— experience.

21

IT WAS EIGHT o'clock Sunday night when the phone rang in Jacob's suite in the Shoreham.

Arlene, who had come down to Washington for the weekend and was preparing to take the eleven-o'clock shuttle flight back to New York, answered it and said, "Sy is on the line."

Jacob put the Washington *Post* down, and walking over to where Arlene was, took the phone from her. "How are you, Sy?" he asked.

"I guess I'm okay, Dad," Sy answered. "Everything down here has been canceled until after the President's funeral."

"More or less the same thing has happened here in Washington," Jacob responded. He settled in a chair next to the phone.

"Sad . . . it's hard not to be."

"Do you know whether or not you'll remain on the President's staff?"

"I doubt it," Jacob answered. "President Johnson will want his own people."

"Dad, would you mind if I ask what you would have told President Kennedy?" Sy asked.

Jacob considered the question for a moment.

"Dad . . ."

"I'm still here," Jacob said. "I was just trying to find the right words. Certainly I would have given him an accurate description—that is to say, as accurate and as objective a description as possible—of everything I saw."

"But what if he'd asked for your recommendation? I mean—"

"Whether we stay there and become more involved, or get out and let the chips, so to speak, fall where they will."

"Yes."

"If we could change the government to truly reflect the will of the people, I'd have recommended that we stay . . . but if the government remains only a government that remains corrupt and doesn't care about the majority of its people, then I would have recommended that our men be pulled out. Does that satisfy you?"

"Most of the people around here think if we go in with some muscle, the VC will vanish," Sy said.

"Each man to his own opinion," Jacob answered. Though he had responded to Sy's question, he really wasn't in the mood to carry on a conversation about Nam. He still had nightmares about what he had seen Chu do to the woman prisoner. And now with Kennedy's death, he was more concerned about what would happen to the United States than he was about the civil war in Vietnam.

"I have another question," Sy said.

"Not about Nam, I hope."

Sy told him about his going to the synagogue for the Saturday-morning service with two other midshipmen.

Not altogether surprised by it, Jacob said, "If it gave you what you wanted and needed, then you're ahead of the game. . . . Did it?"

Sy hesitated; then he said, "The rabbi asked me to ask you if you remember a ship named the *Pelican*."

Jacob was on his feet. "What?"

"The *Pelican*, a Liberian—"

Pacing back and forth, Jacob questioned, "The rabbi asked that?"

"He said he recognized your picture when it was in the newspaper after the fire aboard the *Concord*."

"What's his name?"

"Stikosky."

The name didn't mean anything to Jacob. But then, it wouldn't. Most of the men aboard the *Pelican* hadn't used their real names. His own name had been Steven Karole, and Warren, who never had a name, had commanded the operation.

"What's wrong?" Arlene asked in a whisper.

Jacob shook his head, and then to Sy he said, "The *Pelican* was kind of a command ship during the Israeli war for independence in 1948."

Arlene moved closer to him.

"What did you have to do with that?" Sy asked.

"I was the fighter-control officer aboard the *Pelican*."

"But—"

"It was a special operation," Jacob explained. "Uncle Warren was in command of it. . . . Someday I'll tell you the whole story. Your rabbi was probably a member of the ship's crew."

"Then you fought—"

"We didn't do any fighting," Jacob said. "Our job—my job—was to vector in fighters from various bases if the need arose. The need never arose."

"Does anyone else know this besides Uncle Warren?"

"No."

"Did Mom?"

"No. It was highly classified . . . might still be,

which is why you're not to tell anyone about it. If you ever see the rabbi again—"

"I'm certainly going to see him again," Sy said.

"Oh?" Jacob suddenly found himself wondering if Sy's visit to the synagogue had a deeper source than just the temporary need for solace.

"I'm in love with his niece, Heather."

Jacob came to an abrupt halt. "Did you say what I think you said?"

"Yes, sir, I did. She doesn't know it yet, but she's going to fall in love with me."

Suddenly Jacob laughed so hard his stomach hurt.

"I'm serious," Sy said.

Still laughing and enjoying the fact that he could find something to laugh at, Jacob answered, "I know you, and that's why I'm laughing."

Then all at once Sy began to laugh too.

Jacob reached over to where Arlene was standing, and wrapping his arm around her waist, he drew her very close to him. "Sy is in love," he told her, caressing the sensuous curve of her buttock. "Sy is in love." Then, turning and lowering his voice, he said, "And so am I . . . and so am I!"

22

BEFORE THE YEAR was out, Jacob made flag rank and received orders assigning him to the staff of the deputy chief of naval operations (air), where he was assigned to the planning section. This reassignment had very little effect on his routine. He continued to spend most weekends in New York, and those that he didn't, either Arlene joined him at the Shoreham or he'd fly the two of them somewhere else.

The rumors about President Johnson's willingness to become more involved in the civil war in Vietnam were quickly changing from rumor to actualities, so that by the first of May he was using intelligence data gathered from a variety of sources, including highly detailed photographs of Hanoi and Haiphong, to plan strikes from a carrier force positioned at a place, already dubbed Yankee Station, off the Vietnamese coast.

Jacob, though absorbed in the technical aspects of his assignment, hoped that the United States would maintain a discreet distance from an actual military commitment. But because his view on the situation would have isolated him from his fellow officers, all of whom favored American intervention, he did not discuss it with them. He was paid to carry out government policy, not make it.

Then early one drizzly Saturday afternoon at the end of May, when he and Arlene were at the Plaza, and Arlene needed to be alone for several hours in order to mark a final examination she had given to her class the previous day, he went out to Staten Island to visit with his sister and brother-in-law, Tony.

He and Tony sat on wooden rocking chairs in the rec room while Miriam prepared sandwiches.

A fire was going in the fireplace and Jacob commented about how comfortable he felt, but then he added, with an unmistakable sadness in his voice, "I have a gut feeling that it's all going to change."

Tony looked at him questioningly.

"We're going to become involved in Vietnam," Jacob said.

"The sooner the better," Tony responded.

Jacob stood up, walked to the sliding glass doors, and looked out at the green lawn. "If we do, it's going to be the wrong war, in the wrong place, at the wrong time."

"That's not the way I see it," Tony answered.

Jacob faced him. "The French lost there and so will we."

"The French." Tony sneered. "Tell me, what the hell do they know about fighting? We had to bail them out of two wars . . . Christ, Jacob, more than half their troops in Nam were former members of the Afrika Korps . . ."

Jacob filled his pipe and lighted it before he said, "I was there during one of their coups—"

"Yes . . . yes, I know that . . . I know that their government stinks . . . but corruption is a way of life . . . it's not going to change."

Jacob puffed on his pipe and realized it was a mistake to become involved in a discussion, even with Tony, about Nam. But having started it, he couldn't just say, *Let's not talk about it* and expect Tony to disengage, so to speak.

"I'll tell you what I think," Tony said. "I think we have to go in there, because if we don't, we'll lose all of Southeast Asia and maybe more . . . maybe even Indonesia and the Philippines. You should be able to see that." He was on his feet now too.

"It's ten thousand miles away from here. The war is a civil war."

"It's our call," Tony answered. "Who the hell do you think is supplying the—" He was going to say *Charlie*, but he caught himself and said, ". . . the Vietcong? . . . Russia, that's who."

"It's not our war," Jacob responded.

"Sure it is. Any war where one side is communistic and the other isn't, is our war."

"Tony, we have sons who are going into the military—"

"By God, I'd want him to fight against the Commies. Jacob, I have contacts all over that part of the world. They're just waiting for us to come in and clean up the mess France and England left there after the Second World War."

Carrying a tray of delicatessen, Miriam entered the room. "I could hear the two of you all the way in the kitchen."

"Jacob doesn't understand that it's up to us to make the world safe for democracy," Tony aswered.

Miriam set the tray down on a small plastic table. "Go ahead, help yourselves."

"I'm not hungry," Tony snapped.

Jacob had had no idea that his brother-in-law's feelings were so rabidly anticommunist.

"All right, don't eat, if you think that will help the war against communisim," Miriam said. "But if you ask me—and I know you won't—I'd let those people out there solve their own problems."

"We do that and their problems will become our problems," Tony said, his face now red with anger.

"Tony, Tony, you're getting yourself all worked up for nothing," Miriam said. "Johnson is too smart a man to become involved in a war. Now, why don't the two of you sit down and have something to eat."

"Sure, why not?" Jacob responded with a smile. "Tony?"

"Okay."

Jacob sat down, picked up a sandwich, bit into it, and nodding, said, "Miriam, you can make a sandwich for me anytime." But even as he spoke, he realized that this had been the first time in all the years he had known Tony that they had disagreed on anything.

23

THOUGH TONY HAD called the Company immediately after he had recognized Jack Ruby, it was not until the middle of May that he was questioned by two federal agents, John Wolk and Brian Hicks, in the Bureau's New York office.

The room where the questioning took place was located on the eighth floor. It was small and windowless. The three of them sat at a table, Wolk on one end, Hicks on the other, Tony between them.

Wolk, the shorter of the two, said, "We know quite a lot about you, Mr. Trapasso, from the time between your resignation from the Navy and your present association."

"I knew you would," Tony answered.

"You've been doing a lot of work in Hong Kong," Hicks commented.

"Yes." Obviously they had no information on his real activities.

"How well did you know Mr. Ruby?" Wolk asked.

"I met him in Chicago, about two years before I became involved with my present association."

"Did you have any direct dealings with him?"

"None."

"Exactly where did you meet him?" Hicks asked.

"At a party . . . Giorgio Scalifani—"

"He's a pretty big gun—"

"He called me," Tony said. "I didn't call him. My operation was not only legal but also making money—lots of money."

"Tell us about Ruby," Wolk said.

"He was introduced to me by Scalifani, who said that if I ever had dealings in Dallas or New Orleans, then Ruby would be a good man to contact."

"Was he telling you to hire Ruby?" Hicks questioned.

"No one ever told me who to hire," Tony said sharply.

"Did you intend to extend your range of businesses into those areas?"

"No."

"All right, Ruby was introduced to you. Did you spend any time with him?"

"Not then. But later in the evening he came up to me and told me that he had some very interesting connections in Central and South America."

"Did he mention Cuba?" Wolk asked.

Tony shook his head. "He wasn't specific."

"Did you think he meant Cuba?"

Annoyed, Tony responded, "I already told you what he said, and what he said doesn't imply Cuba, at least it doesn't to me."

"What was your answer to him?" Hicks asked.

"I told him that I would keep that in mind."

"Did you have a specific impression of him?"

"Someone on the sidelines who wants to get into the center of things," Tony responded.

The questioning continued for another forty minutes, during which Wolk and Hicks asked the same questions in several different ways, and at the end of that time Hicks said, "I have just one more question, Mr. Trapasso, before you may leave."

"Shoot," Tony said."

"Did you know Lee Harvey Oswald?"

Tony looked at him for a long moment before he shifted his eyes to Wolk. From the expression on their faces, Tony realized they were waiting for him to reply. He rubbed his chin for a moment; then he said, "I'll let you answer that one yourselves. I'm sorry I wasted my time and yours." And he stood up.

"Just where the hell do you think you're going?" Hicks demanded to know.

"I'm leaving, gentlemen, and if either of you attempts to stop me, I'll have your fucking body nailed to the front door of this building. I don't know how you're conducting your investigation but I do know, at least from what happened here today, that you're playing games, and I just don't want to play."

24

ON THE FIFTH of June, Sy and Andrew graduated from the Naval Academy. After a month's leave, Andrew was ordered to report to the Pensacola Naval Air Station for flight training and Sy was ordered to the destroyer *Munson*, which operated out of Iwakuni, Japan.

That same month Mike graduated from the University of Pennsylvania, and having completed the Naval Reserve Training Program, he too was commissioned a lieutenant (jg) and was ordered to the Pensacola Naval Air Station for flight training.

On a Friday evening, two days into their leaves, the three friends met for dinner at the Plaza, where Jacob maintained a suite. Wearing their service whites, they sat at a table in the Bull and Bear.

"You'll be the one with the experience," Mike said, looking at Sy, "while me and Andrew will still be going to school."

"God, another two years of it at least," Andrew commented, shaking his head.

"And four more years after that," Sy said.

Andrew downed the rest of his martini in one gulp. "You two really planning to go the thirty-year route?"

"That's too far ahead to even think about," Sy answered. "Right now . . . well, now is now, and—"

"Speaking about now and making the most of it," Mike interrupted, "did you ever get anywhere with . . . what's her name? The biochemist you told me about?"

"Have you been holding out on me?" Andrew asked, feigning anger. "If I told you once, I told you a couple of hundred times, when it comes to dealing with women, it pays to ask your old friend Andrew."

Sy laughed.

"Well, what's the problem?" Andrew asked. Theatrically he raised his hand to his brow. "No, don't tell me: the young lady in question won't cooperate . . . she won't accompany you to not even the bedroom door, let alone the bed, where you, being the altruist that you are, want to transport her into the realm of sexual ecstasy."

"C'mon," Mike urged. "What's happening between the two of you?"

"Zippo," Sy admitted, looking down on the white tablecloth.

"Zippo . . . zippo," Andrew repeated. "That is not an acceptable score for an officer—"

"And a gentleman," Mike added.

"That too," Andrew said. "It's a stain on the escutcheon of our honor—we do have one of those escutcheons, don't we?"

"Sure we do," Mike responded.

Andrew nodded. "There, now, you can't stain that. What's this young lady's name?"

Sy hesitated to name her.

"Oh, ye of little faith," Andrew said, pointing a finger at Sy. "Name or no name, let me tell you to be bold in your approach, throw caution to the winds, and make her your own."

"Some advice!" Sy responded sarcastically.

"Be bold, yet tender—that any better?"

"I could have told him the same thing," Mike said, "and I never claimed to be the cocksman that you claim to be."

"Cocksman? I never had, nor would I ever have, that laurel upon my head. Gentlemen, I am a lover . . . a lover—and if there was a laurel given for that, I would proudly wear it for my crown."

"Seriously, have you seen her lately?" Mike asked.

"I called her a few times," Sy said. "We went out for coffee, and . . . well, she was just being sociable."

"Like the man said, 'zippo,' " Andrew commented.

"When was the last time you saw her?" Mike asked.

"April, when I was up here for a couple of days during Easter."

"You let all this time go by without seeing her?"

"I bet he didn't call her either," Andrew said.

Sy glanced at him. "How did you know?"

"Because, buddy, I know you," Andrew answered; then, pointing his finger at Sy, he said, "Mike, our lifelong friend here, is just too damn . . . Mike, what the hell is he 'too damn'?"

"Too damn much of a nice guy," Mike said. "C'mon, Sy, maybe she wants to hear from you as much as you want to call her."

"Nah, she's going to marry a guy named Ralph and live in a beautiful house and be—"

"Hell, man, you have enough money to give a woman anything she wants," Andrew said. "You just don't think of yourself as the son of a multimillionaire. You don't even have to stay in this man's navy, once your time is up. You don't have to do a fucking thing except clip coupons and enjoy yourself."

"Call her," Mike said, putting his hand on his friend's arm. "Call her."

Sy nodded. "I will."

"I want a full report on Operation Heather," Andrew said, "when we meet at Mike's house for the Fourth of July."

"How full a report?" Mike asked.

With a leer, Andrew answered, "All the lovely sexual details."

"Just that you called, okay?" Mike said.

"I said I would," Sy replied.

"Well, now, that kind of determination certainly calls for another round of drinks," Andrew commented as he looked around for the waiter.

"Then let's order dinner," Mike said. "All this talk about women has made me hungry."

25

THE FOLLOWING MORNING Sy phoned Heather. "Listen," he said, "I'm in town—for the weekend. I'd like to see you."

"I don't know—"

"Sure you know," he told her. "I mean, we'll just spend a day out-of-doors . . . nothing very formal . . . a walk in the park, maybe."

After some hesitation she agreed to meet him that afternoon at two o'clock.

"I'll pick you up at your place—"

"I have some work to do in the lab," she said. "I'll be on the corner of Sixty-eighth Street and York Avenue."

"I'll be there," Sy told her.

Without saying another word, Heather hung up.

Sy looked at the phone. "Well, thank you for the invitation!" he exclaimed aloud, and was about to rent a car for the afternoon, when he decided against it. He was almost sorry he had made the date, and considered canceling it. But because he decided that would be the easy way out, he didn't. This time, he wanted her to tell him straight out that he was wasting his time.

Sy planned to be at least five minutes late, but he couldn't bring himself to do it and somehow managed to be at the corner of Sixty-eighth and York Avenue ten minutes early. Wearing a pair of chinos, a white polo shirt, dark amber-colored sunglasses, and long beaked blue hat, he stood back against the iron fence that isolated the Rockefeller Institute from the street.

The day had turned out to be a real New York-style summer sizzler. Though it wasn't even the Fourth yet, now and then there was the crack of an exploding firecracker.

It was ten after two when he saw Heather walking around the corner on the other side of York Avenue. She wore light blue slacks, a red blouse, and her long brown hair was tied back with a red ribbon.

She stopped for the red light, saw him, and waved.

Sy waved back, and when they finally came together she said, "I had a last-minute phone call."

"That sometimes happens," he told her as they started to walk.

After a few moments she said, "This is the first time I've seen you out of uniform. You look different."

"Good different or bad different?"

She turned her face toward him. "Different, that's all."

They walked almost a full block without speaking; then both of them started at the same time.

"You first," Sy told her.

She asked where they were going.

"How about Central Park?"

"On a day like this it will be jammed with people."

"All right, you choose the place," he said as they came up to a red light and stopped.

"Someplace where it's cool."

The light went green and they crossed the street.

Sy waited a few moments for her to come up with a definite suggestion. When she didn't, he decided to follow Andrew's advice and be bold. "We could go back to the hotel," he said, trying desperately to make the tone of his voice sound as ordinary as if he were suggesting they stop for coffee.

They continued to walk.

Sy was beginning to think that she hadn't heard him; then suddenly she stopped short, and facing him, said, "I just don't get it. I don't understand what you want from me."

Her green eyes flashed with light.

"Oh, I know you want to go to bed with me," Heather said. "I knew that the moment my uncle introduced us."

"You're right, I want to go to bed with you. I also want to love you and be loved in return by you."

Her cheeks and neck turned red.

Sy took hold of her hand and began to walk again.

"Ralph and I are almost engaged," she said. "He was very annoyed when I told him that I was going to meet you."

"That was the phone call?" Sy asked, not looking as her.

She nodded.

"Was it?" he pressed, still holding on to her hand.

"Yes."

He thought for a moment before he said, "Can't fault him for that. If you were my girl and you were going to spend the afternoon with another man, I'd be annoyed as hell . . . no, I'd be furious."

Heather laughed. "You don't strike me as the jealous type."

"I'm not . . . but I would be where you're concerned."

They stopped for another light and Sy saw a Good

Humor ice-cream man on the corner diagonally opposite from where they were. "Come," he said when the
light changed. "It's time for ice cream." He took hold
of her hand and began to run.

"You'll get us killed!" she cried, pulled along by
him.

"Never," he answered as they made it to the safety
of the far sidewalk; then to the ice cream man he said,
"Two large vanilla Dixies."

"Suppose I didn't like vanilla and wanted a different
flavor?" Heather questioned, once they started to walk
again.

Sy shook his head.

"What's that supposed to mean?"

"It's not the kind of question I care to answer,"
he said with mock sternness.

For several minutes they concentrated on eating
their ice cream; then Heather asked, "What would
you have done if I had not agreed to meet you?"

"Probably killed myself," Sy said, crushing the empty
ice-cream cup.

"Be serious."

Sy spotted a litter basket and deftly tossed the crushed
cup into it. "Okay, I'll be serious. At the end of this
month I'll be aboard the *Munson*, and—"

"What's a *Munson*?" she asked.

"It's a destroyer and it's based in Japan."

She stopped. "You're going to Japan? I thought you
were still in Annapolis."

He shook his head. "I graduated. I'm a lieutenant
(jg) and I'm assigned to the *Munson* for the next six to
seven months at least."

"What are you going to do?"

"I won't know until I'm aboard."

She turned her head toward him. "My God, you're an officer and . . ."

The way she looked at him . . . the way she looked made him stop. In an instant his arms were around her and his lips on hers.

She struggled to free herself.

He pressed her close to him, feeling the softness of her breasts against his chest, tasting her lips and inhaling the light scent of her perfume. Finally he eased his hold.

"Are you crazy?" she gasped.

"I love you," he answered, keeping her in his arms. "Tell me that you never want to see me again and I'll walk away from you now."

"You *are* crazy!"

Sy shook his head. "Marry me," he said.

"Marry you?" she screeched. "Marry you, I don't even know you. You don't know me. This is insane. Ralph—"

"I know—your uncle told me—you've known him for years and years and he's going to be a doctor and . . . and right here and now, I'm asking you to marry me."

"You're serious, aren't you?"

"More serious than I've ever been in my life," he answered; then, gently caressing the side of her face, he said, "I never, ever asked a woman to marry me before and I never want to again."

"But—"

He kissed her again.

This time Heather didn't struggle to free herself, and when they separated, she whispered, "Take me back to the hotel, Sy."

"You're going to be a beautiful bride," he told her, putting his arm around her narrow waist.

*   *   *

Sy had always been with Jacob when he saw his mother. But because he thought it was important for her to meet his future wife, the very next day he rented a white convertible and drove out with Heather to see her.

On the way there, Sy told Heather what had happened to his mother and how his Aunt Miriam had actually raised him.

"I'm lucky," she said. "My parents are still alive and well. I phoned them last night—"

"I don't remember that," he said, looking at her.

She laughed. "When you were asleep. I told them that I'm getting married."

"I bet they thought you were going to marry Ralph."

She nodded. "They're flying in on the fifth."

"You know, I don't even know where you were born and raised," Sy said, stopping to pay the toll as they came out of the Queens Midtown Tunnel.

"Here—I mean Brooklyn. But my folks live in Florida. My dad is retired. He was a house painter."

"You're joking. . . . You're not joking?"

"Absolutely not joking," she answered.

Sy laughed. "The daughter of a Brooklyn house painter and the son of a career naval officer—I can't begin to guess who our children will take after."

"Your father—at least according to my uncle—is a hero," Heather said. "I mean, a real hero."

"He doesn't think of himself that way," Sy answered, switching lanes. "But he's done some remarkable things and he's really a very remarkable man."

She lightly placed her hand on his. "You love him very much, don't you?"

Sy nodded. "He's really the only one I had to love. My mother—"

"And now you have me," Heather told him softly.

Glancing at her, Sy responded, "Yes, and now I have you."

An hour after leaving the city, Sy drove slowly up the cul-de-sac and eased into a parking spot.

"Are you sure you want me to go in with you?" Heather asked as they left the car and walked up the broad front steps.

"Absolutely. It's the reason why I drove out here," he said. "Maybe knowing that she will soon have a daughter-in-law will make her feel a bit happier."

"Your mother is expecting you, Ensign Miller," the director said after Sy introduced Heather to him. "She's in the main sitting room."

"How has she been?"

"Splendid. Her paintings are quite beautiful," the man answered. "You know your way, don't you?"

"Yes," Sy said, and taking Heather's hand, he left the director's office.

"Your mother paints?" Heather asked.

"Pictures," he responded. "Not walls."

Heather stuck out her tongue.

Entering the main sitting room, Sy said, "Imagine what your uncle would say if he had seen that."

"Only that you deserved it."

"There's my mother at the window. She probably saw us getting out of the car," he said, letting go of Heather's hand and advancing in front of her. "Mother?" he called softly. "Mother."

Tara turned from the window, looked at them for several moments, and then smiled.

"God, she's beautiful!" Heather exclaimed in a whisper.

Embracing her, Sy suddenly found he had a lump in

throat. "Mom," he said, "Mom, it's so good to see you again."

She touched his face.

He took hold of her hand and kissed the tips of her fingers. "I brought someone to meet you," he said.

"Yes, I saw the two of you from the window," Tara told him. She smiled, stepped slightly away from Sy, and looked at Heather.

"Mom, Miss Heather Gershon . . . Heather, my mother." As he spoke, Sy moved his eyes from his mother to Heather and then back to his mother.

Tara studied her for several moments; then, speaking in a soft, gentle voice, she said, "Love him dearly, Heather . . . he's all I have." Then she removed her own gold wedding band, and holding it between the thumb and first finger of her right hand, she took hold of Heather's left hand. "With my ring, I do wed my only beloved son to thee." And she slipped the ring onto the third finger. "There, it's done . . . you're now married." She embraced Heather and then turned to Sy. "The moment I saw her from the window, I knew you were bringing her here to marry."

Sy hugged her fiercely to him.

"I want to see grandchildren," Tara said.

"Yes, Mom."

"Well, I think I'd like to go to my room now," Tara said. "I'm very tired."

"Would you like us to go with you?" Sy asked.

Tara shook her head, smiled wistfully at Heather, and with her head bowed, walked slowly away.

Wiping his eyes with a handkerchief, Sy said, "She's gone . . . gone."

Heather linked her arm with his. "She loves you very much," she told him.

He bit his lower lip, nodded, and started to walk toward the door of the sitting room.

"Can you drive?" Heather asked as they reentered the car.

"Yes," Sy answered, switching on the ignition and backing out of the parking slot. It wasn't until they were heading back to the city on the Long Island Expressway that he said, "I'm all right."

"Are you sure?"

"Absolutely," he answered; then, taking hold of her left hand, he ran his fingers over the ring.

"I want to be married with it," Heather told him.

"Thank you," he whispered. "It's the only thing she ever gave me."

"You're wrong, Sy," Heather told him. "She gave you part of yourself . . . part of what you are comes from her."

Suddenly Sy's vision began to blur. He pulled over to the right side of the road, stopped the car, and burying his face in his arms, he wept.

Heather turned him toward her and held his head against her breasts.

"I never expected her to do something like that," Sy said haltingly. "Never."

"She loves you," Heather answered.

"And I love her." Sy raised his head. "Do you think she knows I love her?"

"Yes, she knows," Heather replied. She held her ringed finger in front of him. "This is proof that she knows."

Sitting up, Sy wiped his eyes, blew his nose, and started the car again. After he slipped the car into the stream of traffic, he said, "I'd like you to go and see her when I'm away."

"Certainly I will," Heather answered, pressing his arm against her breast.

He smiled gratefully at her.

The wedding was hastily put together and was finally held in the evening of the second Saturday in July on the lawn of Tony's house. Despite the short notice, there were a hundred and fifty people there.

The weather cooperated. It was one of those lovely July evenings, with low humidity and a cool breeze that was just strong enough to rustle the leaves of the trees.

Before the ceremony, Sy introduced his father to Rabbi Stikosky, and though Jacob did not immediately recognize him, as they spoke, the face of a younger man began to materialize out of his memory, especially when the rabbi saw Warren and said, "He was in charge . . . he was the real skipper of the *Pelican*."

In a matter of minutes the three of them were talking about the *Pelican* and the other men who had been aboard her. The three of them went to one of the three bars set up on the lawn and drank a toast to the *Pelican*'s crew.

The actual ceremony took place under a portable canopy held—over Heather and Sy; Heather's parents; Jacob and Miriam, who was standing in for Tara; Mike, the best man; and Nina, Heather's maid of honor—by Warren, Andrew, and Tony.

When the rabbi took the wedding ring from the best man, he held it up for all of the guests to see, and then, lowering it, he said, "For years, I thought about this time, the time when I would perform the wedding service for my niece, Heather. But this ring has changed all of that. The presence of this ring would make anything I planned to say about my special love for my niece superfluous. This is no ordinary ring. This ring did not come from a jeweler's showcase, not for this occasion. This ring is full of the wonderful magic of love, a mother's love.

"Some days ago, immediately after Simon and Heather agreed to share their lives, he did a remarkable thing. He took his future bride to see his mother —to share, if you will, the love he feels for her and to have her share in his happiness. His mother, as result of suffering a terrible trauma when he was just a small boy, has only known him through his visits to her, and yet she never ceased loving him."

He lifted the ring again. "This belonged to her, and she removed it from her finger, and putting it on Heather's, she said, 'With my ring, I do wed my only beloved son to thee.' That was the real marriage ceremony. What I do here is only a pale imitation of what your beloved mother did, Sy. Nothing I say or do, and I will say and do what is prescribed by the laws of our faith and the civil laws of the state in which we live, will sanctify your union more than your mother's love already has. And it is with great humility that I now perform those additional rites which will bind the two of you in holy wedlock. . . ."

Jacob had had no idea that Sy had visited Tara and was deeply touched by what the rabbi had said. Not too many prospective bridegrooms would take a future bride to meet an institutionalized mother. He was very proud of him . . . but at the same time, he was concerned about Arlene's reaction to it, and as the rabbi had spoken about the ring, he had glanced at her several times. She appeared to have been as moved by the story as any of the other guests. . . .

Finally the ceremony concluded with Sy stomping on a wineglass, and then hugs, handshakes and *mazel tovs* were exchanged by everyone in the bridal party.

It was only after the last guest shook Jacob's hand and he could leave the receiving line that he joined Arlene, who was sitting at a table with Carol.

"Where's Warren?" he asked.

"Answering a call of nature," Carol answered.

Jacob sat down and took hold of Arlene's hand. "There's an immense amount of food just about ready," he said.

"The hors d'oeuvres are scrumptious," Carol said. "There must be at least sixteen waiters moving around with trays of them."

Jacob said, "I haven't had a chance to sample one. Have you had any, Arlene?"

"Too many," she laughed.

A band set up on the side began to play a slow fox-trot.

"Dance?" Jacob asked.

"Why, yes," Arlene answered.

"Please excuse us," Jacob said, "we have some serious dancing to do."

"Sure . . . I'm going to take a look at what I'm going to eat," Carol said as she stood up. "And find Warren, though I'm not sure which I'll do first."

Jacob led Arlene closer to the music, and taking her in his arms, began to dance with her. "Are you upset?" he asked as they moved in a small circle to the rhythm of the music.

"No . . . not really . . . I shouldn't be."

"But you are."

Arlene nodded. "This was the first time I realized that you're still a married man."

He took hold of her hand and led her to the far end of the lawn before he said, "Tara is my wife in name only. I love you, but I won't divorce Tara."

"I know that," Arlene answered.

They faced each other without speaking.

"I know you love me, and I love you," Arlene said in a low, breathy voice, "but I'm not sure that . . . that I'm willing to continue to be your 'lady friend,' which is a polite way of referring to me."

He tried to put his arms around her.

"No," she said gently. "If you hold me, I'll never be able to say what I want to say."

Jacob took a small step backward. "There. . . . Say whatever it is you want to say."

"I need some time to think," she told him.

"Meaning that you don't want to see me," he said, unable to speak without forcing the words out.

She nodded.

"My son's marriage and my separation—an even score, and all in the same night."

"Jacob—"

"This is your tune, Arlene," he said bitterly.

"Yes, it is my tune," she answered.

"Will you stay the rest of the evening?" Jacob asked.

"Yes," Arlene answered. "Jacob—"

"You said what you had to . . . there isn't any reason to say any more." He looked toward the house, where the light from a dozen flambeaux wavered across the lawn. "I have to go back to the guests," he said.

She fell in alongside him.

"Give me a chance to—"

Too angry and hurt to speak, Jacob quickened his pace.

26

ON AUGUST 2, the first Sunday in the month, Sy was junior officer of the watch, assisting Lieutenant Commander Nansen, OOD for the *Munson*'s forenoon bridge watch, who stood on the port side with hands clasped behind him. Less than a dozen feet away, to his right, Captain John Murry, the ship's skipper, sat calmly in his swivel chair.

Sy, on the starboard side, swept the mirrorlike surface of the sea with a pair of high-powered binoculars. The *Munson*, steaming on station, was ten miles below the Red River Delta, close to its northern turnaround point.

The ship was in a Condition Two of readiness, which it had gone to at the beginning of the watch, after having been at GQ from 0200, when it encountered hundreds of North Vietnamese junks, and fearing they might be armed, the skipper had ordered battle stations. The ship was part of a much larger operation, which the skipper had alluded to on several occasions—and none too happily—but did not define.

Sy was the assistant gunnery officer, but in the short time aboard he'd made friends with several of the other junior officers. Several were assigned to the

Combat Information Center or to the radar/sonar section.

At breakfast that morning in the wardroom, the discussion at the table had been about the previous night's activities. The men agreed that the skipper had done the only thing he could do; then one of the other junior officers assigned to radar had said, "We've been picking up one heck of a lot of activity coming from the south. The NNV uses very fast boats for hit-and-run raids in the north. One of the chiefs told me they were called swifts."

"We've been sending a lot of coded stuff to CIN-PACFLT and to Seventh Fleet," another man had said.

"What I'd really like to know is what we're doing out here," a third officer commented.

"Hell, man, we're here to give those northern gooks a problem," the fourth man commented in a broad western drawl. "Kind of like teasin' a rattler with a stick, but havin' somethin' handy to take his head off with."

Sy hadn't cared much for the analogy when he had first heard it, and now, thinking about it several hours later, he cared even less for it. Though he never had had any direct experience with rattlesnakes, he knew by their reputation that they were highly nervous creatures and very dangerous. Almost as soon as this thought entered his brain, one of the bridge phones rang.

The OOD glanced at him and nodded.

Sy picked up the phone. "Bridge, here," he said.

"Three PCFs moving out of the estuary," the voice said. "Heading toward Hon Me."

"Stand by," Sy said, and instantly repeated the report to the captain.

Murry was on his feet.

"PCFs behind the island," the voice reported.

"PCFs moved behind Hon Me;" Sy said.

Another phone rang.

"Bridge, here," Sy said, answering it.

"We've picked up radio orders to the PCFs to refuel and attack," the communications officer said.

"Communications picked up orders to refuel and attack," Sy said.

"Sound general quarters," Murry calmly ordered.

The next instant the Klaxon screamed; then the OOD switched on the ship's 1MC. "General quarters . . . general quarters . . . all hands, man your battle stations . . . all hands, man your battle stations."

Sy raced to his position in the ship's gun director.

At flank speed, the *Munson* turned toward the open sea. But the gunboats followed in hot pursuit.

"Mounts one, two, and three ready," Sy reported to the gunnery officer.

"Mounts one, two, and three, stand by to fire at ten thousand yards," the gunnery officer responded from the CIC.

Radar-directed, the two forward guns swiveled around in opposite directions: mount number one covered the starboard side, mount number two the port side.

The North Vietnamese motor torpedo boats were closing fast, and Sy realized that the skipper was trying to put as much distance between them and the *Munson* as possible and as quickly as possible.

But the PCFs had twice the speed of the *Munson*.

Sy called out the bearing, range, and speed to the gunnery officer.

"Commence firing!" the gunnery officer ordered.

"Commence firing," Sy repeated.

The dual five-inches barked. The explosions were

deafening. The screaming rounds crashed into the sea's mirrorlike surface, causing the eruption of huge plumes of water that for a few moments, before they fell back and reformed the sun-glinting surface, hung in the air and looked like slender leafless trees.

Round after round was pumped out of the five-inches. And moment by moment the azimuth, range, and distance continually changed.

"Five thousand yards and closing," Sy reported to the gunnery officer.

Sy, his shirt soaked through with sweat, and the sharp stink of burnt cordite in his nostrils, urged the gun captains on the mounts to quicken the firing.

Aware of little else than the blips on the scope, he glimpsed through the one of the director's slits.

A PCF was veering in toward the *Munson*.

"Torpedo, zero-six-five," one of the bridge officers shouted over the 1MC.

The next instant the PCF was bracketed by two plumes of water. Its bow rose up and the entire boat seemed to have come to an abrupt halt. A fraction of moment later, it burst into flame and fell back into the water.

The *Munson*'s rudder was hard over to the right, and as she answered the rudder, she heeled sharply to the left.

"Three thousand yards . . . three thousand yards and closing," Sy called out. "Get those fucking rounds out!" he shouted to the gun captains, forcing himself not to think about the oncoming torpedo.

"Torpedo, two-five-zero," a voice yelled over the 1MC.

Sy brushed his arm across his brow.

The *Munson*'s helm went hard to the right. Suddenly a loud clang came from below her water line.

"A fucking dud!" Sy heard someone in the CIC yell.

Moments later, the sky was filled with the roar of American jets.

"Jesus, Mary, and Joseph, look at those beauties," one of the gun captains shouted.

"And look at those fucking gook boats turn and run," someone answered.

"Cease firing . . . cease firing . . . all guns, cease firing," the gunnery officer ordered.

Sy took a deep breath and leaned back into the chair. Wet with sweat, he felt as if he had become older by an indeterminate number of years. Being in action was nothing like he'd imagined; nothing like he'd been taught; nothing like anything he'd ever experienced before.

Jacob, roused from uneasy sleep by the persistent ring of the phone, reached over to the night table and picked it up. "Captain Miller, here."

"Jacob, the *Munson* has been involved in an action against the North Vietnamese," Warren said.

Instantly wide-awake, Jacob pushed himself up against the bed's headboard. "Any casualties?"

"No reports yet," Warren answered.

"How do you know about it?"

"I was called to the office almost as soon as it began," Warren said.

"How long did it last?"

"Twenty minutes, maybe twenty-two. The *Munson* sank two of the PCFs. Two torpedoes were launched against it. One hit, but was a dud, and the second missed. The *Munson*'s skipper radioed the *Sumter* for air support. When the Crusaders showed up, the PCFs broke off contact."

Jacob broke out in a cold sweat.

"The White House has called an early-morning press conference," Warren told him. "All the Chiefs of Staff will be there. Looks like there's going to be a response."

"You mean a strike?"

"I don't know. Another destroyer, the *C. William Day*, and the carrier *Murphy* were ordered to join up with the *Sumter*. All our troops are going to be placed on yellow alert."

Jacob took a deep breath and held it for a few moments before letting out a ragged sigh. "How the hell did you get all of this so fast?"

"I have connections," Warren answered.

Jacob didn't respond. His friend's evasive answer meant he was referring to his former tie to the ONI and wouldn't divulge his source of information.

"I suspect that Johnson will pull out all stops on this one to get what he wants," Warren said.

"I'm not at all sure that what he wants now will be what he wants if he should actually get it," Jacob said. "There's enough of a problem here with the racial unrest for a President to deal with. But maybe he thinks that taking a tough stand against the Communists in Southeast Asia, coupled to his concept of the Great Society, will help win him the presidency in November "

"He's a hard hitter when it comes to politics," Warren said. "He's probably got the angles on anything he does figured nine ways from Sunday."

"Probably," Jacob agreed. "But politics here isn't the same as politics there. He may think he has a winning hand, but the other guy may be holding all the aces."

"That's something only time will tell," Warren answered.

"For sure," Jacob said.

"I wouldn't wander too far from your phone today," Warren said. "I suspect you'll be ordered to report."

"I hadn't planned on going anywhere," Jacob answered. He hadn't gone anywhere since Sy's wedding, when he and Arlene had agreed to end their relationship. "Thanks for the call, Warren, and give my best to Carol."

"I'll be in touch," Warren answered, and clicked off.

Jacob put the phone back in its cradle and found himself wondering whether Kennedy would have baited the North Vietnamese had he lived, the way Johnson was apparently doing.

Sy and the other *Munson* officers were gathered in the wardroom, where Captain Murry had ordered them. As soon as he entered, one of the men called, "Attention."

Those officers who were seated, immediately started to stand, while the others came to attention.

"As you were, gentlemen," Murry told them, making his way forward. "Smoke if you've got them." He sat down at one of the tables and faced his officers. "Before I get to the main reason why I asked all of you to be here, I want to take a few moments to congratulate Lieutenant (jg) Simon Miller on his excellent performance under enemy fire. . . .Congratulations, Lieutenant Miller."

Sy felt his cheeks turn beet red.

"I mentioned you by name in my report to CINPACFLT and in the final version of the ship's log."

A burst of applause erupted from Sy's fellow officers.

"And now to the main business at hand," Murry

said. "Our ship and the *C. William Day* have been given the task of playing chicken with the North Vietnamese PCFs, or anything else they might throw against us. We are within eight miles of their coast and we have been ordered to stage direct runs to, in the words of President Johnson, 'assert the right of freedom of the seas.' Or stated another way by Rear Admiral Raymond L. Krauss, commander of the carrier group, 'The North Vietnamese have thrown down the gauntlet and should be treated as belligerents from the first detection.' And that means, gentlemen, we fire first."

A low buzz of conversation quickly skittered through the wardroom and in a matter of moments lapsed into silence.

"Until we are told to the contrary," Murry said, "the men in this ship and the other ships operating in this area are at a state of war with the North Vietnamese."

Another momentary buzz of muted conversation filled the wardroom.

"Are there any questions," Murry asked. "None—"

"Sir," one of the officers said, raising his hand.

Murray acknowledged him with a nod.

"Sir, I don't know if this question is out of line or not," the officer said, speaking with a slow, southern accent, "but doesn't the power to declare a war rest with the Congress?"

A smile almost creased Murry's lips before he answered, "Lieutenant Rice, the fine points of government don't enter into it. We're here, and if the North Vietnamese try to make us leave, we'll just have to prove to them that if here is where we want to be, we'll be here, even if we have to fight to be here."

"Yes, sir, I understand that . . . but I guess what I'm asking is whether we should be here at all."

"The fact that we're already here, Lieutenant, negates that question," Murry answered. "Any more questions? None. . . . Good. I know I can rely on all of you to do your best. Thank you, gentlemen." And he stood up.

Shortly after the skipper's speech, huge black monsoon clouds boiled up on the eastern horizon, covering the whole face of the sky. The placid waters of the Tonkin Gulf turned into a raging sea. Slashing rain beat down on the *Munson* as she plowed her way through the prematurely inky blackness that should have been the characteristic brief twilight of the tropics.

Back on the bridge as the OOD's assistant, Sy peered into the blackness, punctuated with jagged flashes of lightning. Murry was on the port side, a dead cigar clamped between his teeth. The OOD stood close to the port-side gyro repeater, while he himself was near the phone bank.

Ever since the action the previous day, Sy had wondered what his father's reaction had been to his own first combat experience. His was a combination of fear and exhilaration—after all, it was his gun crew that blasted the PCF. But he also knew that during the whole action his bowels churned so hard he was afraid he'd drop a load right there. He had heard that many guys did that the first time under fire. He also couldn't help thinking about Heather, and because he had been in action, he wondered if their marriage hadn't been a mistake. Perhaps they should have waited. But for what? He intended to be a career officer. He almost shook his head. He couldn't wait for her. He loved her too much to wait. And in that instant the physical need for her became so intense that it came close to being pain. He had never felt anything like that before. For an instant he closed his eyes and let the image of her naked body fill his brain. Then, opening them, he continued to stare in the pitch-black night.

A sudden bolt of lightning flashed downward not a dozen feet from the ship, illuminating the entire vessel with a bright white light. Within an instant the explosive roar of thunder slammed down on the *Munson*, making her tremble from stem to stern.

"Christ, did you feel that!" one of the yeomen of the watch exclaimed.

And before anyone could answer, another streak of white-hot lightning slashed down directly in front of the *Munson*'s bow just as it was digging into a huge wave. This time the burst of thunder caught the ship when she was struggling to break free of the wave.

"Between the fucking waves and the fucking thunder, we're like a fucking cork," the helmsman muttered, struggling to hold the ship on her course.

Murry glanced at him. "Mind your helm," he said.

The bridge was no place for idle chatter, even if it did help relieve the tension.

Suddenly the *Munson*'s stern was out of the water. Her twin propellers grabbed air, sending shuddering vibration through the struggling vessel. Within moments her stern slammed down into the heaving sea.

Murry checked his radar and shook his head.

A phone rang.

Sy answered it with, "Bridge, here."

"The *Day* reports multiple targets, bearing zero-four-eight, range fifteen thousand yards," the communications officer said.

"Roger," Sy answered, and putting down the phone, repeated the report to Murry.

"Get our radar on that bearing," Murry said.

The OOD looked at Sy. "Give the bearing and range."

Sy picked up the phone. "Bridge, here," he answered as soon as radar answered. "The skipper wants you to slew to zero-four-eight at fifteen thousand yards. . . . The *Day* reports multiple targets out there."

"Wilco," radar responded.

Murry waited a few moments; then, looking at his radar display, he asked the OOD, "What do you see?"

The phone from radar rang.

"Bridge, here," Sy said, answering it.

"We don't pick up anything," the voice on the other end said. "There's a lot of clutter from wave action and a lot of atmospheric interference."

"Stand by," Sy said, and gave the report to the skipper.

"God damn, if we can't tell a target from a fucking wave, we're in deep shit," Murry exploded.

"They look like targets to me," the OOD said.

"Tell radar I want confirmation," Murry growled, "and I want it now!"

"Confirm target," Sy told radar.

There was a momentary pause before the man answered, "Wilco."

Murry pointed to the radar display, and chomping down on the dead cigar, he said, "The *Day* is four thousand yards astern, yet they were able to—"

The phone rang again.

"Radar reports multiple targets, bearing zero-four-eight, range nine thousand yards, speed forty knots, closing fast."

"Sound general quarters," Murry ordered.

The Klaxon screamed for several moments. The

OOD's voice came over the 1MC, "Battle stations . . . battle stations . . . all hands, battle stations."

Sy raced up to the gun director, making his way up the steep steps as quickly as possible, despite the pitching and rolling of the vessel, to the small cubicle perched on top of the ship's bridge.

As each mount reported "ready," Sy relayed its status to the senior gunnery officer. He watched the target indications on the radar; they were indistinct and difficult to track.

The *Day* began firing.

The gun mounts were turned toward the targets.

"Commence firing," the gunnery officer ordered.

"Commence firing," Sy told the gun captains.

A burst of red flames shot out of the *Munson*'s five-inch guns.

Suddenly she went hard over to the port and the mounts were automatically slewed around to correct for the change in the ship's position.

Within minutes the *Munson* changed course again, this time going into a hard right turn.

Despite the damp coldness that the rain brought, Sy was sweating. Because of the heavy seas, he knew that the gun crew had difficulty keeping their footing, and the sudden changes in the ship's course caused her to heel sharply each time she was turned, making it even more difficult for them.

There was no letup in her fire, or the fire from the *Day*.

Then suddenly the order came to cease fire.

"Cease fire . . . cease fire," Sy told his gun crews.

And almost immediately the roar of jets filled the night.

Aware that the storm had ended as quickly as it had begun, Sy rested against the back of his chair. Every

muscle in his body ached . . . for now the shooting
was over, but there wasn't any doubt in his mind that
this was just the beginning.

The following morning, Murry assembled in the wardroom the officers of the bridge, radar, and sonar watches
who had been on duty before and during the previous
night's action. Again he told them, "Smoke if you
have them." Then he said, "Gentlemen, the results of
last night's action have prompted me to bring you
here."

Sy rested his elbows on the table.

The officer next to him whispered, "A guy in sonar
told me we dodged twenty-two torpedoes."

"He's probably pulling your chain," Sy whispered
back.

"The question I've had to ask," Murry said, "is
whether or not we were shooting at targets or at
distortions on our radar resulting from the weather
conditions." He paused to light a fresh cigar, and once
it was drawing to his satisfaction, he continued. "All
of you played some part before and during the time
we were firing and taking evasive actions against reported torpedoes; therefore, I'm going to ask each of
you to present in writing to me at this time as precise a
recollection as to what occurred as you possibly can.
None of your statements need be signed." He turned
to the master chief standing by and said, "Would you
please distribute the necessary paper to the officers."

"Aye, aye, sir," the master chief answered.

"You may confer with one another," Murry said.

The radar officers to whom Sy had spoken before
general quarters were sounded said, "The skipper
wanted target confirmation, and that's what we gave
him. We had something on the scope, but what the

hell that something was, we hadn't the slightest god-
dam idea."

As he wrote his explanation and listened to some of
the comments made by the men around him, Sy came
to the conclusion that they and the *Day* had expended
a "hell of a lot of ammo on nothing."

After Murry had asked the master chief to collect
the papers, he said, "From what I have just heard and
from what I am sure I will read in your reports, it
seems obvious to me that a superabundant amount of
anxiousness on my part combined with extraordinarily
difficult weather conditions to produce a nonexistent
enemy."

"Captain, I confirmed what you saw on the radar,"
said the OOD of the previous night's watch.

Murry nodded. "That's because I wanted confirmation," he said. "I take sole responsibility for what
occurred . . . but it is important that Washington knows
what actually happened and how it happened. Thank
you for your cooperation. We . . . I don't want to be
responsible for starting a war." He stood up.

Someone called out, "Atten' hut!"

The men stood up.

"As you were, gentlemen," Murry said, and left the
wardroom. As soon as he was gone, the XO dismissed
the men.

27

IT WAS SIX o'clock in the evening when Jacob in his suite at the Shoreham turned on the TV, and like tens of millions of other Americans, listened to the Pentagon spokesman declare that "a second deliberate attack" had taken place against American destroyers operating in the Tonkin Gulf. But unlike the millions who watched and heard this mild-looking man with horn-rimmed glasses, Jacob had been involved in determining the retaliatory strike against four North Vietnamese patrol-boat bases and an oil-storage depot. That strike was being carried out, even as the six-o'clock news was being presented, by planes from the carriers *Ticonderoga* and *Constellation*.

Shortly afterward, President Johnson came on TV. In a solemn voice he said, "Repeated acts of violence against the armed forces of the United States must be met not only with alert defense, but with a positive reply. That reply is being given as I speak to you tonight. . . ."

Jacob stood up, crossed the room to the TV, shut it off, and began to pace. He had not only helped plan those strikes but also read transcriptions of the conversations that had taken place between the Crusader pilots from the *Ticonderoga* and the skipper of the *Munson*. There was no doubt in his mind, or in the minds of the other staff officers involved in planning the strike, that the North Vietnamese had not committed any hostile act against either the *Munson* or the *Day*. The result of this strike would only deepen America's role in the Vietnamese conflict.

Knowing something about President Johnson's ability to make the members of Congress come around to his way of thinking, Jacob was sure that he would manage to get them to vote him broad powers to deal with the situation.

His phone rang and he immediately picked it up. "Captain Miller, here," he announced.

"I miss you, Jacob," Arlene said.

He was too surprised to speak. His heart skipped a beat and began to race. "I miss you too," he finally responded. "I miss you very much."

"I—"

"There's no need for you to explain," he told her.

She began to cry softly.

"Arlene?"

"Yes."

"I love you," Jacob told her.

"I love you," she answered. "I was so afraid that something had happened to Sy . . . Oh, Jacob, I'm sorry. I behaved so badly. But now, tonight, as I watched the news . . . I know how much Sy means to you, and I—"

"Can you come to Washington tomorrow?"

"Yes, my love," she answered. "I'll take the eight A.M. flight down."

"There'll be a car waiting for you," Jacob told her. "I don't know when I'll be finished at the office, but I'll call you to let you know."

"Yes, Jacob."

"Good night, love," Jacob said.

"Good night, my love," Arlene responded.

Jacob put the phone down; then, crossing the room, he went to the desk, picked up a pipe, and filled it with tobacco. As he smoked, he stood at the window and looked at the illuminated dome of the Capitol. He knew that what he had seen and heard on TV was completely disingenuous and that President Johnson for all his alleged political savvy had commenced the biggest political blunder of his professional career. There were men like himself, who know that no matter what Johnson would say about keeping us out of a Southeast Asian war, that was exactly the kind of war he would involve the country in. Jacob blew a column of smoke toward the ceiling, turned, and decided to go down to the bar for a drink. "At least," he said aloud, "by tomorrow night you won't be alone. . . ."

28

MIKE AND ANDREW sat together in the rear of ready room four and listened intently to the briefing officer. They were *nuggets*, the Navy's way of saying they were the "new guys" on the street and would have to prove themselves to the "old-timers." For some of those "old-timers," this would be their second tour. But for Andrew and Mike it was going to be their first mission Up North, the vernacular for North Vietnam.

Immediately after having completed their training at the Pensacola Naval Air Station, Andrew and Mike had been assigned to VF-10, which was deployed on the *Boon*, an Essex-class carrier that was returning to Task Force 77, after having been back in the States for a refitting. They and the rest of Fighter-Squadron 10 landed on the *Boon* after she had sailed from Alameda, California, and had cleared the twelve-mile limit. That had been ten days before. Now, on the last day of January 1966, after having successfully made the required number of daylight and night landings, their names were put on the flight schedule and they would finally fly their first combat mission as part of Task Force 77, on Yankee Station off the coast of North Vietnam.

"A few words to the nuggets with us, especially the fighter jocks," the briefing officer said. "Play it safe. Show the rest of us how good you are by doing your job."

Almost everyone in the ready room swiveled around to look at Andrew and Mike. Some grinned, while others rolled their eyes.

"Let's give them something to look at," Andrew whispered, grinning back. He'd made several quick sketches of some of the nearby men while the briefing was in progress.

"Like what?" Mike asked.

"Like this," Andrew said, standing up and bowing from the waist. "Seldom have so few had so much attention from just a few more." And as he sat down, he said out of the side of his mouth, "Your turn, sport."

Mike stood up. "Gentlemen, my sidekick tells me it's my 'turn' to demonstrate my affection for all of you; therefore it gives me great pleasure to offer you this . . ." And he began to sing. When he was finished, the men began to clap and cheer. Even the briefing officer had a smile on his face.

"Well, doesn't that beat all hell," Lieutenant Commander Dwight Harrison, the air group commander, said, standing up and looking at Andrew and Mike. "One mouthy nugget and the other a singin' one. Let's all pray they have the necessary talents to stay alive."

"CAG, we have talents you wouldn't believe," Mike answered flippantly.

Harrison shook his head. "I've heard that one before."

"Gentlemen," the briefing officer said, "the time is

now eleven-thirty. The first launch will be at eleven-forty-five. Good luck." He took a few moments to collect his charts, papers, and reconnaissance photographs before he stepped off the small platform and left the ready room.

"I don't think we scored high marks with the CAG," Mike commented, looking at Harrison, who was now speaking to two of the men in the fighter squadron, but looking at him and Andrew.

Andrew shrugged. "That's his problem."

"It damn well might be ours," Mike said. "We're going to have some company."

Two fighter pilots came up to them. The taller one, Lieutenant Charles Korale, said in a flat dry tone, "Troost, the CAG says you're my wingman."

The other pilot, a jg named Peter Hahn, pointed to Mike. "You're on me, canary."

"The two of you listen, and listen real good, to what I'm saying," Korale said. "You do what we do and nothing more, understand?"

"Do what you do," Andrew responded.

"I want to hear it from you, canary," Hahn said, his eyes hard on Mike.

"I have a name and a rank. Use one or both, Lieutenant," Mike fired back.

Hahn glared at him. "Just do it," he snapped, turned abruptly around, and walked away.

"That's not the way to win friends and influence people," Korale said, looking at Mike. "And out there, you need all the friends you can get." Then he too turned around and walked away.

'I'd say we made an impression, wouldn't you?" Andrew laughed.

"One of us has to go," Mike responded.

As if he were praying, Andrew put his hands together. "Dear God," he said, "I promise to be a good pilot and not make any more funnies, if you—"

The 1MC came on and the already familiar voice of the air boss sounded throughout the ship. "All hands, now hear this . . . all hands, now hear this. Stand by to launch aircraft. . . . Pilots, man your aircraft . . . pilots, man your aircraft."

"Time to get dressed and go to work," Mike said as they went to suit up.

"This certainly isn't what I call style," Andrew commented, zipping up his G-suit.

"Couldn't agree more," Mike answered. They rode the escalator up one level below the flight deck. Wearing twenty pounds of gear, which consisted of torso harness, a Mae West, and a survival kit and a helmet, they, and all of the other pilots, looked like and walked like creatures from another world.

Korale and Hahn were behind them.

"Check your beeper," Korale said.

"Did," Andrew answered.

"Do it again," Korale ordered.

Andrew made sure the PRC-63 was operating.

"Do the same, canary," Hahn said.

Mike was about to tell the jg to take a flying fuck, but instead muttered what the hell and checked the beeper. "It's good," he reported.

Hahn didn't answer.

They reached the top of the escalator, then went slowly up a flight of steps and finally out to a continuing crescendo of noise on the sun-baked flight deck.

Strapped into their A-4 Skyhawks by separate yellow-shirted plane captains, Mike and Andrew went through a checklist to make sure all of the plane's systems were operating. Then they waited for the launch to begin.

Inside the G-suits they sweated, while the *Boon*'s skipper brought her sixty degrees around to have the necessary combination of ship's speed and wind for the launch.

Though it was against the regs, Andrew slipped off his helmet and wiped the sweat from his eyes. This launch, he told himself, was going to be like any other. But the words wouldn't hold. It wasn't like any other. He was part of a twenty-plane Alpha strike force that was going to fly over enemy territory, in Route Pack V, to destroy, if possible, a bridge. The Alpha strike targets in Route Packs V and VI were always called by either the Department of Defense or the White House and passed down through the chain of command to CTF-77 and then to the CarDiv commanders. This wasn't a game. The enemy was real: his AA defenses were real. The MIGs that would try to jump you were real, and his mounting fear was real.

"Christ," he swore, "I can't remember a fucking thing the BO said." Then he told himself to think of something else. He put his helmet back on and closed his eyes. . . . The leave time he had had before joining the squadron, he had spent in New York and in northern Italy, at a hotel on Lake Garda, where he had done some painting, working mainly in acrylics.

But when he had returned to New York, with just three full days left to his leave, he had met Helena Vogel, a tall, slender, almost girlishly built woman with corn-silk hair, lovely blue eyes, and a delicately chiseled face. Of German extraction—her father, she said, had been a sergeant in the German Army and had fought at Stalingrad. Both she and an older sister had been born in Rochester, New York, where her parents had settled after having come to the United States. . . .

"What the hell am I thinking about? . . . I should be remembering—"

Over the 1MC the air boss said, "Stand by to start aircraft. Check all wheel chocks and tie down. Stand clear of jet intakes and tail pipes."

While the air boss paused to give the plane handlers time to follow his instructions, Andrew squirmed restlessly in his sweat-soaked G-suit and craned his neck to look at Mike, whose aircraft was directly behind his.

"Start engines," the air boss called.

The starter jeeps, with small jet engines, were hooked up to the aircraft, switched on, and turned up to a predetermined RPM; the aircraft engines caught on and, idling, blasted out heat waves from their exhausts with an ear-splitting roar.

Andrew now concentrated on the planes that were being launched at intervals of one minute, give or take a few seconds.

"Stand by, number eight," the air boss said.

"Standing by," Andrew radioed, his lips and throat already parched.

"Move into position, number eight."

Andrew watched the barrier come down and he taxied up to the catapult. The plane was hooked up to the cat shuttle by tow cable at the front and by a hold-back cable at the rear.

The launch captain signaled that he was ready to launch.

Andrew pushed the throttle forward, giving the aircraft maximum power. The plane shuddered, straining to move. Andrew saluted the launch captain, who returned the gesture, dropped to his right knee, and flung his right hand toward the bow.

The cat fired and Andrew's A-4 was hurled into the

air. Moving from zero to 110 knots in three seconds, the G-force pushed him hard against the back of the seat, and pulling on his face, distorted it. In seconds it was over and he was climbing to the marshaling altitude of twenty-two thousand feet.

Mike checked the sky around him. To his left it was empty; to his right and slightly below him were the various groupings of aircraft that made up the strike force: sixteen A-4s and four F-8s. Two A-4 Iron Hands and their Crusader escorts were on either side of the strike birds. Two TarCAPs flew on the right, where the MIGs were most likely to come from, if any came at all. Four F-8s were below him to suppress flak. And flying behind was the MiGCAP. There were other aircraft involved to provide electronic support, tankers for refueling after the strike, and two helos were on the search-and-rescue station.

The coast of North Vietnam came into view.

Mike was beginning to regret the incident in the ready room. He'd come off a wiseass, no doubt. But that was not the way he wanted to be known.

"Feet dry," the strike leader radioed tersely.

Mike made sure his ordnance was "hot." In moments he was over the land. He checked his instrument panel. Everything was normal. Ahead, the strike leader had already begun his slow descent toward the target to allow the attack aircraft to get to the target as quickly as possible, minimizing the risk of being hit by a SAM, surface-to-air missile, or antiaircraft fire.

The target was in sight, and the SAMs, looking like flying telephone poles, started coming up. Up to this moment, radio silence had been maintained, but now no-rad was useless.

The A-4 flak-suppressing section streaked in. Immediately after them, the A-4 and F-8 bombers went to work on the target.

Mike watched the huge plumes on every side of the bridge grow and die in seconds. Then suddenly the high-pitched warning tones of Fansong filled his ears. A SAM was coming toward him.

"Two SAMS, one o'clock low. Break right. Break right!"

Mike kicked the plane into a sharp right turn. There seemed to be SAMs all over the sky. He saw one coming up in front of him. He lightly thumbed his trigger. The twin Colt 20mm cannon fired. The SAM turned into a ball of flames.

"Took a hit . . . took a hit!" a pilot shouted.

Mike came out of the turn. An F-8, three o'clock low, trailed smoke.

"Can you make it to the crash site?" the strike leader asked.

"Will try," the pilot answered.

The next moment, the Crusader staggered, then dissolved into black smoke.

Mike swallowed hard. He'd never seen a plane shot down before.

"Jesus, did you see that!" a pilot exclaimed.

Mike recognized Andrew's voice, but didn't answer. The sweat dripped into his eyes, forcing him to blink to clear his vision. His bowels twisted. He felt as if he was going to drop a load.

Suddenly the fighter-direction ship in the gulf called, "Blue Bandits airborne at Bull's-eye." MIGs had been scrambled.

"Everyone, look sharp," the strike leader called out.

The last section of bombers was going in on the target.

Mike spotted Andrew on the far right just as he was completing a 180-degree turn.

The strike planes were coming up to twenty thousand feet and reforming into a formation.

The MIGs hadn't showed up yet.

"Let's go to *Boon* town," the strike leader said.

The entire strike force turned east, and as soon as they passed over the beach, the strike leader radioed, "Feet wet."

Now Mike and the other pilots visually checked one another for any damage, leaking fuel, or hung ordnance.

"Okay, guys," the strike leader said, "the tankers are waiting for us. You new guys, go in nice and easy . . . no slam, bang, thank you, ma'am. Use loving tenderness."

"You're talking to an expert on loving tenderness," Andrew answered.

Mike had to smile. But there was some truth to it—Andrew was truly the only cocksman he had ever known.

"Your turn, twenty," the flight leader said, calling Mike by the number painted on his plane.

"Wilco," Mike answered, sweating more profusely as he swung in toward the tail of the KA-3 tanker and slowed to the tanker's speed. He took a deep breath, and as he exhaled he slowly eased his aircraft to engage the weaving basket on the end of the fuel boom with the fuel probe jutting out on the right side of the A-4. "Got it!" he exclaimed, advancing the throttle. He watched the fuel-gauge needle rewind. "Full," he radioed.

"Roger," the boom operator answered.

Mike eased the throttle back, unplugged from the fuel boom, and making a slow right turn, headed back to the marshal—the entry to the landing pattern above the ship—before being recovered.

After the debriefing, Mike and Andrew went into the wardroom and helped themselves to coffee and sat down at a table to drink it. Lunch had been prepared for the returning pilots, but most of them, like Mike and Andrew, preferred coffee to anything else.

"The worst damn thing," Andrew said, lighting a cigarette and taking a deep drag on it, "was the sweat. I kept wanting to take my fucking helmet off and wipe the stuff out of my eyes."

Mike agreed, and said, "I felt as if I was going to crap and there was nothing I could do to stop."

Andrew nodded vigorously. "That's one fucking feeling to have."

Both of them laughed.

Then, looking past Mike, Andrew commented, "Your friend is coming our way."

Mike glanced over his shoulder: Hahn was approaching the table. "Let's keep it straight," he said, facing Andrew again.

"Yeah, why not?" Andrew responded.

"You guys did all right Up North," Hahn told them. "I saw you get that SAM, Mike . . . that was good shooting."

"Why don't you join us," Mike said. He was prepared to apologize for the way he'd acted earlier.

Hahn hesitated.

"Join us," Andrew said.

"Sure, why the hell not," Hahn said, breaking into a grin.

"Why didn't those MIGs come after us?" Mike asked. "They weren't that far away."

"They wanted you to make the mistake of going

after them," Hahn answered, taking out a corncob pipe and filling it with tobacco. "We go off chasing them, and then their buddies come in on the strike force." He lit the pipe, and once he had it drawing to his satisfaction, he puffed out three perfect smoke rings.

"That was you who called out those two SAMs at one o'clock low," Mike said, sure that he recognized the voice, now that he'd heard Hahn speak.

The jg nodded. "Have to take care of you nuggets," he said, "or there won't be anyone left to fight this war."

Mike grinned. "Thanks," he said. "Thanks a lot!"

"Who was the guy who punched out over the target?" Andrew asked.

"Bill McGinn," Hahn answered. "This was his second tour. During his last one, he was pulled out of the drink by a SAR helo after having part of his left wing shot away by AA fire. Had he been rescued again, he'd have been on his way home. Regs—two downs resulting from enemy fire and you go back to the States for good."

"That's a risky way to get out of this war," Andrew commented.

Hahn shrugged. "I never heard of anyone doing it on purpose, but I guess there's always a first time for that as well as anything else . . . right?"

"Right," Andrew echoed.

Hahn started to stand. "You guys better shower down after you finish your coffee."

"I was wondering if we smell," Mike said.

Hahn nodded. "Everyone does after a mission. It comes with the job. See you around." And he walked away.

Andrew drained the last of the coffee in the cup.

"Guess what I was thinking about while we were waiting to launch?"

"Getting laid."

"Close . . . close. I was trying to remember the last
time I was with Helena and—"

"She's the new one, isn't she?"

"Yeah. But I couldn't," Andrew answered. "I kept
thinking about facts and then the air boss came on and
that was the end of it."

Mike clicked his tongue sympathetically. "I'm going
to shower, what about you?"

"Why not," Andrew answered. "I don't have anything else to do, and besides, I'm beginning to realize
just how tired I am." He shook his head. "Seven
fucking months out here is going to be a ball-buster,
and that's even with going to Subic Bay for a few days'
R&R."

They collected their cups and saucers and carried
them to the designated place outside the ship's galley.

Their cabin, which they shared with six other pilots,
was on the oh-four deck, below the arresting wires.
Every time a plane touched down on the flight deck,
they could hear a hammerlike blow and the grinding
pull of the arresting gear, if the aircraft actually landed.

They made their way down through a combination
of steep flights of steps and a maze of narrow, brilliantly lit passageways. Below deck it was hellishly hot
and humid.

"You know," Andrew said before they reached the
cabin, "there's a hell of a lot of feeling against the war
in the States."

"I know, but we're here and they're there," Mike
answered. They had spoken a great deal about the war
on the way out to the gulf. His position was the same as
the government's: let Nam go to the Communists,

then the rest of Southeast Asia will go down like dominoes. "A line has to be drawn somewhere," he said. "And here is as good as any other place."

"Maybe, maybe not," Andrew replied. "This line happens to be ten thousand miles away from us."

"Wrong," Mike said. "This line is only as far from this ship as it takes the strike leader to radio 'feet dry.'"

"That's one way of looking at it," Andrew answered as he opened the door to the cabin.

"Like I said before, we're here and the peaceniks aren't."

Andrew didn't answer.

"Besides," Mike said, "it's easy to chant 'Make love, not war,' when no one's shooting at you."

"That's just the point: why should we have people shooting at us?"

"Because," another pilot injected, "they're the fucking enemy; that's why."

"He said it, I didn't," Mike said.

"That's the same thing as saying, 'We're here because we're here.'"

Mike stripped off his shirt. "We're here because we're needed here."

"That's exactly what those peaceniks are questioning."

"Commies," commented the pilot who had spoken before.

"Maybe not all of them," Mike said, "but certainly 'fellow travelers.'"

"Commies," the pilot repeated. "Fucking Commies!"

The weeks rolled by, then the months. The missions were more or less the same. MIGs were scarce, but the number of SAMs increased substantially, and this forced the planes to lower altitudes, where they became targets for conventional radar-directed antiaircraft guns, even small-arms fire, if they were flying low enough.

Then one morning, with three weeks left to their first tour, Andrew, flying wingman to Lieutenant Korale, was giving support fire to a battalion of marines.

"I'll drop orange smoke where I want you to lay your eggs," the forward air controller said.

"Wilco," Korale acknowledged.

Andrew spotted the FAC's plane, a single-engine job that looked like a toy. He checked his altimeter. He was at fifteen thousand feet.

"Blue Two," Korale called. "Follow close. I'll break right on my climb, you go left."

Andrew acknowledged Korale's order.

"Orange smoke, three o'clock," Korale called.

Andrew kicked his aircraft over and started down, behind Korale. Each of them carried four five-hundred-pound bombs.

They were going in fast and steep.

The altimeter's needle unwound . . . Andrew was passing through eight thousand feet.

"Lookin' good," the FAC called.

The altimeter's needle indicated five thousand feet. The ground was coming up fast.

Suddenly black puffs began to erupt close by.

"Thirty-seven mm," Korale said tightly.

Andrew didn't answer.

"Do it at five hundred," Korale said.

They were at fifteen hundred feet.

Andrew saw nothing but trees, the mirrorlike surface of a curved swath of a river, and the orange smoke, now lying over the green of the jungle below.

"Bombs away!" Korale yelled.

Andrew's fingers flipped the pickle switch and he

pulled back on the stick. The Gs pushed him back against the seat and he could feel his face distort.

As he climbed, he felt the shock waves from the explosions of eight five-hundred-pound bombs. The aircraft shuddered and screamed as he climbed almost straight up.

"Good work," the FAC radioed. "Damn good work."

Andrew was starting to break to the left.

"I'll put down white smoke for you guys to follow up with some fancy shooting," the FAC said. "We want to push Charlie back across the river."

"We'll hit them from both sides," Korale said. "I'll make the first pass."

The antiaircraft fire was becoming more intense.

"One run only," Korale told the FAC.

"What the hell are we shooting at?" Andrew asked. He was at five thousand feet and leveling off. He couldn't see anything.

"Follow the smoke," Korale answered.

A ribbon of white smoke began to spin out and touch the top of the trees.

"It's all yours, Blue One," the FAC said.

"Going in," Korale radioed.

Andrew saw him come in, low and fast; then he started his run, thumbing the red trigger button as he closed with the white snakelike smoke.

The 20mm shells spewed out of the wing cannon.

He glanced at the altimeter—five hundred feet. He lifted his thumb off the red trigger button and pulled sharply back on the stick. The aircraft's nose went up.

"Angels twenty," Korale called.

"Wilco," Andrew answered, aware that he was sweating and breathing hard. He wanted to be out of there, and it seemed to take too long for him to gain altitude. There were black puffs all around him.

Suddenly Andrew felt his plane jounce, but the next instant it continued its climb.

"Blue One, thanks for the help," the FAC called.

"Hope it did some good," Korale answered.

"My boys own this side of the river. Thanks again, over and out," the FAC said.

They were still over land. Minutes away was the smooth, glinting surface of the gulf.

Andrew had just reached twenty thousand feet and was leveling off when suddenly he felt another sharp jounce. But this time the plane didn't resume its normal operation. The jouncing continued.

"Blue One, I have a problem," Andrew reported. "Have violent bucking."

Korale swung around and went below him to check out the plane. "You're leaking fluid . . . you're smoking. . . . Bail out, Troost . . . bail out!"

Smoke filled the cockpit.

The unthinkable, the stuff that his nightmares were made of, was suddenly a reality. He was coughing . . . his vision was blurred.

"Troost . . . Troost, get the fuck out!" Korale shouted.

Andrew was dizzy. He knew the aircraft was falling.

"Troost, eject . . . eject!"

Andrew lifted his hands, took hold of the face mask, and using what strength he had left, pulled it down. . . .

Minutes after Andrew went down, Mike was on an Air-Sea Rescue H-3 helo, flying low over the VC-held territory.

"We've got a beeper signal," the helo pilot said. "But we've got to get a voice ID before we go in."

Mike nodded. "Let me use the radio," he said.

The pilot nodded and handed him the mike.

"Beeper, beeper, voice up," Mike called, using the standard signal. "Beeper, beeper, voice up."

"Nothing coming up," the pilot said.

Mike repeated the call.

"I see you," Andrew answered. "Charlie might be nearby."

Mike grinned. "I got him," he told the pilot. "Beeper, beeper, voice up."

Andrew ID'd himself and gave his location with respect to the helo.

"Tell him we're coming down," the pilot said.

Mike relayed the message.

The helo banked to the right, and as it came in for a landing, the gunners at both doors fired several long bursts.

The helo was down.

Andrew left the cover of the trees and hopped and skipped toward it.

Two corpsmen ran to him, and shouldering him between them, brought him onto the helo.

"Broken?" Mike asked, pointing to Andrew's left leg.

"Sprained, probably," Andrew answered.

"Christ, I heard you go down over the ship's radio . . . I didn't think you'd make it."

"Nearly didn't. That cockpit filled with smoke so fast I was beginning to lose consciousness."

"Korale said you ejected at about fifteen thousand."

Andrew shook his head. "I don't even remember ejecting . . . I came down hard." Then he looked questioningly at Mike. "How the hell are you here?"

"When the helo left, I went with it . . . no one tried to stop me."

Andrew grinned. "The old man is going to rag your ass. You're not supposed to be here."

"Yeah, but I am."

Andrew grabbed hold of Mike's hand. "I'm glad you're here . . . I'm real glad."

29

WARREN, WHO HAD made flag rank at the end of 1964, was standing in the door of the bedroom watching Carol pack his valise. He'd been reassigned from the Pentagon to naval headquarters in Saigon, where he would plan and coordinate air and sea strikes against selected targets on the coast of North Vietnam, or in support of U.S. Army operations in the south.

"The time will go quickly," he said, trying to reassure Carol, who couldn't hide the way she felt about his leaving her. "And when I come up for R&R, we can meet in Japan. The Kurokachis would be delighted to have us visit them."

Carol finished packing, closed the valise, and after setting it aside, she turned toward him. The movement caused her right breast to come free from her red housecoat. "You may be an admiral," she said, "but that wouldn't stop you from being killed."

"I'll be fine," he said, going to her and caressing her bare breast. She couldn't begin to realize how much he would miss her, even if he could find the right words to tell her.

She looked down at his hand, then, taking her own,

placed it hard over his. "I never thought I could love you the way I do," she whispered.

"Nor I you," Warren answered, gently squeezing her breast.

Carol looked up at him. "I wish . . . I wish I could have given you a child."

"You've given me you," he said, gathering her in his arms. "It's more than I dared hope for." He kissed her lips, gently at first, then with increasing passion.

Carol opened her mouth and gave him her tongue. "You still have two hours before you have to leave," she whispered.

Warren nodded. Slipping the red robe off her shoulders, he took hold of her hand and led her to the bed.

Tony put down Truman Capote's *In Cold Blood*, and looked at his watch. It was eleven P.M. He was just about to go over to the TV and turn it on for the late Sunday news when he heard a car come up to the cul-de-sac and then stop.

He left the chair, went straight to the front door, and opening it, saw Ruth. She was coming toward him. Her cab was already pulling away.

He stepped back to let her enter the house.

She looked at him, bit her lower lip, and shook her head.

"Who's there?" Miriam called from the top of the stairs.

"Ruth," Tony called.

"Are you all right, Ruth?" Miriam called out.

"Tell her I'm all right," Ruth said, putting down a small brown leather valise.

"She's all right," Tony answered, helping his daughter out of her wraparound tweed coat.

"I'm coming down," Miriam said.

Ruth left her valise in the foyer near the door and walked into the living room.

Very concerned, Tony followed. Though Ruth was a mature woman and well on her way to becoming a pediatric surgeon, he couldn't help wondering if she'd come home to tell them she was pregnant and Steve wouldn't marry her. If that was the situation . . .

Miriam padded into the room and immediately embraced Ruth.

"Suppose we sit down," Tony said, "and let Ruth tell us why she's here."

"Have you had dinner?" Miriam asked.

Ruth shook her head. "I'm not hungry, Momma." She bit her lip.

"I have half a cold chicken—"

"She said she's not hungry," Tony snapped.

Ruth settled down on the edge of the couch, clasped her hands together, and looking down at the Oriental rug, said in a quiet voice, "It's over between me and Steve."

Tony almost breathed a sigh of relief. He'd never particularly thought that Steve was the kind of man Ruth should have chosen. But love, he knew all too well, was blind, and he had kept his mouth shut until now. "He's the loser, not you," he said.

Miriam sat down in one of the club chairs and adjusted her bathrobe over her legs.

"It's all because of this stupid war," Ruth suddenly flared up. "This war that no one wants."

Tony considered sitting down on the arm of the chair occupied by Miriam. He regretted having been sharp with her. That wasn't the way he usually treated her.

"What has the war to do with the two of you?" Miriam asked.

"He wants to leave the country . . . go to Canada or Sweden."

"What?" Tony almost yelled.

Ruth nodded.

"You mean he wants to dodge the draft!" Tony exclaimed.

"He doesn't want to kill anyone," Ruth said.

Tony began to pace. "Guys like that make me want to puke," he said vehemently. "No one wants to kill— unless they're sick. But the Commies have to be stopped!"

"Oh, Daddy, that's such a primitive attitude," Ruth answered.

Tony halted. "Force is the only way," he said tightly. "It's the only language they understand."

Ruth shook her head. "I can't and won't believe that."

"Is Steve going to Canada?" Miriam asked.

"Sweden," Ruth answered, burying her face in her hands and sobbing. "Sweden, after we've been together all these years. Oh, Momma, I told him I couldn't go."

"Good for you," Tony said.

Ruth lifted her tearstained face. "Daddy, I don't believe in the war . . . I believe just the way he does . . . but Mike is out there fighting. I couldn't do that to my own brother. I'd never be able to live with myself afterward if something should happen to him and I left the country."

Miriam left the club chair, and sitting down beside Ruth, she cradled her daughter in her arms.

Tony bent over them and stroked his daughter's hair. "You're better off without him," he said gently.

"I love him," she wept. "I love him . . . but I can't do anything that will hurt my brother." Then suddenly

she pulled away from her mother. "The war is wrong
. . . it's wrong in every way."

Tony felt his anger rising and backed away. He'd
never told anyone either in or out of the family about
his involvement in Vietnam, and he seldom voiced his
feeling about it, but now he said, with more passion in
his voice than his wife and daughter were used to
hearing, "If I were younger, that's where I'd want to
be, and I'm proud that Mike is there . . . very proud!"

Jacob held Tara's hand as they walked in the garden
behind the main building. It was a perfect day—the
kind of days that late April and a good part of May
are famous for in the New York area.

"I received a wonderful letter from Sy," Tara said,
"with pictures of baby Ann-Sophie. Sy said that sometime early next year he'll be able to come here to visit,
and he will bring the baby to me."

"She'll be able to walk and talk by then," Jacob
responded. Sy and Heather were living in the San
Diego area. After Sy had returned from his tour of
duty aboard the *Munson*, he was transferred to a small
boat unit for training, then reassignment to Nam with
the River Patrol Force, Task Force 116. That reassignment was actually in progress. Sy, now a full lieutenant, was already on his way back to Nam. He'd left
the day before yesterday.

"Sy said he'd be going back to the war again," Tara
said sadly.

"He has already left," Jacob told her. Instantly he
felt her grip tighten. "The thirteen months will pass
quickly." The pressure eased on his hand.

They moved to a swing seat and sat down on it.

"I follow the war," Tara told him. "I read about

it in the newspapers and I watch it on the TV. It's very strange to see a war on TV."

"Yes, that's very strange," Jacob agreed.

"The other night I actually saw someone—a marine—get shot," she said.

He was surprised that the patients were permitted to watch that kind of program.

"Most of the people here know I have a son over there," she said; then, with a hint of a smile on her lips, she added, "And they all know you're a naval officer."

He smiled too, more at the pride in her voice than anything else.

Then she said, "But this war isn't like the wars that you fought, is it?"

"It's very different," he answered, amazed at her ability to perceive that there was a difference between Nam, World War Two, and even a difference between it and Korea.

"You've been there—what do you think about it? Do you think we'll win it?" she asked, her blue eyes looking straight into his eyes.

"I don't know," Jacob answered. "It's not easy to predict the outcome."

She pursed her lips and a shadow came into her eyes. "I don't know either," she said in a low voice. "I usually know about such things."

Jacob was suddenly afraid that she'd retreat into herself again and he'd lose contact. But then the shadow left her eyes and she said, "We're still married, aren't we?"

"Yes," Jacob answered.

"You've been a good husband."

"Well, thank you . . . it's nice to be appreciated."

"Jacob, I know I haven't really been a wife—"

"You are my wife," he told her.

Shaking her head, Tara said, "No, I haven't. . . . I've been talking to my doctor about it. I can't do it with you ever again . . . I can't have sex with you." Her voice went low and intense. "And I probably won't ever be able to leave this place."

"Tara—"

"The doctor says that I have to face the reality of the situation . . . I have to talk about it to you."

Jacob held her hand. "There's no need to," he said. "I—"

"You need someone who can be a real wife to you," Tara said, her blue eyes bright with light. "I never wanted to think about that, but now that the doctor made me, I know you do."

Jacob was too stunned to speak.

"You need someone who can give you what I can't," Tara said, casting her eyes down to the bottom of the swing. "You know what I mean, don't you?"

"Yes, I know," Jacob answered, his throat in a tight knot.

Her eyes went to his. "You know I love you, Jacob."

"I know," he said. "I love you too, Tara."

She gave him a thin smile. "Yes, I know that." Then, taking a deep breath, in a more resolute voice she said, "It would be easier if you divorced me—"

"Tara—"

"Let me say what has taken me so many years to say. Please."

"All right."

"I know you would never do that," Tara told him.

Jacob nodded.

"But that shouldn't stop you from finding someone who would . . . you know what I mean, Jacob. You're a handsome man and it shouldn't be hard for you to find—"

Suddenly he put his arms around her, and before he could speak, Tara began to scream, "No . . . no . . . not me . . . I didn't mean me!"

Jacob let go of her. "It's all right, Tara. I just wanted to hug you. That's all, Tara."

But she sat stiff and mute.

30

IN 1972 PRESIDENT Nixon was running for a second term and the war in Vietnam was still going on. Despite the opposition to the war in the United States, hundreds of thousands of men had been drafted between the years 1964 and the present and eventually sent to Nam for a thirteen-month tour of duty.

But men like Mike and Andrew, who were professionals, were returned to Vietnam for more than one tour. At the beginning of February, Andrew and Mike had started their third tour, this time deployed aboard the carrier *Harrison*, a seventy-seven-thousand-ton modified Forrestal-class vessel. Both were lieutenant commanders. Both had gone through Top Gun, the Navy fighter-pilot school at Miramar, California. They were considered by their peers and superiors to be seasoned fighter pilots, though neither one had downed an enemy plane. Each had taken his share of flak and small-arms hits, and except for Andrew having had to eject after having been hit, they had managed to be physically unscathed.

After his previous tour, Mike had married Barbara, and within a year they had a son, whom they named George, and now Barbara was pregnant again and was due to give birth just about the time he was scheduled to return to the States.

Andrew was still technically a bachelor, though he and Helena lived together whenever he returned to the States.

Each of them had a "nugget" for his wingman. Andrew pulled Jessy Wright, a black man, whose father was a professor of law at Yale. Mike's wingman, Pierce Branigan, was born and raised on a farm in Nebraska.

Two previous tours had taught Andrew and Mike not to get emotionally close to any of the "nuggets," at least not until they had managed to survive at least half the deployment on Yankee Station.

They met Jessy and Pierce in the ready room the second day out from San Diego after a routine briefing by the ship's skipper.

Andrew let Mike be spokesman for both of them when they first met Jessy and Pierce, and he said, "I don't have anything to tell you, except two things. We cover each other. You leave me uncovered and when I get you down on the deck, I'll kick the shit out of you." He looked at Pierce. "You understand that?"

"Yes, sir," Pierce snapped.

Mike's eyes fastened on Jessy. "You got that, mister?"

"Got it, sir."

"You do what I do and what Commander Troost does. You do what we tell you to do, and maybe, just maybe, you'll get back to the States in one piece. Any fancy flying, save until you're in bed with some broad."

Mike dismissed them, turned to Andrew, and said, "These guys are going to be hard to handle."

"What makes you think so?"

"Each of them gave me a snappy 'Yes, sir,' but there

was a goddamn twinkle in their eyes that said, 'Fuck you, I'm a goddamn hotshot fighter pilot, not a goddamn Boy Scout.''

Andrew shrugged. "Then they'll have to learn the hard way. We did, and so did all of the other drivers on the ship.''

The outward-bound voyage took eight days and was filled with day and night FLTOPs. Jessy and Pierce were good pilots, but Jessy seemed to be the more aggressive of the two.

The *Harrison* laid over at Subic Bay for two days for replenishment and Andrew and Mike went across the bay to the Cubi Point O Club, also known as the Zoo, to have a few drinks and dinner ashore.

It was crowded, noisy, and so filled with smoke that layers of it drifted just below the ceiling.

Mike and Andrew were at the bar, working on their third double Scotch, when Andrew suggested they go to Olongapo, Po City, for some "feminine companionship.''

"Meaning you want to get steamed, reamed, and cleaned," Mike answered.

Andrew shook his head. "Just want to get laid.''

"Go if you want to," Mike answered. "I'm a family man . . . my wife would object strenuously.''

Andrew was about to object, when he suddenly saw the reflections of Jessy and Pierce in the mirror behind the bar. Jessy was as tall and as black as a Masai warrior, while Pierce was a redheaded, wiry man. They made an incongruous-looking pair. "Heads up, we're about to have a courtesy call from our not-too-sober wingmen.''

"Glad to see you here, sir," Pierce said, looking at Mike.

Mike nodded.

"I told you, Jessy, they can't be all bad . . . they even drink like us, and we're not bad."

"Better get your friend out of here," Andrew said to Jessy, "before he gets into more trouble than he ever believed existed."

Jessy rolled his eyes. "Commander, I just want to know one thing. Why the hell are you in this war? . . . I mean, everyone knows that you don't give a flying fuck for it."

The alcoholic mist that swirled through Andrew's brain instantly lifted. His eyes darted to Mike.

"Why don't you guys—" Mike started to say, but Andrew cut him short. "I'm here because I wear these," he said, touching his wings. "If I had a damn choice, I wouldn't be here. This is not my fucking war . . . it's not our fucking war."

"And what about bringing freedom to people who want it?" Jessy questioned.

"Or just beating the Commies at their own game?" Pierce asked.

"That's just bullshit," Andrew answered.

Several of the other men at the bar joined in the argument, and soon everyone involved was shouting.

"Let's get the hell out of here," Andrew said, "before somebody starts throwing punches." He dropped a five-dollar bill on the bar.

Mike did the same.

"Got to make a pit stop," Andrew said, pushing his way through the knot of men in front of him.

Mike followed, and when they were in the street, he said, "Next time we might not be able to get out."

Andrew didn't answer.

"You're talking too much about the war. . . . Just do what you're supposed to do."

Andrew stopped. "Listen, I'll see you aboard ship. I'm going to Po City."

"You can't fuck the war away," Mike said.

"I can sure try," Andrew answered, turned, and walked away.

The *Harrison* arrived on Yankee Station at 0600 and the first strike mission was scheduled for 1200 the same day.

The air wing commander was the overall strike-group leader, and by 1000 all of the air-wing pilots were assembled in Strike Operations.

"Gentlemen, the target is the bridge at Co Trai, outside the town of Phu Ly," the AWC said.

"Christ, that damn bridge was taken out twice before," one of the men complained.

"It has to be taken out again."

Andrew and Mike glanced at each other. They had flown strikes against the bridge before and knew that there'd be more SAMs than before, and more flak.

The briefing took the better part of an hour. They were given the latest weather info, including what kind of cloud cover they could expect to find over the target area.

The rendezvous altitude for Andrew's and Mike's fighter group was fifteen thousand feet. They were going to go ashore at twenty thousand feet, trading off altitude for speed on the run in. Flak suppressors were ordered to move in ahead of the main bombing force. Andrew, Mike, and the other fighter pilots were told to peel off and head west for five miles, to cover for inbound MIGs. Only one run would be made on the target.

As soon as the main briefing was over, the pilots went to their individual ready rooms, where their CAGs continued to brief them. At 1130 a voice came over the 1MC ordering the pilots to man their planes.

Mike and Andrew suited up and went up to the flight deck together, with Jessy and Pierce following. Though none of the four men had mentioned the incident that had happened in the Zoo, the two wingmen kept their distance from their "mentors."

Just before the four of them separated to go to their own planes, Andrew stopped and said to them, "You guys take care up there. Watch your asses." Then he shook Jessy's and Pierce's hands. "Take care," he said to Mike.

"You too," Mike answered.

Andrew highballed him and went to his plane.

The launch went smoothly. At angels fifteen Jessy was on his starboard wing. The other fighters were contained in a tight box of sky. As soon as the F-8s were refueled, the AWC's voice came up on the radio, ordering them on a heading that would take them to shore.

Inbound there was no talk on the radio.

Andrew was conscious of the sky's intense blue and the glint of the sun off the water.

"Hot guns," the AWC said.

Andrew lifted the red switch cover and pushed the switch to its On position.

Minutes later, even before the AWC called "feet dry," the high-pitched whine of the Fansong began— they were being tracked on North Vietnamese radar.

"Target, ten o'clock," the AWC called.

Andrew watched the flak suppressors—A-4s with four five-hundred-pound bombs under their wings— angle down toward the bridge. They went in fast, and in moments, balls of fire erupted like giant red flowers on both sides of the silver ribbon of river.

"Fighters out," the AWC called; then to the A-8 drivers he said, "We're going in. Follow me, bomb in my smoke."

Andrew continued to fly west.

"Okay, guys, we'll orbit here," his CAG said.

Andrew banked to the right . . . Jessy followed. In the distance, Andrew could see Mike and Pierce.

"SAMs ten o'clock," one of the pilots called.

"SAMs three o'clock," Mike radioed.

The sky was beginning to fill with flying "telephone poles."

From the shouting on the radio, Andrew knew that the A-8 drivers were taking very heavy flak.

"Break left, Micky . . . break left," a fighter pilot called to another in the squadron.

Andrew glanced left. An A-4 was trying to get out of a SAM's flight path. It failed and became a mass of flame.

"Jesus, did you see that!" Jessy exclaimed.

There were more calls for upcoming missiles.

"I'm hit . . . I'm hit," the AWC radioed.

"Can you make it to the coast?" his wingman called.

"Negative."

Andrew caught sight of two SAMs. "SAMs eleven o'clock," he called, banking to the right.

"Those guys down there are getting creamed," Mike radioed.

"Let's go to angels ten," the CAG said.

Andrew pushed the stick forward.

"Jessy, you have SAM coming up under you. Pull up . . . pull up," a pilot called.

Andrew pushed his plane into a roll. For a few moments he lost sight of Jessy's plane, and when he saw it again, it was burning. "Eject," he shouted. "Jessy, get out!"

"Can't," answered the small, frightened voice. "Can't. . . . Punching out."

The A-4 went into a momentary nosedive before it exploded.

"This is Commander Ryerson. Call it a day. . . . Angels eighteen . . . head for the marshal . . . fighters trail the rest of us."

Ryerson was the deputy air wing commander.

"Wilco," the two CAGs answered.

With his jaws clamped tightly together, Andrew began to climb again. The flak was still intense. He flew over the bridge: it was down. . . .

31

SY, NOW A lieutenant commander, commanded squadron 105, consisting of six "Nastys," and the officers and men necessary to man them. The squadron operated in the north, on the Cua Viet River, not far from the border between South and North Vietnam.

On this particular morning, Sy stood in front of the squadron's officers in the briefing room, which was one end of a rectangular wooden shack that also served as headquarters and squadron radio room. Behind him was a large map of the river area from the coast to a point fifteen miles inland, along the twisting river, but only six miles in a straight line from where their base was.

"This morning we received word from an NNV spotter that Charlie is moving a lot of supplies across the river at this point," Sy said, touching the map with the end of a sharpened stick. "That's a good four clicks beyond our most distant operating point."

"That's really bad Indian Country," one of the men commented. "The banks go straight up three or four feet, and the river is less than fifty yards across there, even now with the waters up."

"That's about right," Sy responded. "But that's where we're going. Saigon wants that traffic stopped."

He moved a step away from the map. Thin, almost gaunt now, with dark semicircles under his eyes, Sy didn't like the mission any more than the man who said it was bad Indian Country. "We're going to go in just before dark. We'll have two dozen marines with us. They'll be ferried here by helos by late afternoon. There will be two sweeps by four helo gunships before we attack, and there will be two A-4s in the area, if we need them. . . . Any questions?"

"Skipper, if there's going to be a Marine attack, why do we have to attack?" one of the newly assigned jgs asked.

"The marines will drive them toward the river and we'll be waiting for them. The plan is to drop the marines off four clicks downstream, make sure they're in position; then we come full throttle upriver, like the U.S. cavalry. At the same time, the gunships begin their sweep. If everything goes according to plan, the operation shouldn't take more than seven, eight minutes . . . twelve at the most. We'll pick up the marines two clicks downstream." He paused, asked for questions, and when there were none, turned the rest of the briefing over to the squadron's XO, who would give them whatever additional information they would need.

The marines, under the command of a tall captain nicknamed Hawke, arrived thirty minutes after Sy left the briefing area.

"This is a piece of cake for my men," Hawke said after a more formal conversation. "A piece of cake. All you have to do, Commander, is, as the expression goes, 'cover the waterfront.' "

Sy admired his confidence, and he could see from

the looks of his men that they were battle-hardened and confident.

They arranged call signals. Hawke was Hawke. Sy was Fish One. The gunships were designated Trouble One and Trouble Two. The flight commander was Strike One. The call signals were radioed to the TAC, aboard the carrier *Bunker Hill*, which was steaming off the coast on Yankee Station.

The officers and men spent the remainder of the day readying their boats for the operation. Every gun was tested. Every engine was started. Additional cases of .37mm, and .50-caliber ammo were brought aboard each boat. Fuel tanks were topped and radio equipment checked before the men knocked off for lunch.

Hours later, at 1630, the marines divided into groups of four and boarded the six Nastys.

Hawke and three other marines were aboard Sy's boat. The Nasty, a Swedish-made boat, drew very little water and moved at twenty-five knots with the throttle pushed fully forward. But now it was moving slowly up the river, and even this slow its powerful engines were loud enough to limit conversation between the men on board and could be heard for at least three clicks in any direction along the river.

"Skipper," the radioman said, "number nineteen's engine is running rough and requests permission to return to base."

Sy picked up his field glasses and looked back over the stern, past the 37mm mount and the towheaded young man from Deadwood, South Dakota, who manned it.

Nineteen was three hundred yards behind and just coming around the bend on the narrow river. There were, counting his boat, six swifts in his squadron. But operating in the jungle took a high toll of equipment, as well as men. Both were subject to frequent breakdowns.

When nineteen finally rounded the bend, it was trailing black smoke.

Sy lowered his glasses and said, "Permission granted."

"Aye, aye, skipper," the radioman answered.

Facing the bow, Sy looked automatically toward the .50-caliber machine gun mounted on the forward part of the deck, where the gunner, a young black man from Newark, New Jersey, was intently scanning the riverbanks. The river was narrowing to less than two hundred yards.

"Don't much like it here," the helmsman commented.

"Ease back on the throttle," Sy told him. He didn't "much like it" either. The banks were very high; the men were already past their furthest previous operating point.

"Easing back on the throttle, eight knots," the helmsman answered.

Sy dipped his head and looked into the radio room, a small closetlike space. "Pass the word to the other boats to slow to five knots, and tell them to keep a sharp lookout," Sy told the radioman.

As soon as the boat slowed, Sy became aware of the hot, humid air again. Sweat poured out from under his helmet. Removing his sunglasses, he drew his bare, deeply tanned arm across his face. He looked back at the boats following him. All of them had reduced speed. This was his second tour in-country, and, he had promised Heather, his last. Even if he hadn't made the promise to Heather, it would probably be his last. The burden of the fighting was being shifted to the Vietnamese, and the riverboat squadrons were going to be turned over to the VNN. But he, like so many other officers in and out of the Navy, knew that the South Vietnamese would never be able to "cut it" alone; they needed the Americans to fight for them. Unlike the North Vietnamese, they didn't have a cause worth dying for.

"We gonna be heard, skip, long before we there," the forward gunner shouted, looking back at Sy.

Sy nodded. Though he was the squadron commander, there was a friendly relationship between him and the rest of the men in the unit. His squadron and other riverboat units didn't maintain the distinction between the enlisted men and the officers that was characteristic of other units. Sy much preferred the camaraderie of the riverboat force to what he'd experienced aboard the *Munson*.

The forward gunner started to point and called, "Skipper—"

A burst of machine-gun fire stitched across his chest, throwing him to the deck.

Sy hit the Klaxon.

Fire was coming from both banks.

The rear gunner was firing at the right bank.

Sy ran to the twin fifties and sprayed the left bank.

The other boats were taking their share of heavy fire.

"Call for close air support," Sy shouted to the radioman. Hawke and the other marines on deck returned fire.

"Air support confirmed," the radioman yelled back.

"They got ropes up," another man shouted.

The narrow neck of the river was blocked by rope nets.

Suddenly the boat veered sharply to the left.

Sy glanced back. The helmsman was headless. Blood was still pumping out of his neck. "The helm," Sy shouted. "Get the helm." He started back to the cockpit. But the boat plowed into the bank, knocking him off his feet. He started to stand, and was thrown down again. But this time his feet were knocked out from under him.

When Sy looked, he saw that his two legs were in one place and the rest of him was in another. He tried to move, but found he couldn't. He knew he was bleeding to death. Then suddenly he saw two NVA soldiers look down at him.

"Shoot me," he pleaded. "For the love of God, shoot me."

One of them put the muzzle of an AK-47 against his forehead.

The other said something.

The muzzle was pulled back, one of them tore the watch off Sy's wrist, and then the two of them rolled him over.

"Oh, God, no!" Sy screamed.

They laughed and kicked him over the side.

Sy died, knowing he was drowning.

Jacob entered Tara's room. The drawn shades created a gray light. She sat in the corner on a straight-back chair. Her eyes were wide open.

"This is the way she sits," the director whispered to Jacob from behind him, "since she read your son's name in the casualty lists a few days ago."

"I'd appreciate being alone with her," Jacob said.

"Yes, of course," the director answered, stepping back.

Jacob waited until he heard the door close before he started toward Tara, but suddenly seeing her paintings, he stopped. She'd covered every one of them with smears of black. "Oh, Tara," he whispered against the tight knot in his throat. "Oh, Tara!" Going to her, he knelt in front of her and took hold of her hands.

She stiffened.

He let go of her and slowly stood up. The war had taken the small piece of the world she had left, and now she had nothing, only a gray room in which to live out the rest of her life. He tried to speak, but could find neither the voice nor the words that somehow would ease her pain as well as his.

After a few minutes Jacob left Tara's room. It would be a long time before he visited her again.

32

ON MAY 8, orders came from Washington to mine Haiphong harbor. The mining would be accomplished by A-6s and A-7s, operating off the *Harrison* and two other carriers.

Mike listened to the briefing officer as intently as he could, though his thoughts were almost completely centered on Andrew, who was sitting next to him, as he always was during briefing.

"This time we expect fighter opposition," the briefing officer said. "It's not going to take them long to figure out that Haiphong is being mined. We expect them to commit as many MIGs as they can put in the air. But for this evolution the Air Force will stage a show of its own in an effort to draw the fighters away from the Haiphong area. . . ." He continued to explain what kind of flak the pilots could expect in terms of SAMs and then in terms of conventional AA fire.

When he finished, the met officer, Calvin Finch, a tall thin black man with a reputation for having a good sense of humor, took his place and said, "There's a storm front moving in from the east—"

A groan went up from the pilots, and one of them asked, "When isn't there a storm front moving in?"

Cal, as he was called by the men, held up his hands, pinkish-white palms out. "I don't make the storms," he answered. "I just report them."

"Some of us think you do voodoo and bring them on," another officer said. " 'Cause you-all don't care for us white boys."

"Lawd help me," Cal answered, rolling his eyes, "I got me a maggot in front of me . . . a bigot would be bad enough, but a maggot aboard this ship is too much, even for a man like me."

"I saw you do your little dance step," the same officer said. "That's not your black rhythm, that's your ordinary black voodoo."

"Harrison," Cal replied, using the pilot's surname to identify him to everyone, though everyone already knew him, since he and Cal engaged in the same kind of playful exchange at almost every briefing as a way of reducing the tension. If one didn't start, the other did. "Harrison . . ."

"You already said that."

"Harrison, if I did voodoo, it would be to shut your big fat mouth," Cal responded.

That response drew a laugh from the men.

"All right, gentlemen," the CAG said, getting up, "let's get on with this."

The men became silent.

"We expect heavy rain, winds of fifteen per, with gusts as high as twenty-five. That means that we're going to have a damn high sea running and we'll be doing a lot of pitching and rolling. Any of you have been hit and can't put your plane down, let us know. We'll notify Da Nang to expect you. But there's a bright side to all of this: the weather inbound to the target area will be excellent, with unlimited visibility and scattered clouds at nine thousand feet. Are there any questions? None. Good." He left the podium and turned the remainder of the briefing back to the briefing officer.

Mike glanced at Andrew and whispered, "Listen, if you're not feeling well enough to fly—"

Andrew shook his head. "I'll fly. But this is the last fucking mission I'm going on."

"What?" Mike questioned loud enough to cause everyone in the room to turn around and look at him. "Sorry," he quickly apologized. "That just popped out."

As soon as the briefing was over and they were suiting up, Mike pushed Andrew for an explanation.

"I don't want any more," he said. "I want out. I wrote to my father and told him what I intend to do: I'm going to turn in my wings. I don't believe in this fucking war . . . I never did. Last time we were in the States, I even took part in that protest march to Washington."

Mike shook his head and pursed his lips. He hated the people who protested the war. They didn't understand—

"My mother even spoke to my father the last time I was home. She pleaded with him to pull some strings and have me reassigned. Christ, he's a fucking admiral now. He could have done it. But he wouldn't."

"She should have known he wouldn't. Even Jacob wouldn't do that for Sy, and he's also, as you put it, 'a fucking admiral now.' That's not the way those two think."

"Yeah, Sy's back for another tour too . . . this time up north."

The air boss came on 1MC and ordered the pilots to "man your planes . . . pilots, man your planes."

"We'll talk about this later," Mike said as they went up to the flight deck.

"Nothing to talk about," Andrew answered. "I've been thinking about doing this for a long time. I don't want to make a career of this."

"There's a lot to talk about, but not now. Now you have to concentrate on flying."

"Like I said, friend, there's nothing to talk about."

"Sure there is. You can't just throw away—"

Andrew uttered a forced laugh. "I threw away my life the moment I agreed to go the Academy. And now, goddamn it, Mike, I want my life back."

Just before they stepped on the flight deck, Mike grabbed hold of Andrew's elbow and pulled him back. "Then why the fuck are you going on this mission?"

Andrew pulled his arm free. "C'mon, you know the fucking reason—I'm not a coward," he said, and walked out onto the noisy flight deck.

Mike went after him. "No one ever said you were," he called out, instantly realizing that Andrew couldn't hear him.

Each carrier was sending its air wing on the strike. A total of eighty-four aircraft, in three different groups, would be involved. The group from the *Harrison*, code-designated Flying Jacks for the mission, would be the second strike group. The first strike group would come in from the east, the Flying Jacks from the south, and the third from the west. The TOT, time over the target, for each strike group would be three minutes.

"Feet dry," the strike leader radioed.

Mike saw the coast of North Vietnam come up on the horizon and checked his ordnance to make sure it was "hot." Then he glanced to his left—he was flying on the right of the strike group—at Andrew. "Just don't do anything stupid," he whispered.

The familiar rhythmic beats of Firecan, the North Vietnamese tracking radar, came into Mike's earphones. Within moments he was over the beach and small black clouds of AA fire began to puff out below him, where the attack bombers were flying. For this strike, because of the anticipated MIG activity, there were four TarCAP fighters on each side of the strike group. Andrew was his wingman, and a pilot named Chris Burke, on his second tour, and his wingman, a "nugget" with a Polish-sounding name, were behind them.

"Turning," the strike leader radioed.

Mike eased his A-4 into a ninety-degree turn.

The strike leader began to descend toward the target area. Huge columns of black smoke were already pushing into the sky, while the quick dark blooms of bursting antiaircraft shells became more numerous.

The bombers in all three groups were divided into those that would drop mines into the harbor and those that would go after specific targets in the harbor area.

The flak suppressors peeled off from the formation and started their attack.

"Ah, shit!" a pilot yelled over the radio.

Mike saw one of the flak suppressors suddenly pull to the right.

"I can't control her," the same pilot shouted. "I can't—"

The A-4 plowed into a clump of trees and became a rolling ball of fire.

Mike heard the high-pitched tones of Fansong and then Andrew warned, "SAM, nine o'clock low."

Mike kicked his plane into a half left turn.

The SAM passed him by, expended its short burn rocket, and began to fall.

The bombers were into their run—those that were dropping mines and those that were going for the railyards and oil-storage tanks around the harbor.

"Holy Mother of God," someone yelled.

"Jim, are you all right?" the strike leader called, identifying the man.

"Negative . . . I'm hit."

The Fansong began to wail.

"Sixteen . . . Sixteen, two SAMs coming up at four o'clock," an unfamiliar voice shouted.

Andrew was sixteen.

Mike glanced over at him. Andrew slipped to the right and dropped below them.

The last of the bombers were pulling away from the target. On afterburners they screamed upward at more than a sixty-degree angle.

Now there were SAMs almost everywhere. The high pitch of the Fansong never stopped.

The pilots shouted warnings to one another.

"SAM on your tail, Greek," the strike leader yelled. "Break right . . . break right."

Mike couldn't follow the swirling action that banded the sky over Haiphong with thin white contrails.

"Red Bandits airborne at Bull's-eye," the fighter-direction ship called.

The bombers were coming up to altitude.

"Bandits . . . Bandits . . . eight o'clock high," a pilot called.

"We'll take them," the MIGCAP leader said.

Mike glanced over his shoulder. The fighters guarding the rear were already turning.

"Bandits . . . Bandits, three o'clock high," the nugget shouted.

"Here we go!" Mike yelled, kicking his A-4 into a left turn. "There's six."

A call from another pilot indicated eight more MIGs attacking from the south.

Mike climbed. "Andrew, stay close."

Burke and the nugget were coming up behind them. The NVAF pilots pulled their noses up.

Mike pushed his stick slightly forward. The MIG's belly came into view. He fired two Sidewinder missiles. A slight jolt shook the plane.

An instant later, the MIG flashed into flames and began to fall.

Mike rolled into a left turn.

The MIGS were trying to fight their way past the Skyhawks and Phantoms to get at the slower attack planes.

Mike glimpsed a MIG streaking down to his left and kicked his A-4 toward it. This time he was on the MIG's tail. He cut in the afterburner, and thumbing the cannon trigger, gave him a short burst.

The MIG's right wing seemed to bend; then it tore away. The plane spiraled downward.

"Got the bastard!" Mike yelled.

"Two up for the day," Burke answered.

The radio was busy with pilots either shouting or talking.

Mike pulled up to twenty-two thousand feet and was positioning himself for another dive when suddenly the strike leader called out, "All fighters, reform . . . all fighters, reform . . . Red Bandits are breaking off . . . Red Bandits are breaking off . . . all fighters, reform. . . . Anyone else got two or more Bandits? . . . No. . . . That makes you high man for the day, Mike."

"How does it feel to be high man, Mike?" a voice asked.

"That's got to be our own air CAG," Mike answered, trying to keep the excitement under control. Few pilots ever managed to get "one kill," but "two kills" in a single engagement almost verged on the extraordinary.

"I'll tell you when I'm aboard," Mike answered; then, looking at his fuel gauge, he added, "That's if I *get* aboard . . . I've got about ten minutes more in the air before I'm dry."

"Those afterburners will do it every time," the strike leader said. "Better go get yourself some fuel . . . you're the first at the tit."

"Thanks," Mike responded.

Within two minutes the KA-3A tanker came into view.

"Go get it, tiger," the flight leader said.

"Going," Mike answered, and began to maneuver his aircraft to couple with the boom. Twice he tried to engage and twice he failed.

"Take it easy," Andrew said. "Take it very easy, Mike."

"Yeah, easy," Mike responded, lining up with the fuel boom again and easing the throttle forward. He had been waiting to hear Andrew's voice, and now that Andrew had spoken, he somehow felt much better. The F-4 plugged in and began to suck up fuel.

With his fuel tank full, Mike unplugged, slowed down, and turned away from the tail end of the tanker. But only when he was flying toward the *Harrison* did he realize there was a carpet of dense clouds below him. He switched on his radio and spoke to the strike controller aboard the carrier. "Dealer, this is Blackjack Two-zero."

"Go ahead, Blackjack Two-zero," the SC answered.

"Inbound from Haiphong . . . eighty miles at zero-eight-five."

"Roger, Blackjack Two-zero. Proceed to five-zero miles and switch marshal."

"Wilco," Mike answered. Every plane in the strike group went through the same procedure and every pilot listened intently to the instructions he'd receive from the SC and then the marshal.

Mike switched his instruments, and at fifty miles out from the *Harrison* he switched radio frequencies and reported his position to the marshal.

"Roger. Come two-zero-seven-five degrees."

"Wilco," Mike answered, and began changing his course. "Say type of recovery."

"Case three," the marshal answered.

"Roger," Mike answered. A case-three recovery meant that the weather below was very bad and he'd be flying his instruments all the way down until he broke out of the clouds and saw the ship. The final approach, as it always was, would be visual, regardless of the weather.

Ten miles out, Mike reported his position again.

"Have you on radar. Switch tower," the marshal responded.

Mike eased the stick forward, dropping the A-4's nose. In moments he crashed through the top of the clouds and quickly found himself in a world of rapidly fading light.

His eyes were riveted to the red-illuminated instruments.

"Correct zero-two right," a voice calmly said over the radio.

Mike made the correction and watched his position change on the glide-slope indicator.

"Looking good," the voice said.

Mike was sweating. He was three miles out and still hadn't broken out of the cloud cover. Straining to see the ship, he suddenly had a horrific vision of crashing into its stern. Then he broke out of the clouds and saw the ship illuminated with red lights.

He rolled his A-4 into the groove off the carrier's stern and looked for the ball between the two banks of green datum lights. In a moment he saw it. "I have the ball," Mike radioed, and started for the deck. Ahead he saw the quick flash of the green cut light and pushed the throttle forward. The next instant he slammed down on the deck and grabbed the wire. The sudden stop jolted him and the aircraft; then one of the rain-soaked handlers signaled him to cut the engine. Within moments the plane was hooked to a small yellow tractor and moved out of the way to make it possible for the next plane, which was already off the stern, to land.

As soon as the aircraft was parked, Mike unbuckled his harness and climbed out of the cockpit and down onto the deck, where he was immediately congratulated on his two "kills" by the plane captain and the other men who handled the aircraft. There were also congratulations by the debriefing officer, who said, "Tomorrow you'll be flown to Saigon and be presented to members of the press at the daily five-o'clock news briefing, better known as the five-o'clock follies."

"You're joking? . . . C'mon, tell me you're joking," Mike pleaded.

"Orders from CINPACFLT," the debriefing officer said. "You're an authentic American hero."

"Isn't there any way—"

"None. It won't be all that bad."

"It's bad enough."

"In addition to being on TV, you'll also have three glorious days in wonderfully exciting Saigon," the briefing officer said.

"I'm safer on a strike than I am in Saigon," Mike said.

"Some of us are born heroes; some of us make ourselves heroes. Luckily, I fall into neither category, but you, Lieutenant Trapasso, made yourself a hero and, therefore, you must suffer the consequences. Matter closed."

The debriefing finished, Mike and Andrew headed directly for their quarters.

"That was good flying and shooting," Andrew said as they entered the cabin.

"I thought you'd never notice," Mike answered facetiously.

"Yeah, I noticed. A couple of the other guys scored hits, but none of them bagged anything."

Mike dropped down on his bunk.

"I'm going to shower, then go see the air wing skipper," Andrew said in a toneless voice.

Mike jumped to his feet. "Just what the hell is wrong with you?"

"Nothing. I just came back from a mission where I watched my best friend kill two other guys—maybe they were best friends too—and a couple of our guys get knocked out of the fucking sky."

"Those fuckers would have burned my tail if they had the chance!"

"That's just it, Mike, they would have. That's just what doesn't make any sense," Andrew said, stripping off his shirt.

Mike shook his head.

Andrew stripped off the rest of his clothing, wrapped a towel around his waist, and padded off to the shower.

Mike lit a cigarette and sat down on his bunk. He did and didn't understand Andrew's attitude. He did at times, especially when he was back in the States with Barbara and the baby. But this war was also his life.

Andrew came back to the cabin and finished drying himself. He commented, "Not only did I have to shower with salt water, I'm already just as sweaty as I was when I went into the shower."

"You know what this will do to your father?" Mike asked, blowing smoke from his nostrils.

"It doesn't mater anymore. He's on his own; I'm on my own. That's the way it has to be," Andrew said, taking a clean uniform out of the closet.

Mike stubbed out the cigarette in a hammered-copper ashtray. "I can't stop you," he said.

"Don't feel bad about it—no one can," Andrew answered, offering Mike his hand.

Mike shook it.

"See you around," Andrew said.

"You know you'll be hustled off the ship?"

"I know."

"Are you prepared for what will follow?"

Andrew nodded. "The sooner I'm free of the Navy and the Navy is free of me, the happier I know I'll be."

"Suppose the brass press for a court-martial?" Mike questioned.

"Not a chance," Andrew answered. "Not with the way public opinion is today. The war is unpopular, Mike. You don't see it that way, because you don't want to."

The two men shook hands again.

"Good luck, Andrew," Mike said.

"Good luck to you," Andrew answered. "Enjoy Saigon." He winked, turned, and left the cabin.

Engulfed by a sudden wave of weariness, Mike sat

down on his bunk again. Several moments passed before he realized he was shaking with fear. "I could have been the one to punch out," he whispered. "I could have been killed. . . ."

33

ANDREW NEVER RETURNED to the cabin. Two marines came down to collect his clothing and personal belongings and the following morning as Mike was boarding a helo for Saigon, Andrew was boarding a twin-engine COD, carrier on board delivery aircraft, that would fly him off the carrier, possibly to Camranh Bay.

At Hotel Three in Tan So Nhut Airport, Mike was met by several Navy PR officers, including Phil Sands, a captain, a short stocky man with horn-rimmed glasses and a sweaty handshake.

"We've got a limo waiting," Sands told him, "and on the way to your hotel, I'll go over your schedule for the next few days."

As they approached the limo, a sailor saluted and opened the rear door.

Mike returned the salute, thanked him, and then sat down in the rear seat. Sands sat next to him and two of the other officers used the jump seats.

"This afternoon you'll be lunching with the American ambassador and the President of South Vietnam, General Thieu, and other South Vietnamese government officials."

Mike quickly sized Sands up and came to the conclusion that he was a civilian wearing a uniform, rather than a professional like himself.

"The reporters will ask all sorts of questions—"

"Listen, Captain, first things first," Mike said. "And the first thing I want to do is shower with fresh water; then I want to phone my wife, and finally I want to eat something not prepared by Navy cooks."

Sands grinned. "No problem. . . . Oh, by the way, did you bring your service whites with you? . . . Never mind, we'll treat you to a new set."

There were reporters waiting for them when they reached the Hotel Majestic. But Sands and his two assistants pushed their way through them and moved quickly across the ornate lobby, complete with marble floor and gilt-framed paintings on the walls.

The elevator was a cage, practically open on all sides, except for some ornamental ironwork.

"Your suite is on the fourth floor," Sands told him as they moved slowly upward. "To make sure that you are not disturbed by members of the press, there will be two marines posted at your door while you're here."

Accepting what he'd just been told, Mike had a momentary vision of Andrew walking between the two marines toward the transport.

The elevator stopped, one of Sands's assistants opened the door, and a short time later the four of them were in the suite.

"Anything you want, Commander, just lift up the phone and call downstairs for it," Sands said.

"Anything?"

Sands went to the phone, and lifting it, said, "Tell me and I'll get it for you."

Straight-faced, Mike answered, "Boom boom."

Sands flushed and began to stammer.

"You said 'anything,' Captain." Mike turned to the two other officers. "You heard him. Four months without a woman—well, you guys know how it is."

Finally Sands regained enough poise to say, "Within limits, Commander, Food, drink—even newspapers, magazines, and books. But—"

"Don't sweat it, Captain," Mike told him with a smile. "I'll settle for a phone call to my wife."

Sands laughed. "You must be one hell of a mean poker player, Commander."

"I am," Mike said with unabashed straightforwardness. "And either call me Mike or Trapasso." He nodded to the other two officers. "That goes for you as well." Then he gave Barbara's telephone number to Sands.

"It will be a while before we get through."

"Yeah, I know. I'm going to shower. After you put through the call to my wife, I'd appreciate a bottle of Scotch—"

"There's a full bar here," one of the other officers said as he went to the side of the room and opened the bottom of a cabinet. "Even a small refrigerator for ice and whatnot."

Mike helped himself to a double Scotch, neat; then he showered. He thoroughly enjoyed the combination of hot fresh water pouring over him and perfumed soap that produced a rich lather. Then, as he dried himself, Sands called out, "Your wife is on the line, Mike."

Towel wrapped around his waist, Mike left the steamy bathroom and took the phone from Sands.

"Where are you?" Barbara asked.

"Saigon. . . . I'm fine. How's George?"

"Wonderful. He misses his father," Barbara said, "and so do I."

"I miss you too," Mike told her, and asked after his mother and father.

"Dad is back in Hong Kong," she said.

They spoke for several minutes more about family things and then Barbara said, "You still haven't told me why you're in Saigon."

"I . . ." He hesitated.

"You're okay, aren't you?" she questioned.

"Yes . . . yes, I'm fine. I'm here for a press conference. I shot down two enemy planes yesterday."

He could hear her gasp; then she said, "Thank God you're safe. I . . ."

"Listen, there's no need to cry."

"I can't help it. I try not to think about it, but if anything should happen to you . . ." She began to sob.

"Barbara."

"Yes . . . yes, I'm here."

"I'll call tomorrow," he told her, and looked questioningly at Sands, who nodded.

"I forgot to ask you how Andrew is," she said.

Mike hesitated. He wasn't certain whether Sands and his assistants knew what Andrew had done; if they did, how much.

"He's all right, isn't he?" she asked, her tone full of alarm.

"Yes."

Barbara was momentarily silent.

"He's all right," Mike assured her, and before she could ask any more questions, he told her again that he'd phone every day while he was in Saigon.

"I love you," Barbara told him.

"I love you," he answered.

After the initial five o'clock briefing in the theater of the Rex Hotel, given by Mr. Horace Cunningham, the civilian representative of the information service for the American forces in Vietnam, Mike was presented to the members of the press and received a standing ovation.

"Commander, will you please describe for the ladies and gentlemen of the press how you downed the two MIGs," Cunningham said.

"I got the first with a missile," Mike answered. "I had a perfect shot at his belly . . . and the second one I got with cannon fire . . . I hit his right wing, coming at him from above and behind."

"Are these your first two kills?" another report asked.

"Yes. MIGs don't usually come out and fight, unless they can jump you."

"Why do you think they came out to fight this time?" someone asked.

"Because we were going after a major port."

"Was the strike successful?" one of the women reporters asked.

"I could see many fires when I left the target area," Mike answered, aware that she was beautiful.

Mike fielded the questions as fast as they came. Some he thought were stupid, and several were repetitive; then the woman who had asked him if the strike was successful stood up and said, "Commander, would you tell us what you know about Commander Troost's refusal to fly another mission?"

Cunningham immediately stepped forward. "Commander Trapasso is not prepared to comment—"

"The commander can speak for himself," a man with a distinct French accent said.

Mike looked at Cunningham and said, "I'd like to answer the question."

There was a burst of applause.

Cunningham stepped back.

"Commander Andrew Troost is my best friend," he said, looking straight into the TV cameras, "and while I do not happen to share some of his views, he is certainly entitled to them. He is, as everyone who has ever flown wingman with him knows, a highly skilled fighter pilot and has served his country with dedication and courage."

"Is he the son of Admiral Warren Troost?" one of the men called out.

"Yes."

Still standing, the woman asked, "Can you give us some insight as to why he turned in his wings?"

"Yes, but I won't," Mike answered. "When the time comes, Commander Troost will explain his actions."

"Do you think he should be court-martialed?" she pressed.

"That decision is not up to me," Mike answered.

"I'm asking for your opinion, Commander Trapasso," she said.

Mike hesitated and Cunningham started forward again. "It's all right. My opinion in this matter doesn't matter. What you really want to know is whether I agree with what he did. Since I'm standing here in front of you, the answer should be obvious."

The woman sat down.

There were a few more questions, all of which Mike answered without hesitation.

34

WARREN WAS DOZING on the couch in the rec room. He'd come home from the office early and had told Carol he felt as if he were "coming down with the flu."

A single ring of the phone entered his light sleep, but it didn't ring again. Then suddenly he heard Carol call his name. Opening his eyes, he looked up at her and was about to ask if someone had just phoned, when she said, "Hilary is on her way here."

He bolted into a sitting position. "What?" Until a few months ago, he hadn't seen or spoken to her on the phone for almost four years.

"She called from the airport."

Warren stood up and ran his fingers through his hair. The last time he had seen her she had pleaded with him to "pull strings for Andrew" to remain in the States. He had never told Carol about that visit. At the time, he was too embarrassed to speak about it to anyone. "Did she say why she was coming?" he asked.

"No."

Warren looked at his watch. "It's four-thirty, and—"

"Should I set another place for dinner?" Carol asked.

"Hilary doesn't usually eat until nine, often later,"

he said. "Put out some crackers and cheese, or anything else that you think will serve the purpose."

Carol nodded, then asked, "Are you feeling any better?"

"Worse, now that I know she's on her way here," he answered.

Carol went up to him and placed the palm of her hand on his forehead. "I think you might have some fever."

"I'm sure I do. Whenever I have fever, my head aches and my eyes become very sensitive to light." He made a face. "I really don't want to see her."

"I could tell her you're ill."

"Too late," Warren said. "I'll just have to see her and find out what she wants. But right now, I'm going to lie down on the couch, close my eyes, and rest."

"You do that, hon," Carol replied.

Warren returned to the couch, and stretching out on it, he said, "After Hilary leaves, remind me to tell you about her visit to me a few months ago."

"You never mentioned that she visited you."

"I didn't want to talk about it," he said.

"Why—"

"I don't want to talk about it now," he told her as he put his arm over his eyes. "I'll tell you all about it later. Now I want to rest."

Carol brushed her lips over the top of his head.

He took hold of her hand and kissed the back of it. "You have her beat by ten miles," he told her.

"Rest," she responded, and padded out of the room.

Warren shifted his position. He hoped she wasn't going to ask him again to pull strings for Andrew. . . .

The sound of the bell woke Warren, and within a matter of moments he heard Carol and Hilary speaking. His head still hurt and his eyes were still sensitive to light and now he felt the ache associated with the flu in his joints.

Both women entered the room just as Warren managed to pull himself up into a sitting position.

"I'm sorry to disturb you," Hilary said.

Warren nodded and invited her to sit down. Despite the fact that she was well made up and wearing a very expensive-looking white suit, she looked ill herself.

"Hilary, would you care for something to drink?" Carol asked. "Something cold, perhaps?"

"A double shot of vodka on the rocks would be fine," Hilary answered.

Carol glanced questioningly at Warren, who said, "We don't stock anything stronger than soda."

"Nothing, then," Hilary said.

"Will you stay for dinner?" Carol asked.

"No, I want to catch an early shuttle flight back to New York," she answered. "I have a meeting with my lawyers first thing tomorrow morning."

"I hope it has nothing to do with our legal settlement," Warren said sourly. "I thought that was all settled years ago."

Hilary took a deep breath, and when she finally exhaled, she said, "Andrew handed in his wings."

Warren's jaw went slack. He began to tremble. He tried to speak, but couldn't form the words.

Carol sat down next to him and took hold of his hand.

"It probably will be on this evening's news," Hilary said, now wiping her eyes with a tissue. "I flew down to—"

"Is that why you're meeting with your lawyers?" Warren asked.

"He's being held under hack in Subic Bay. He phoned

me and said that he will be shipped back to the United States in a matter of days."

Warren looked at his watch. "It's almost five. . . . Carol, would you please turn on the TV." He spoke in a flat clipped tone.

"I know you blame me," Hilary said.

"Blame," Warren repeated as the TV came on. "I blame myself for putting Andrew where he should never have been put."

The anchorman came on. "This is John Gault with the five o'clock evening news. First, from South Vietnam we have two juxtaposed stories: one about a hero and one about . . . well, we'll let you decide."

Suddenly Warren found himself looking at Mike.

"Lieutenant Commander Michael Trapasso successful downed two MIG 21s in a dogfight over the North Vietnamese port of Haiphong during yesterday's strike. During eight years of war with thousands of strikes flown off the various carriers on Yankee Station, Lieutenant Commander Trapasso is one of the few of a group of American fighter pilots who have managed to shoot down an enemy plane. But he not only bagged one, he got a second kill during the same engagement. Our correspondent Chuck Ryan has the story. . . ."

Leaning forward, Warren listened intently. "His family will be proud of him, real proud . . . and they should be."

Warren looked at Hilary. "Tony told me some time ago that the reason why Ruth and her boyfriend split up was that he was going to avoid the draft by going to either Canada or Sweden and wanted her to go with him. But she wouldn't . . . she wouldn't because she couldn't betray her brother . . . couldn't betray Mike."

Carol returned to Warren's side.

"And now to our other story," Gault said, and

Andrew's picture filled the screen. "Though there is no official word yet, we have information from reliable sources that Lieutenant Commander Andrew Troost, the son of Admiral Warren Troost and grandson of the man whom he was named after, Admiral Andrew Troost, has refused to fly another combat mission. Lieutenant Commander Troost handed in his wings after having taken part in the strike against Haiphong. Ironically, both men fly from the same carrier and, from what we understand, they have been lifelong friends. Both Commander Troost's father and grandfather were World War Two heroes. The Troost naval tradition—"

Warren leapt to his feet and switched of the TV. "Enough," he growled. "Enough!" He began to pace.

"Come back here and sit down," Carol said. "You'll only make yourself sicker."

"I couldn't feel any worse than I feel now," Warren answered, but he returned to the couch, and locking his hands together, said, "It's over for Andrew and it's over for me."

"Oh, Warren!" Carol exclaimed.

" 'The sins of the fathers shall be visited on the sons.' Well, this is the reverse: the sins of the sons shall be visited on the fathers—only it's one son and one father." His voice reduced to a tight whisper. "It's my son, and the Navy can be terribly unforgiving, especially in a situation like this one."

"What can happen to him?" Hilary asked.

Warren was on his feet again, pacing. "I don't know . . . I don't know the circumstances. At least he did it after the strike and not before."

The phone jangled, drawing everyone's attention to it.

"I'll get it," Warren said, and striding over to the

phone, he picked it up and immediately identified himself. "Jacob," he told the others; then, speaking into the phone, he said, "Hilary is here now . . . the first I heard about it was from her."

"I'll see what information I can get," Jacob said. "Whatever help you need, you can count on me—that goes for any legal fees."

"Thank you, Jacob," Warren said. "It's—"

"I'll be in touch," Jacob told him.

The line went dead.

Warren pursed his lips, shook his head, but said nothing. As soon as he put the phone down, it rang again. "Admiral Troost, here," he answered.

"Warren, it's Tony."

"You must have heard about Andrew."

"Yeah, it's all over the Hong Kong newspapers," Tony told him. "Listen, I've already put through calls to some of my friends in Washington . . . you know the kind I mean."

"Yes, I do," Warren answered.

"I also called my legal people in New York, and—"

"Hilary is meeting with her lawyers tomorrow morning," Warren said.

"Listen, you know my feelings about the war. I'd like to kick the shit out of Andrew, but he's your son and you and I go back to another time and another war. Don't worry, nothing will happen to Andrew, that I promise you."

"Jacob is trying to get more information about what happened," Warren said.

"Good. Now, I want you to listen to me very carefully and do what I tell you to do."

"But—"

"Warren, don't argue with me!"

"Tell me what you want me to do," Warren said.

"I have already phoned a few people. They'll be at your house within the next couple of hours. They're going to move you and Carol to another house. You'll live there until the dust on this thing settles."

"Are you sure that's the way to go?" Warren asked.

"Certain. There are too many crazies out there for and against what Andrew did . . . and one of them just might be crazy enough to try to hurt either you or Carol, or the both of you."

For several moments Warren considered what Tony had just told him; then he said, "We're in your hands, Tony."

"Tell Hilary not to stay in her apartment, but to move to a hotel. I'll have some friends guard her. I'm flying home tonight. I'll see you soon."

"Yes, see you soon," Warren answered, and put the phone down and disconnected it. "It's necessary," he said; then, going to Carol, he took hold of her hands and explained what Tony wanted them to do; then he turned to Hilary and did the same.

Neither woman objected.

"This is a hell of a way for a man to act near the end of his career," Warren commented; then, his voice sad and tired, he added, "I didn't even have the presence of mind to congratulate Tony."

"I'm sure he knows that you meant to," Carol said gently.

Warren nodded, and despite his effort to stop them, tears welled up in his eyes and rolled down his cheeks.

"I'm sorry, Warren," Hilary said, her voice breaking. "I never thought he'd do something like this."

Warren shrugged, buried his face in his hands, and wept.

35

IT WAS NOT yet dawn when Jacob, now a vice-admiral, came onto the flag bridge of the carrier *Anzio*, the command ship for the evacuation of all American personnel from Saigon. He hadn't had more than two hours' sleep in the last thirty-six hours, but neither had any of his staff, or the men who flew the shuttle runs between the *Anzio* and the *Trenton*, the other carrier involved in the evolution.

Jacob nodded to the watch officer.

"Sir, units of the NVA are shelling the outskirts of Saigon," the WO said.

"How many more people are in the embassy compound?" Jacob asked. It was his responsibility to get everyone out. The wives and children of embassy personnel had already been airlifted out.

"Several thousand," the WO answered. "Most of them Vietnamese who worked with us."

Jacob paced the deck for several moments before he asked, "When will we be ready to launch?"

"The ship's XO called just before you came onto the bridge. The first helo should be . . ." The WO checked his watch. "In two minutes, sir."

"Good," Jacob answered, rubbing his hands. He sat

down in the command chair. This was the end of South Vietnam. The last of the American troops had left in 1973, and now, in April 1975, the last two days of the month, a little over sixteen months after the war between the two Vietnams began again, South Vietnam ceased to exist.

The 1MC came on. The voice on it gave clear, sharp orders for the launch of the first helo, and even as he spoke, the ship's high-intensity lights came on, silvering the black surface of the water.

Two dozen choppers were in the air in a matter of minutes.

Both carriers had taken additional helos aboard for the evacuation when they laid over at Subic Bay for twenty-four hours.

Jacob had foreseen this disaster during his first visit to Vietnam, when he had been sent by President Kennedy to evaluate the situation, and later he had been commander of a carrier battle group on Yankee Station for the usual seven months. Then, because of the policies in Washington under the Nixon administration, his pilots spent more time playing cards than they did fighting the enemy. And when they did engage, they weren't permitted to hit those targets—specifically missile sites under construction—because those sites were being built by Russian engineers. It didn't seem to matter to the politicians in Washington that when those sites became operational they'd kill his men. From the very beginning, as far as he was concerned, it was the wrong war, in the wrong place, at the wrong time. And now, with Nixon forced to resign because of his implication in the Watergate break-in, and Ford, the former Vice-President, now President, the war was coming to its natural conclusion.

The 1MC signaled the changing of the watch.

Jacob turned and acknowledged the new WO.

The very next moment, the phone rang.

"Sir," one of Jacob's aides said, "Captain Grant is reporting that some of our helos have taken ground fire."

"Is the fire confirmed?" Jacob asked.

The aide asked the question, listened for a few moments, and then said, "Yes, sir, it's confirmed."

Jacob was hoping that the NVA would not fire on the helos. He didn't want to risk even a minor incident that would eventuate in an exchange of fire between the men under his command and the NVA. "Launch fighter squadron one-oh-six. They'll fly protective cover. They're not to fire on NVAs unless the NVAs are firing at them or our helos."

The aide relayed the order.

The 1MC blared, "One-oh-six pilots to the ready room . . . one-oh-six pilots to the ready room . . . launch in ten minutes."

Jacob sat down again.

The squadron's planes were already coming up on the elevator and rolling into position for the pilots.

"Helo inbound," came from the 1MC.

The phone rang.

"Sir, the captain requests permission to recover the helo before commencing the launch," the WO said.

"Reason?" Jacob asked, leaving the chair again.

"Sir, the helo is carrying more than its capacity."

The air boss came on the 1MC. "On deck, stand by to recover helo."

The Huey came toward the carrier on her port side, maneuvered over the deck, and slowly set down. Almost immediately, civilians bent low began to leave the helo, and listening to a man giving directions over a bullhorn, ran to the open bulkhead door in the island.